A DARKNESS OF THE HEART

A DARKNESS OF THE HEART

A JOANNE KILBOURN MYSTERY

GAIL
BOWEN

McCLELLAND & STEWART

Library and Archives Canada Cataloguing in Publication data is available upon request

ISBN: 978-0-7710-0975-4
ebook ISBN: 978-0-7710-0976-1

Published simultaneously in the United States of America by McClelland & Stewart, a division of Penguin Random House Canada, a Penguin Random House Company

Library of Congress Control Number is available upon request

Typeset in Trump Mediaeval by M&S, Toronto
Designed by Leah Springate
Cover image: © Anton Belovodchenko / iStock photo / Getty Images

Printed and bound in Canada

McClelland & Stewart,
a division of Penguin Random House Canada Limited,
a Penguin Random House Company
www.penguinrandomhouse.ca

1   2   3   4   5   22   21   20   19   18

Penguin
Random House
McCLELLAND & STEWART

For Hildy Wren Bowen, Brett Bell, Max Bowen,
Carrie Bowen, and Nathaniel Bowen
with gratitude for your support,
your laughter, and your love

CHAPTER

1

I have always found the slyly botched logic of Lewis Carroll's *Alice's Adventures in Wonderland* appealing, not just because of its playfulness, but because for much of my life, like Alice, the grasp I've had on my own identity has been slippery. On the December morning when I learned that the circumstances surrounding my conception were very different from what I had always believed, I was sixty years old. My four children were healthy and excited about their lives, and my five-year-long marriage to Zack Shreve had made me happier than I had ever imagined I could be. My professional life as an academic and political adviser had been engrossing and often rewarding, and in early retirement, I was enjoying time spent with my grandchildren and pursuing projects I hadn't had time for when I was at work. My life was full, and I was content.

But the previous year and a half had been a struggle. The sudden deaths of three people who had been an intrinsic part of our family's lives had left us swimming for the surface. In the months immediately following the tragedy, it seemed that every time we were able to see light, a tidal wave of grief would engulf us and we would sink back into darkness.

But as this year moved inexorably towards its end, I was feeling optimistic about the future. Zack had finished his term as mayor of Regina in November and had returned to his position as senior partner in the firm he and his four closest friends from law school had opened the day after they were called to the bar; our youngest daughter, Taylor, high school diploma in hand, had decided to take a gap year, staying with Zack and me while she considered her options; and for the first time in memory, there was nothing I was obliged to do. Free to choose my path, like the knights in Middle English romances, I felt ready to take "the adventure God sent me."

But the news delivered on the morning of December 1 knocked a fundamental building block of my identity out from under me, and I was faced with what Alice called "the great puzzle": Who in the world was I?

The sequence of events that led to the revelation about how I came into being began with the sudden, fatal heart attack of a man named Lev-Aaron Sloane, whose partner of fourteen years, Roy Brodnitz, was a brilliant, mercurial writer of Broadway shows. When the love of his life died, Brodnitz was thrown into a downward spiral of grief and depression. The birds no longer sang. Desperate, his friends and colleagues tried everything to help him out of the depths but he was unreachable. It was as if he couldn't remember how to live. One morning, Brodnitz found himself standing in front of a small art gallery on West 25th Street in Manhattan. Drawn by a shimmering abstract in the gallery's window, he went inside and asked to see the painting.

Later, when I came to know Roy, he told me his grandmother used to chide him for too often letting his heart run away with his head, but that morning Roy's heart led him exactly where he needed to go.

The painting, oil on canvas, was large: 160 by 130 centimetres. At the top of the canvas, a luminous white glow appeared to undulate like a sheet in the wind. As the eye moved downward, the radiant light mutated into pulsing bands of colour: yellow-green, indigo, violet, and finally a deep, vibrant red.

Brodnitz bought the work, titled *Aurora*, and had it delivered immediately to his loft in Tribeca. As he watched the late-afternoon light play on the painting's bands of colour, Roy Brodnitz once again heard the birds sing. That night he began writing a script for a play that would be called *The Happiest Girl*, a dark and deeply moving musical about the power of redemptive love. After more than two years on Broadway, the show was still playing to packed houses.

Grateful for his resurrection, Brodnitz decided to co-curate an exhibition of work by the Canadian artist who had painted *Aurora*, Desmond Love. The show, held at a mid-sized gallery in Brooklyn, was enthusiastically received. After many years, Desmond Love had finally emerged from the shadow of his daughter, Sally Love, who had been a wildly successful and controversial artist, and also my lifelong friend.

Like her father, Sally died young. After her death, I had adopted her four-year-old daughter, Taylor. When Roy Brodnitz learned that Desmond Love had a then-seventeen-year-old granddaughter, he invited our family to the opening of his exhibition, *Aurora: The Art of Desmond Love*, and to be his guests for a performance of *The Happiest Girl*. On the day after Taylor's graduation, we flew to New York City. Taylor slept from the moment we boarded the plane till we landed at JFK. Except for an occasional catnap, that sleep was the last she had until we boarded the flight back to Regina four days later.

Roy Brodnitz had been the consummate host: he knew the city, and he knew how to dazzle. We saw art at MoMA and the Chelsea galleries, art and gardens at the Met Cloisters and the Botanical Gardens in the Bronx. We ate smoked fish and watched the rowboats float by at Loeb Boathouse in Central Park; we savoured the tasting menu at Gramercy Tavern and sampled a half-dozen flavours at Van Leeuwen Artisan Ice Cream; we visited the top of the Rock, the Statue of Liberty, and the National September 11 Memorial. And we went to shows, on and off Broadway. By far our favourite was Roy's musical. *The Happiest Girl* followed the journey of a fourteen-year-old searching the Canadian arctic for answers about her grandmother's mysterious disappearance. The production's message—that death is not the end—was balm for our spirits.

Aurora: The Art of Desmond Love was also a gift. Roy had tracked down a modest but impressive collection of Des's work, including four other paintings in the *Aurora* series. The five *Aurora* paintings were hung together in a single gallery room. To stand in that cool, quiet space and absorb the ancient power of the northern lights that the paintings seemed to emit was to know peace.

After our trip to New York, two things happened: Desmond Love became a significant presence in our family's life, and Roy Brodnitz's world intersected with ours, with results that were both seductive and unsettling.

The Happiest Girl was being produced as a movie, and the filming was taking place at the Saskatchewan Film Production Studios in Regina. During Zack's tenure as mayor, he had lobbied aggressively to bring the industry back to our city. Gabe Vickers, a veteran producer often described as a "big gun," had been at the opening of *The Happiest Girl* two years earlier, and from the moment the curtain fell, the play became what he called "his passion project." Vickers's production company, Living Skies, had moved its offices to Regina at the beginning of the year. His first task had been to secure financing for *The Happiest Girl*, but before he approached backers, Vickers had put together an impressive creative team: Roy Brodnitz would write the script; Ainsley Blair, the choreographer and director of the stage play and Roy's long-time collaborator, would direct; Rosemond Burke, an acclaimed eighty-year-old British actor, would play the grandmother; and Vale Frazier, a seventeen-year-old actress who had starred in the show on Broadway and had already been nominated for a Tony, would play the lead. Gabe's reputation as a producer with a genius for coordinating writing, directing, and editing would do the rest. Acquiring a clutch of eager backers, including a Reginian with deep pockets and a penchant for anonymity, was not a problem.

When we'd said goodbye to Roy in New York in June, he said he expected pre-production would begin in Regina around Labour Day. He was right on the money. The official start took place on the Tuesday after Labour Day. It was a media event on a slow news day, and Living Skies' trendy retro-Brutalist-style offices were crowded with politicians eager to take credit; creatives eager to establish availability for jobs; media eager to get clips for a feel-good story; and Living Skies employees eager to charm. As mayor, Zack's attendance at the opening was a given, and Taylor and I had tagged along because we thought it would be fun. Rumour also had it that Living Skies' craft services' cinnamon buns were to die for.

Not surprisingly, at the kickoff Gabe Vickers was surrounded, but he was at ease, accustomed to being the centre of attention. Tall and heavy-set, he wore jeans, a black T-shirt, and a black calfskin leather jacket that fit him like a second skin. His greying blond hair was thick and as shaggy as that of a boy overdue for a haircut; his ready smile revealed a gap between his front teeth that was as winningly boyish as his tousled hair, but as I watched him field questions, I noticed that Gabe Vickers's easy smile never quite reached his cool and assessing grey eyes.

When he spotted Zack, Gabe wrapped up the interview he was giving and approached. As Zack introduced us, Gabe took Taylor's hand. "I was hoping you'd be here this morning," he said. "You and I didn't have much time to talk in New York. We'll have time to come to know each other while I'm here."

A faint flush rose from Taylor's neck to her face. "I'd like that," she said.

"So would I," Gabe said, and then he turned his attention to me. Political insiders use the term *royal jelly* to refer to the intangible element that marks those born to be leaders. In all the years I had been politically active, I met two men and two women with the uncanny ability to draw people into their orbit and direct them wherever he or she wanted them to go. Gabe Vickers wasn't a politician, but he had the royal jelly, and for several seconds too long, I stood with his hand in mine, struck by the aura of power around him. When Zack noticed, he cleared his throat. "Gabe, I can see by all this activity at Living Skies that your team is already hard at work."

Gabe's response was casual but authoritative. "Abe Lincoln said, 'If I had nine hours to chop down a tree, I'd spend the first six sharpening my ax.' The same logic applies to the film industry. Every hour we spend in pre-production saves us countless hours and a whack of money down the line."

"'Measure twice, cut once' is solid advice in every field," I said.

Gabe's eyes met mine. "Exactly," he said. "If you cut a piece of fabric improperly, it's ruined. Pre-production is when we design every step of the film. If it's not done properly, all we can do is salvage what we've lost." His attention shifted back to Taylor. "You're a visual artist," he said. "You're lucky. You get to work on a clean canvas—no need to cover up past mistakes."

Before Taylor had a chance to respond, an assistant summoned Gabe. His eyes remained fixed on Taylor. "I have to take off, but let's talk again. I'm interested in learning how it feels to have as many chances as you need to get it right."

The three of us watched as Gabe strode out of hearing range, and then Zack gave me a lopsided grin. "So, what just happened?" he said.

"I think I learned how Gabe Vickers can put together the financing for a multimillion-dollar movie without breaking a sweat," I said. "If you're concerned about our chequing account or my virtue, don't leave me alone with him."

Zack grinned, but Taylor seemed perplexed. "He *is* compelling," she said.

"I didn't realize you'd met Gabe in New York," I said.

"He was in Vale's dressing room when Roy took me backstage to introduce us. You and Dad were still talking to the actor who played Ursula's mother. I was only with Gabe for a few minutes, but he left an impression."

"Good or bad?" Zack said.

Taylor still seemed puzzled. "I don't know," she said. "I just knew he was a person I'd never forget."

During pre-production, Gabe flew back and forth to New York weekly. It was a punishing schedule. When I suggested that a barbecue with our family might offer Gabe a respite, Zack, usually the most hospitable of men, vetoed the idea.

I was surprised. "Why not?"

"I don't like him."

"He seemed pleasant enough when we talked to him at the production office's opening."

"The next time I saw Gabe Vickers, he didn't seem so pleasant. He invited me to lunch, and after we'd finished our Arctic char, he signalled to the server to bring the bill. Then he told me he had distinctive sexual preferences and asked for the contact information for someone who could hook him up."

"Wow. Did he tell you what he's into?"

"No, and in my experience, sometimes it's better not to know specifics if you're going to have future dealings with the guy. Anyway, I deliberated for a nanosecond. Gabe reminded me that, given his role in bringing the production of a major film to the studios in Regina, discretion was essential, and I gave him the number of someone who might be able to help him. We sealed the deal with a manly handshake, and I slunk away with my tail between my legs like a beaten dog."

"Don't be hard on yourself," I said. "People like Gabe have a way of knowing which button to push. And he *did* hit the right button. *The Happiest Girl* is going to be marketed as a family movie. Rumours about kinky sex would be bad optics in the eyes of the investors and the general public. But you're right about not inviting him to the house. Let's keep things strictly business with Gabe Vickers."

The following weeks were filled with beginnings and endings. Zack and I both campaigned for mayoralty candidate Lydia Mah, and for a slate of progressive candidates for city council. On election night, Lydia and most of the candidates we supported for city council won, and we celebrated their victory and Zack's liberation from his tenure as mayor.

During the first week in November, Roy Brodnitz and Ainsley Blair arrived in Regina to begin working with the dancers whose movements would be used for the animation of *The Happiest Girl*. The same dancers were also performing in an event Roy and Ainsley were co-hosting to honour Zephyr Winslow. Both of them had grown up in Regina, and Zephyr Winslow had been their dance teacher and mentor before they left the city twenty-five years earlier to begin their careers in New York.

Celebrating Zephyr was taking place the evening of Friday, December 1. Zack, Taylor, and I were planning to meet Roy there and pick up our relationship where it had left off in June. Seemingly, the universe was unfolding as it should, but on the evening of November 30, Roy called, his voice quietly urgent, and said there was something he needed to speak with me about privately. We agreed to meet at my home the next morning when Zack would be in court and Taylor would be at an anatomy class she had enrolled in at the university.

As I arranged the coffee tray for Roy's visit that morning, I was intrigued but not concerned. I was almost certain I knew what he wanted to discuss. Taylor was quickly establishing a reputation as an artist worth watching, and from the moment they met, she and Roy knew they were kindred spirits. Roy ruefully acknowledged that Taylor had "claimed him with a look," and after we returned to Regina, they had stayed in touch.

When, one night at dinner, Taylor casually mentioned that she and Roy were discussing the possibility of her studying in New York, Zack and I exchanged a brief worried glance but offered encouragement. We were a close family, and the idea of Taylor moving away was not easy, but she was dedicated to her work, and Zack and I had been preparing ourselves to accept the inevitable.

Roy arrived at our front door promptly at 10:30. He was a strikingly handsome man in his early forties, mid-height and lean, with deep-set blue-grey eyes, a flawless complexion, and sculpted features. Moving with the lithe grace of the dancer he had always been, Roy removed his watch cap, jacket, and all-weather brogans and slipped into the pair of moccasins he'd brought in his messenger bag.

After I hung up his coat, I held out my arms in greeting. Roy took my hands in his. "I've been looking forward to this," he said.

"So have I," I said. "Come inside. That wind is nasty."

He shuddered. "Tell me about it. I walked here from the hotel."

"I'm impressed," I said. "I have a fire going in the family room. It's just off the kitchen. Why don't you thaw out while I get our coffee?"

"Sounds inviting," Roy said, but it was clear his mind was elsewhere. He had moved towards the painting on the wall facing the door. "Sally Love?" he said.

"You have a good eye," I said. "That *is* Sally's. Given the family connection, we own a number of her paintings, but that one has a special place in my heart. She painted it the summer Des took her to the Saugeen Reserve on Lake Huron. The women there make decorative boxes out of birchbark and porcupine quills, and Des wanted Sally to see the workmanship. The box they brought back for me had the pattern of a loon family on the lid. I still treasure it."

Roy half turned, his gaze intense. He looked like a man about to say something, but when he remained silent, I carried on. "Sally and Des experienced something remarkable that day. They were sitting on a hillside overlooking the lake when a band of wild horses streaked down the hill, heading for the water. The horses were only a few metres away from them. Sally said their hooves barely touched the ground, and their coats were so black they were almost blue." I smiled. "She called that painting *Flying Blue Horses*," I said. "Sally was never big on titles."

"How old was she?"

"The summer she made the painting?" The memory of what came after that time was painful, and I hesitated before answering. "It was the year before Des had his stroke," I said finally. "Sally would have been twelve."

Roy moved closer to the painting. "Twelve," he said softly. "That's incredible."

"It is," I said. "And, as you know, Taylor inherited that talent. I had three children of my own when I adopted her. I was confident about my parenting skills, but raising a child like Taylor has been uncharted territory for me. Luckily, Sally's family and mine had cottages next to each other when we were growing up, and I'd watched how Des was with Sally."

"He was a good father?"

I nodded. "The best," I said. "He knew exactly what Sally needed, and he gave it to her."

"What did she need?"

"The things all kids need—love, family jokes, knowing that someone who cherishes them is always there, ready to answer questions and cheer them on when they're afraid to jump off the high board."

"Encouraging kids to take the leap must be tough for a parent," Roy said.

"It is, especially for someone like me, who prefers safe harbours, but Sally was always a risk-taker. Years later, when I read that Karl Wallenda, the tightrope walker, said that being on the wire is life; the rest is waiting, I thought of Sally."

Roy's smile was thin. "Not long after he said that, Wallenda fell to his death."

"That doesn't change what he believed," I said. "Sally needed the high wire too, and Des was able to stand back and urge her on."

"And you've been able to do that with Taylor?"

"Not always," I said. "But Taylor thrives in spite of me. Come see for yourself. She wanted me to show you her work when she wasn't around. She thought you'd find it easier to focus if you were on your own." I led Roy down the hall into the guest room I used as an office. One of the walls was filled with pieces Taylor had made as she was growing up. I drew Roy's attention to a framed drawing of hula dancers with spiky eyelashes and corkscrew, shoulder-length curls, bumping grass skirts against one another. "Taylor was four when she did this," I said. "Sally said she knew as soon as she saw the drawing that Taylor's life would be making art. She had left Taylor with her father years before, but she was finally ready to be there for Taylor the way Des had been there for her." I swallowed hard. "It wasn't to be," I said.

Roy touched my arm. "But we carry on," he said.

"Because there's no alternative." I took a deep breath. "Now for something completely different." I pointed to a poster in comic book format that Taylor had made when she was in Grade Four. "This one definitely has a narrative," Roy said.

"It does. The Grade Four students at all Regina's public schools had to draw a picture depicting an event in the province's history. This is Taylor's illustration of Mouseland," I said. "Tommy Douglas's story. You're a Saskatchewan boy. You must know it."

Roy raised an eyebrow. "I've lived in New York for twenty-five years," he said. "I could use a refresher."

"Okay," I said. "But Tommy Douglas tells it better. Once upon a time, there was a country called Mouseland. The mice of Mouseland had always been told that only cats had the right to govern them. There were two different factions of cats—sometimes one faction governed; sometimes the other, but whatever faction was in office, the mice suffered. One day, a particularly smart little mouse said, 'Maybe it's time for us mice to take charge of Mouseland.' The cats called him a Bolshevik and threw him into jail. The mouse was philosophical. 'You can lock up a mouse or a person,' he said, 'but you can't lock up an idea.'"

"That's a great line," Roy said. "But Taylor doesn't strike me as political."

"She's not," I said. "But she chose our family's old friend Howard Dowhanuik as her honorary uncle. He was premier of this province for over a decade, and he took his honorary uncle duties seriously. He must have told Taylor that story fifty times. I'm not sure she totally grasped the political message, but she liked the mice and the cats."

Each panel of Taylor's illustration was dense with action, and Roy was rapt as he leaned in and narrowed his eyes to examine them. "Taylor didn't just dash this off," he said. "There's real precision here."

"She won a plaque for that poster," I said. "Our MLA presented it in the rotunda of the legislature. Unfortunately, our MLA was a cat, but it was still a nice moment."

We both laughed and continued the tour. As an older child, Taylor had made many striking pieces of art. Her portrait of the late twin sister of our daughter-in-law, Maisie, at the age of six always moved me. Roy examined each piece with care, but I had saved the work I was sure would resonate most strongly with him for last. Taylor had titled it *Two Painters*.

The scene was an artist's studio, with a floor-to-ceiling window that bathed the subjects in cool, atmospheric, and almost silvery light. The artists had their backs to each other. Both were barefoot. Both wore denim cut-off shorts and men's shirts with rolled-up sleeves. Their bodies, long-limbed and graceful, had the same lines, although Sally's body was more muscular. Both women had their hair tied back from their faces: Sally's blond hair was knotted loosely at her neck; Taylor's dark hair was in a ponytail.

Physically and in their total absorption in the work before them, the kinship between Sally and Taylor was apparent, and yet there was no connection between them. It was clear that, despite their proximity, each woman felt that she was the sole occupant of the space in which she found herself. Propped on an easel between the two women was one of Des Love's bright, joyous abstracts.

"The way Taylor uses her grandfather's canvas to link Sally and her together is a nice touch," Roy said.

"It is," I agreed. "But Des's abstract wasn't part of the original work."

Roy frowned. "What *was* there?"

"Space," I said.

He took a step back to get a wider perspective. "That's a large area," he said.

"It is," I said, "and the space gnawed at me because of what it revealed about Taylor's feelings towards her mother. Taylor told me once that making art allows her to see what she's been thinking all along,"

"And the space showed she felt alienated from Sally," Roy said. "But ultimately she did fill that space."

"She did, and it was a watershed in her relationship with her mother. When Taylor first came to live with my kids and me, she ached for Sally. Not long before she died, Sally gave me one of her paintings. Taylor used to disappear into the room where I'd hung the painting and trace its lines with her finger. She said she felt happy when she touched something her mother had made."

"That's heartbreaking."

"It was, but when Taylor began painting seriously, she wanted to learn more about her mother and, of course, there was plenty about Sally online." My voice was tight.

"That must have been terrible for her," Roy said. "The first time I typed in Desmond Love's name on my laptop and hit Search, the floodgates opened. There wasn't much about Des, but there was certainly plenty about Sally's private life, and it was all salacious."

"No thirteen-year-old wants to think about a parent as a sexual being," I said, "and Sally's affairs with both men and women were catnip for the tabloids. But seeing the stories wasn't the worst of it. There was a TV interview that really tore Taylor apart. The journalist asked Sally if, in retrospect, she felt that leaving her husband and three-month-old baby had been too high a price to pay for her career. Sally appeared genuinely surprised at the question. She said she left her husband and child because family life was choking her, and that before she left the marriage, she destroyed every painting she'd made after Taylor was born. When the interviewer asked about her string of lovers, Sally shrugged and said that she did her best work when she had an interesting partner, and when the partner was no longer interesting, she moved along."

Roy winced. His emotions were unguarded, flying across his face with unnerving transparency. "Why would she say that publicly?"

"Because it was the truth," I said. "Sally was never able to lie. I tried to explain it to Taylor, but I couldn't get through to her. She'd inherited a number of Sally's paintings. After Sally died, many of them were on loan for a retrospective of her work, but when the paintings were finally returned to us, we hung them. After Taylor saw that interview, she took all the paintings down and turned them so they faced the wall. Finally, we put them in storage."

"But Sally's paintings are hanging here now."

"They are. It took time, but Taylor finally realized that her mother did the best she could with the life she'd been given." I took a deep breath. "But that's a long story, and there was something you wanted to talk to me about. The coffee will be ready, and I made ginger scones."

"My favourite," Roy said.

"I noticed you headed straight for the ginger scones the day you took us to brunch at Loeb Boathouse," I said.

I set out the coffee tray on the table overlooking the creek that ran behind our house. On lazy days, Zack and I liked to have breakfast there. No matter what the season, the view of our yard and the creek was soothing, and that morning as the snow fell and the pine siskins fed on the fresh nyjer seeds in our feeder, I was at peace.

Roy had gone back to the hall to pick up his messenger bag. When we sat down, he placed the bag beside his chair and I filled our cups. We each took a scone and settled in. For a few moments, Roy was silent, gathering his thoughts. Finally, he said, "What are your feelings about Des?"

I had steeled myself for a discussion of Taylor's future, and this was a soft lob. "I loved him," I said. "Everybody did."

Roy leaned towards me. "How was Des with you, Joanne?"

Uncertain about the direction of the conversation, I chose my words carefully. "Whenever I saw Des, I was with Sally, so I was peripheral, but he was always kind. I tried to impress him once by saying I knew his paintings were abstracts but I wanted to know what they were 'about.' It was a dopey question, but Des considered it carefully. He told me his work is about the magic of paint. I remember his words so clearly. He said, 'I start with a blank canvas and then gradually where there was nothing, there's colour and movement and life.'"

"A profound answer," Roy said.

"It was," I agreed. "It made me feel that what I thought mattered. It wasn't a feeling I had often, and I was grateful. I still am."

Roy placed his cup in its saucer. "I believe you just gave me the opening I've been hoping for," he said. "Joanne, do you remember Des and Nina Love's house on Russell Hill Road in Toronto?"

"Of course. On school holidays I visited the Loves there, and when Taylor inherited the house, it was put up for sale. As her guardian, I signed the papers." I frowned. "Roy, that was fourteen years ago, is there a problem?"

"Not a problem, but something has been uncovered. The present homeowners have been in touch with me. They wanted to soundproof a room in their basement for their son's garage band. When the workmen were ripping out the walls, they discovered a safe." Roy opened his messenger bag, removed an old office folder, and placed it on the table between us. "There was nothing in the safe but this," he said. "When they read the material inside the folder, they tried to contact the real estate agent with whom they'd dealt when they purchased the property. He died ten years ago, so they got in touch with me."

"Why would they do that?"

Roy moved to the edge of his chair. "Because they'd read about the *Aurora* show and were hoping that, because I'd been a co-curator, I'd have your contact information. When they told me the nature of the material in the file, I suggested they send it to me, so I could hand it to you in person. The package arrived yesterday.

I felt the first stirrings of unease. "Roy, is there something in there that will affect Taylor?"

"This isn't about Taylor," Roy said. "This is about you." He paused, gauging my response, and when I didn't say anything he continued. "There is no easy way to say this, Joanne. It appears Desmond Love is your biological father."

My mind went blank. "That can't be true," I said. "My father was Douglas Ellard. He was a doctor—a general practitioner."

Roy voice was gentle. He tapped the folder with his fore-finger. "You need to look at this. If you'd prefer to be alone, I can let myself out."

"No, stay," I said. "It doesn't matter." And, in truth, at that moment, it didn't matter. I felt nothing. I opened the folder and began leafing through its contents. It contained five letters, all of which were addressed to Desmond Love at the Russell Hill Road address, and they were all from my father. He'd been dead for over forty years, and I seldom thought of him, but the image that flashed through my mind was sharp-edged. In it, he was the man I'd always known: tall and dark-haired with a cool, observant gaze and a smile that came seldom but was worth waiting for.

In many ways, my father was an old-fashioned man. Except when we were at the cottage, he always wore a busi-ness suit. The walls he'd built around his inner self were seldom breached. He rarely expressed his private thoughts in words, but on occasions when his feelings ran deep, my father handwrote a letter. The stationary he used never varied—always buff cotton-fibre with his monogram in block letters. He wrote his final letter to me the morning of my sixteenth birthday, two hours before he died of a heart attack while he was making rounds at the hospital. On his way to work, he'd dropped the letter off at the club where my birthday party was being held and asked that it be hand-delivered to me when I arrived.

Even the sight of my father's elegant cursive handwriting didn't move me. Together, the letters laid out the circum-stances that brought forth my existence, but as I read them through I was numb.

The gist was this: After years of a childless marriage, my father learned that he was sterile. My mother refused to adopt, saying she didn't want to bring a "stranger" into their lives, but my father was adamant. One way or another, there would be a baby in their house. My mother, knowing the results of artificial insemination were unpredictable, refused to waste months, perhaps years, in pursuit of something that might never happen. According to my father's letter to Des, she said she wanted "to get this over with as quickly as possible," so she could get on with her life. The idea of having intercourse with Desmond Love to produce the child my father wanted was hers. Des and my father had been best friends since they were boys, and my parents trusted him to keep the facts around my conception secret.

The next letter was dated four months later. In it, my father told Des that since the first trimester of my mother's pregnancy had been completed successfully, he was optimistic that there would be a child, and he thanked Des "for this great gift."

The third letter came three months after I was born. My father believed in dotting every *i* and crossing every *t*, and the letter reflected my father's determination that Desmond Love possess legal proof that he was my biological father. He thanked Des for submitting to the blood tests and said he had forwarded them to the lab for comparison with mine and that the attached results had been conclusive. The tests were in the file folder. One had my name on the patient line; one had Desmond Love's.

Even a cursory glance at the tests suggested they'd been exhaustive. I checked the dates on the forms. "Those tests are over fifty years old," I said. "The technology must have been rudimentary then. There could have been mistakes."

Roy's voice was calm. "I'm sure there were mistakes," he said. "But these results seem accurate. I looked online for information about paternity tests. DNA testing wasn't a possibility until the late '70s, but these tests were standard for the time. They allow doctors to compare blood markers that are inherited. It looks like the markers on the tests of your blood and Des Love's match up, and they show that you and Des share a relatively rare blood type—AB positive. You'll want to look into it yourself, of course . . ."

"I don't think so," I said. "My father was satisfied there was no mistake, and he was a physician." I picked up the fourth letter. It was written shortly after my second birthday. It was the longest and the hardest for me to read. The handwriting was erratic, and my father had clearly been distraught when he wrote it. He told Des that he had been concerned all along about my mother's attitude towards me, but he had held out hope that she would come to love me. She hadn't. My father said that I was becoming increasingly withdrawn and fearful, and he had finally realized that my best chance for a normal life would be if Des and his new wife, Nina, adopted me. The closing sentence of the note was uncharacteristically emotional. "My heart is breaking."

The final letter was written two days later, and it was very brief. "Caroline is concerned that if Joanne is with you, my loyalties will be 'divided even further.' She asks that I rescind the offer. I am deeply sorry for the pain I have caused you."

The arc of my early childhood in five letters. No matter how often I reread them, the facts didn't change. A new light had been shed on questions that had perplexed me for much of my life, but my thoughts were shifting too quickly for me to form answers. I slipped the letters and the medical reports back into the file folder. Roy Brodnitz was standing at the window watching the creek. When I joined him, he turned to face me.

"Joanne, I don't know you well. But even an outsider could understand that you lost something this morning. For what it's worth, I think when you're able to process this, you'll realize that you've gained something too."

"Zack claims it's always better to know than to not know," I said. "At the moment, I'm just dazed, but this news may explain some pieces of my life that have puzzled me."

"Anything you want to talk about?" Roy said.

"When this news sinks in, I'm guessing there'll be many things I'll want to talk about, but at the moment all I can think of is my decision to adopt Taylor. I have never for a second regretted it, but there were many reasons why taking on another child, especially a child who'd been through what Taylor had been through, could have made me back away. Money was tight in our house. My husband had died suddenly, and we hadn't given much thought to building a financial portfolio. All three of my children were still at home, and I was trying to finish my dissertation so I could get tenure. There was a lot on my plate, but I never hesitated because I was certain Taylor belonged with me."

"Yet you'd only met her a few times . . ."

"And I really knew nothing about her, but I felt this . . . *compulsion*."

"That's a strong word," Roy said.

"The emotion was strong. Now that I've learned that Des was my biological father, I'm wondering if what I felt for Taylor was primal—some sort of blood connection."

"I've been thinking about the blood tie too," Roy said. "When you told me about Des taking Sally to a place where they saw flying blue horses together and then coming back with a token gift for you, I was afraid that when you learned Des was your father, you might feel life had cheated you."

"Because Sally got the magic and I got the porcupine quill box?" I said.

Roy smiled. "Something like that," he said. "But just now when I saw your face as you talked about Taylor, I knew that the sister left behind was the lucky one."

My eyes filled. "The sister left behind knows that too," I said. "It's just going to take her a while to get her head around the rest."

CHAPTER

2

As the two of us stood side by side looking out at the creek behind my house, Roy Brodnitz displayed a capacity for stillness that I welcomed. Sensing my need for calm, he was silent until he apparently felt the time had come to draw me out.

When a neighbour in a slick winter jogging outfit ran along the bike path with her dogs, Roy stepped closer to the window. "Vizslas," he said. "They're great dogs."

"Our dogs are certainly fond of Bela and Zoltan," I said.

Roy laughed softly. "Distinguished Hungarian names for members of a distinguished Hungarian breed."

"Not many people are familiar with Vizslas."

"Lev-Aaron and I owned one," Roy said. "Seeing Bela and Zoltan brings back some happy memories."

"Bela and Zoltan's owner usually just runs them up to the Elphinstone Bridge," I said. "You and I could bundle up and you could get acquainted with the Vizslas when they make their way back. I could use a walk. I'm sure our dogs could too."

Zack and I own a mastiff and a bouvier. Pantera and Esme's daily routine does not include a late-morning walk, but as I took their leashes from the hooks by the back door, they showed they were adaptable.

The wind had died down, and Roy and I weren't the only ones opting for fresh air and sunshine. Our house is five minutes from one of the best sledding hills in the city. That morning the hill was alive with preschoolers in snow gear, cheeks rosy, voices shrill with excitement as they streaked down the hill, while their parents, faces taut with worry and pride, kept watch.

Roy and I were enjoying the postcard perfection of the scene when Bela, Zoltan, and their owner returned. As Roy and the owner exchanged Vizsla stories, the ache in the back of my neck that signalled an oncoming headache disappeared. Chatting about dogs with friends was part of the life I had always known. By the time Roy and I headed home, I wasn't quite on firm ground, but I was getting my footing.

As I filled the dogs' water dishes, Roy stayed by the back door, his eyes on me. "Do you want me to take off?" he said finally.

"Why don't you stay for lunch," I said. "I have some lentil soup in the fridge."

"You're sure you wouldn't rather be alone."

"I'm sure. My grandmother Ellard used to say that I was a girl who enjoyed her own company." I felt a jab of pain. "I guess technically she never really was my grandmother, but whatever the case, this is a day when I could use a friend."

Roy removed his boots and jacket. "I'm here," he said. "Joanne, did you love your grandmother?"

I took out the lentil soup, poured it into a pot on the stove, and ignited the gas under it. "I loved her very much," I said. "And she loved me."

"Then remember the love, and forget the rest," Roy said.

"Don't throw the baby out with the bathwater," I said.

Roy nodded. "Right. Now, how can I help with lunch?"

I pointed towards the pot. "Soup's on," I said, "but if you want to get the dog drool off your hands, the guest bathroom is the first door to your right as you go down the hall."

Over lunch, I told Roy that I'd assumed that the reason he'd wanted to speak with me alone that morning was to suggest that Taylor study in New York. During her Grade Twelve year, our daughter had formed a plan: After graduation, she would spend the summer at the lake with us, painting, swimming, and savouring the lazy days with her long-time friends, Gracie Falconer and Isobel Wainberg, before the three of them went their separate ways to attend university. In September, Gracie was to go to Notre Dame in South Bend, Indiana, on a basketball scholarship; Isobel was heading to Johns Hopkins in Baltimore for pre-med; and Taylor planned to move to Toronto, to share a duplex with her on-again, off-again beau, Declan Hunter, and to attend art school at OCAD University. The plan seemed firmly in place, but when we returned from New York, our daughter informed us she'd decided she needed a year to consider her next move.

Roy wasn't surprised when I told him about my assumption. "Taylor and I have been discussing her future," he said. "So far all she's told me is what she *doesn't* want to do. There are great art schools in New York, but I don't think enrolling as a full-time student is really the answer for her."

"You and Ainsley Blair went to New York together when you were seventeen," I said. "How did you two get started?"

Roy looked sheepish. "By enrolling full-time in a dance school," he said.

I raised an eyebrow. "Do as I say, not as I do?"

"Point taken," Roy said. "But Taylor is a special case. The school Ainsley and I went to wasn't one of the top ten, but neither were we. Like all the students in our classes, Ainsley and I had talent and ambition. But everyone knew it would be years, if ever, before our dreams were realized. Taylor has already achieved what her would-be classmates are still dreaming of."

"And her fellow students would resent her."

Roy shrugged. "It's human nature. Zephyr Winslow has quotations plastered all over the walls of her studio. One of them always stuck with me: 'Fame is a prize that burns the winner.' Taylor's work is already selling to collectors. She's extraordinarily gifted. She's young; she's beautiful; she's Desmond Love's granddaughter and Sally Love's daughter. She's the whole package, and that will make her a target of envy. From what I've read about Sally, she could shrug off the backbiting. But I don't think Taylor has developed a protective layer."

"That's because she never had to," I said. "From the moment I adopted her, I've tried to shield her. The psychiatrist with whom my new daughter and I spent many hours said Taylor had suffered 'an appalling and crushing series of traumas,' and recommended counselling, reassurance, routine, and constant reinforcement of the fact that her new family wasn't going anywhere without her."

"And that worked," Roy said.

"It did, but building trust takes a long time. On Taylor's first day of kindergarten, the children were asked to make a picture of their family. Taylor drew a detailed picture of herself—very small and absolutely alone. I stuck the drawing to the fridge door with a magnet the way I always did with my children's work. At the end of kindergarten, each child in Taylor's class was supposed to draw a picture of him or herself ready for Grade One. Taylor drew another very detailed picture of herself, but this time, she dominated the page and Mieka, her big sister, and Peter and Angus, her brothers, and I were gathered around her. The day I stuck that drawing to our refrigerator door was one of the best days of my life."

When we finished lunch, Roy turned on his phone, checked the messages, and frowned. "There's a problem with one of the dancers. Do you mind if I call Ainsley?"

"Not at all," I said.

Roy made his call in the family room and I cleared away the dishes. It wasn't long before he came back. "I'm going to have to take off," he said. "Are you okay?"

"I am," I said. "Roy, this has been a difficult morning for me. I hope you know how grateful I am that you were here."

"Any time you want to talk, text me," he said. "And I'll see you tonight at the celebration for Zephyr Winslow."

"I'd forgotten about that."

"Considering the news you're dealing with, you might want to skip it," Roy said. "And it won't be our only chance to talk. I'm going to be in town for a while."

"How long is 'a while'?"

"Production will take about sixty days. Ainsley stays till post-production is finished, and she likes having me around. Depending on how other projects pan out, I may be here till summer."

"Good news for the Shreve family," I said. "I mean that, Roy. I'm glad for all of us that you'll be part of our lives."

After Roy left, the house suddenly seemed empty. I'm a twenty-first-century urban woman, but Catherine Parr Traill's *The Canadian Settlers' Guide* written in 1854 contains advice that has carried me through more occasions than I can count. "In cases of emergency," Catherine says, "it is folly to fold up one's hands and sit down to bewail in abject terror: It is better to be up and doing." Discovering that Desmond Love was my biological father was hardly an emergency, and bewailing in abject terror has never been my style, but I am a big fan of being up and doing.

Zack, Taylor, and I were driving out to the country the next day to have lunch and choose Christmas trees with Mieka and Peter and their families. Carrying the tree lights and ornaments in from the garage was exactly the kind of mindless task I needed, and in an hour, I had the ornaments unpacked, the tree lights tested, and everything laid out on a trestle table in the family room.

When I picked up the plastic bag containing the photo ornaments of Taylor—one a year since she'd joined our family—I remembered that I hadn't placed this year's photo in the ornament I'd bought at a craft fair. Both were on the desk in my office. The ornament was simple—a square frame of reclaimed wood with a loop of hunter-green velvet ribbon to attach it to the tree. Zack had taken the photo of Taylor at the lake the previous August. Tanned and dreamy-eyed, her dark hair still wetly glistening from a swim, our daughter was stretched out in a red-and-orange striped hammock, a glorious girl of summer.

I cut the photo to fit the frame, slid it into place, and returned to the family room. As I examined the ornament to make sure Taylor's photo was centred, my mind was flooded by memories of other summers—those I'd spent with the complex, enviable girl I never knew was my sister and the gifted man who, until that morning, I had believed was peripheral to my life.

I had no idea how long I'd been sitting on the couch lost in the remembrance of things past, with Esme and Pantera snoozing on the rug in front of the fireplace, when Zack wheeled into the room. His sudden presence was a shock, and I leapt to my feet. "You're home," I said, and my tone was not welcoming.

Zack chuckled. "Not quite the greeting I hoped for, but yes, I am home. Like the proverbial bad penny, I always turn up." He bent to give the dogs a head scratch. "However, I am early. Madam Justice Gorges came down with the flu, so court was adjourned." He wheeled closer, looked at me, and frowned. "Are you okay?"

I tried to shake myself out of my reverie. "Of course," I said. "What made you think I wasn't?"

"I don't know. Maybe it's just that I don't remember ever coming into a room and finding you doing nothing."

"When she was little, Taylor used to say, 'I'm not doing nothing. I'm thinking.'"

"Fair enough," Zack said. "I'll try again. Is there something special on your mind?"

"Yes," I said. "As a matter of fact, there is."

I told the story of Roy Brodnitz's visit that morning without digression or unnecessary detail. Zack was the most active listener I'd ever known. He soaked up information, taking everything in without questions or the need for clarification. The folder discovered in the safe hidden in the basement was still on the table where Roy and I had taken our coffee. I brought it to Zack. He was methodical as he read through the medical reports and my father's letters. When he'd finished, he replaced everything in the file and handed it back to me.

"This would shake anybody," he said.

I nodded. "When I read it, I felt as if I'd been caught in a riptide," I said.

Zack's voice was deep and comforting. "You've always been a strong swimmer, Jo." He turned his chair so it was parallel to the couch, transferred his body onto it, and said, "Come join me for a while."

For a few minutes we sat close, content just to watch the flames jump and flicker in the fireplace. Finally, Zack broke the silence. "So where do we go from here?" he said.

"Roy says that I'll come to see this as a gain rather than a loss."

Zack began massaging the back of my neck. "I could bounce a dime off those muscles," he said. "I take it that at the moment, balancing gains and losses is tough slogging."

"Boy is it ever," I said. "As far as family goes, I didn't have much to lose. I was a boarder at Bishop Lambeth School from the time I was six till I went to university, so I don't have many memories of my parents. What I remember of my mother was her never-empty highball glass, her over-flowing ashtray, and her non-stop diatribe about how I'd ruined her life. Oddly enough, what I remember most about my father is his office. It was at the front of their house across the hall from the waiting and examining rooms."

"You never mentioned that your father's office was in your home."

I nodded. "My grandfather was a doctor too, and he prac-tised in that same space. When I close my eyes, I can still see my father's desk and his chair. On the wall behind his desk were his medical degree from the University of Toronto, a framed article by Sir William Osler entitled 'Chauvinism in Medicine,' and a reproduction of a painting called *The Doctor* by Sir Luke Fildes. The painting was of a doctor examining a dying child while the child's parents looked on. I always struggled not to cry when I looked at it. When I told my father that, he said the painting made him want to cry too."

"Sounds like a good guy," Zack said. "I wish I'd known him."

"I wish I'd known him better," I said. "I'd just started Grade Eleven when he died, and, of course, I was a boarder. The only time I really spent time with my father was when he came up to the lake to be with my Grandmother Ellard and me in August. He taught me how to canoe and swim, and he grew cherry tomatoes—the kind you like. When I woke up in the morning at the lake, there was always a little bowl of them by my place at the table. He died not long after Des. He and Des had been best friends since they were boys. I've always thought the pain of losing Des killed my father. Anyway, that's about it for my parents."

Zack frowned. "It doesn't make sense. Your father wanted a child so much, and then . . ."

"And then he was absent for most of my life," I said. "Why he abandoned me has nagged at me since I started at Bishop Lambeth. At the end of classes my first day, the other girls were getting ready to go home. I started to get ready too, and one of the teachers took me aside and explained that I was a boarder and that meant that Bishop Lambeth was my home now."

"My God. That's terrible. Hadn't someone told you beforehand?"

"Probably someone did," I said, "and I just didn't understand. Anyway, for the next thirteen years Bishop Lambeth *was* my home. The school was eight blocks from our house on Walmer Road. I once overheard a teacher refer to me once as 'one of those orphans with families.' That stung."

Zack touched my cheek. "Jo, I'm sorry."

"Don't be," I said. A wave of sadness swelled inside me, but I swallowed it down. "I have a great life. No regrets, including my time at Bishop Lambeth. It was a fine school, and given the situation with my parents, it was probably the best place for me. Learning about Des just opened a door I thought I'd closed long ago."

A log sputtered and rolled towards the hearth. I rose, took the poker from the fireplace toolset, and pushed the log back into place.

"Why don't you come back here, so we can talk some more," Zack said.

I curled up on the couch with his arms around me. "This feels good," I said. "But I don't have much more to say. One of the things that drew me to you from the moment we met was your refusal to speculate about 'what ifs.'"

"That's because speculating about what might have been is pointless. People spend their lives lining up all their dominoes in a pattern they're certain will get them where they want to go, and when they're sure everything is in place, Fate comes along and topples the first domino in the line. After that, the sequence continues until everything's knocked down."

"So we start again?" I said.

"That's one option," Zack said. "But if you're smart, you take a look at where all those fallen dominoes have taken you. Sometimes what you end up with is better than what you planned. Look at me. My plan was to become an ace pitcher for a major league baseball team, but after I was sure I'd lined up all my dominoes, I got hit by a drunk driver on my way home from practice and ended up in a wheelchair. So instead of spending every waking hour perfecting my curveball, I went to law school, discovered law is a kick-ass profession, married you, and adopted Taylor. If I'd hung around after practice that night, or if somebody had taken the drunk's car keys away and poured him into a cab, I might have ended up with the life I'd planned, and I would have missed out on what we have."

It was a nice moment, but when I leaned in to kiss my husband, Pantera emitted a long, curiously mellifluous and potent fart. Zack and I groaned and sprang apart. "Want to reconsider your choice?" I said.

"Nope," Zack said. "I'll stick with what we have, but let's get out of here while we can still breathe."

We had decided it would be best if Taylor and I were alone when I told her the news. Zack was in the shower, and Taylor and I were sitting at the kitchen table waiting for the pizza we'd ordered for dinner when I relayed the story about Roy Brodnitz's visit that morning. Like Zack, our daughter listened without question or comment. When I handed her the file, she read the contents carefully, then closed the folder, and looked at me. "There's no possibility of a mistake, is there?" she said.

I shook my head. "No," I said. "Des was my father, so that makes Sally my half-sister and you my niece."

Taylor's smile was ironic. "And your daughter."

I laughed. "Right, and after that, it gets complicated, but nothing fundamental has changed."

"Except now you and I know that we have the same DNA—or at least some of the same DNA." Taylor held out her hand and led me to the living room. A painting Sally had given me not long before she died hung over a low, paint-splattered wooden worktable that had been in her last studio.

Standing so close that our bodies touched, Taylor and I gazed at the painting. "Did I ever tell you about the night Sally delivered this to my house?" I said.

"Yes, but tell me again," Taylor said. "I want to hear all the stories about you and Sally and Des again."

"Okay," I said. "Well, it was bitterly cold. I was in the kitchen working on a lecture for my Political Science 101 class, and suddenly Sally was there with this huge packing case. She ripped it open, propped the painting against the wall, and said, 'It's called *Perfect Circles*. So what do you think?'"

"What *did* you think?" Taylor said.

"I didn't think anything. I was mesmerized," I said. I gazed at the painting. "I still am."

The scene was of a tea party in the clearing down by the water at the Loves' summer cottage. The picture was suffused with summer light, that soft incandescence that comes when heat turns rain to mist. In the foreground there was a round table covered with a snowy cloth. On either side of the table was a wooden chair painted dark green. Nina Love sat in one of the chairs. The eyelet sundress she wore was the colour of a new fern, and her skin was translucent. The light seemed to come through her flesh the way it does through fine china. She was in profile, and the dark curve of her hair balanced exactly the pale line of her features: yin and yang. Across the table from her sat a girl of fifteen, very tanned in a two-piece bathing suit that did nothing to hide a soft layer of baby fat. The girl's braided hair was bleached fair by the sun. Her expression as she watched Nina's graceful hands tilt the Limoges teapot was rapt—and familiar. The girl's face was my own forty-five years earlier, and it glowed with admiration and love.

The woman and girl bending towards each other over the luminous white cloth seemed enclosed in a private world. In the distance beyond them, the lake, blue as cobalt, lapped the shore.

There were other figures in the picture, and I knew them too. Under the water, enclosed in a kind of bubble, were a man and a young girl. I could recall the slope of Desmond Love's shoulders and the sweep of his daughter's blond hair as she bent over the fantastic sandcastle they were building together in their own little world under the waves.

"Even now, when I look at this painting I can feel the heat and the endlessness of those summer days," I said. "Your mother told me *Perfect Circles* was the only painting she ever made of Nina. She said Nina was so beautiful she could almost forgive her."

"I hardly remember my grandmother," Taylor said. "But you do, don't you, Jo?"

"Nina was the centre of my world," I said. "Look at the expression on my face in the painting. Sally told me that the one good thing Nina did in her life was to love me. I've tried to hang on to that."

"Were you able to forget the rest?"

"You mean forget that she killed your grandfather and your mother and father? No. What Nina did to them was inhuman. But I've spent years trying to sort out the evil she did to them from the good she did for me." I pointed at the canvas with my forefinger and described a circle around Nina and me. "Taylor, if Nina hadn't given me a place in her perfect circle, I would have been lost. She was a monster, but she saved me."

Taylor bent towards the canvas and looked more closely at Nina's face. "I understand why Sally wanted to paint her—at least once. Nina's features are flawless, you know. The proportions are exactly right. How could she be so exquisite and so twisted inside?" Taylor shook her head. "There's so much I don't understand."

"Same here," I said.

Taylor put her arm around me and snuggled in. The warmth of her young body was comforting. For a few minutes, the only sounds in the room came from the traffic on our street. The air was heavy with the words my daughter and I longed to say to each other, but before we could begin, the doorbell rang. The words would have to remain unsaid. The pizza man was waiting.

CHAPTER

3

The invitation to *Celebrating Zephyr* had suggested that guests wear "festive attire"—a new dress code category for me, but Google was helpful, directing me to a site that explained the words *festive attire* gave guests "the go-ahead to have fun and play with their look, especially with their accessories."

I've never had fun playing with my look, so I slipped into what the festive attire site referred to as my "Go-To Little Black Dress," added my favourite Navajo silver and turquoise dangly earrings and bracelet, picked up my black clutch, and turned my attention to Zack.

His closet door was open and he was staring meditatively at his tie rack. "How formal is this shindig, anyway?" he said.

"What you're wearing is fine," I said. "A charcoal suit and a white shirt is always acceptable, but the invitation called for 'festive attire.' You're supposed to play with your look and have fun with your accessories."

Zack made a moue of disbelief, spun his tie rack, and selected a silk tie with a swirl of colours that evoked

Scheherazade. He tied it in a Windsor knot, tucked in a matching pocket square, and turned his chair to me. "Good to go?" he said.

"Dazzling," I said.

Taylor always instinctively knew how to dress for an occasion. That night she chose fitted black cigarette pants, a tailored white-silk man-style shirt, hot-pink ankle boots with side zippers and three sets of buckles, and a vintage black-and-white beaded crossbody bag she'd found at a flea market when we were in New York.

Celebrating Zephyr was being held in Sound Stage 1—at 15,000 square feet, the largest of the three sound stages of the Saskatchewan Film Production Studios on College Avenue. As Zack slowed at the building's entrance, Taylor pointed to a banner on the building that read, "Welcome, *The Happiest Girl*!!!"

"There's your sign, Dad," she said.

Zack glanced at it and beamed. "That never gets old," he said, and he had every right to be pleased about the banner which had gone up last January. When his term as mayor ended, Zack had not accomplished everything he'd set out to do, but he had resurrected the moribund Saskatchewan Film Production Studios, and that was good news for the city.

Fifteen years earlier, the fine arts building of the old University of Regina campus had been gutted and reconstructed as a movie and TV studio facility. The production companies came, lured by a lucrative provincial tax credit, a pool of talented people eager to work, and Regina's relatively low cost of living. For almost a decade, the facility flourished, producing B movies and TV series. But when a new and conservative provincial government was elected, it scrapped the tax credit and the bubble burst. Production companies moved to more fiscally hospitable provinces, and the shining, state-of-the art Saskatchewan Film Production Studios became a white elephant.

As mayor, Zack had lobbied aggressively to bring movie making back to the city. When first Caritas, a small production company that had flourished in Regina then decamped, moved back into its old offices, followed in short order by Living Skies, my husband had been one happy guy. The sound stages were once again humming with activity. Film jobs were green and lucrative, and now the provincial government was being pressed to restore the tax credit. The future of the Saskatchewan film industry looked bright.

Throughout her life, Zephyr Winslow had been a tireless advocate and supporter of the arts. Zephyr's seventy-fifth birthday and the fiftieth anniversary of the founding of her dance studio coincided, and Roy and Ainsley had come up with the idea for an evening dedicated to celebrating her contributions to the culture of our city, and especially to the lives of her students. When he was mayor, Zack had pressed for something larger and splashier than a private gathering.

Tonight, after an evening of dazzling performances by dancers from *The Happiest Girl*, my husband's successor, Mayor Lydia Mah, would announce that in recognition of Zephyr Winslow's commitment to creating and sustaining a vibrant cultural life in our city, on the Monday of the May long weekend the Saskatchewan Film Production Studios would be officially renamed the Zephyr Winslow Studios. The occasion would be marked by a city-wide public celebration of the arts: dance, theatre, music, the written word, ceramics, drawing, painting, sculpture, printmaking, design, crafts, photography, filmmaking, architecture, and textile and conceptual art. It was exactly the celebration Zephyr deserved, and we were excited about tonight's public announcement. As soon as we parked, Taylor jumped out of the car, held out her arms, and twirled in a circle. "This is going to be such a great night," she said, "and, Jo, knowing you and I are really family just makes everything better."

Gabe Vickers met us at the entrance. He greeted us warmly, but his focus was solely on Taylor. "I've been waiting for you," he said. "I wanted to escort you to Sound Stage 1 on your first visit."

"That's very thoughtful," Taylor said. When she gave him her most dazzling dimpled smile, I felt a pang.

Gabe bowed his head in acknowledgement. His after-shave was distinctive and pleasant—woody, spicy, and fresh. "It's my pleasure. I know Roy and my wife will be delighted that you're joining us."

"I spent some time with Roy today," I said. "I'm hoping that when the celebration for Zephyr is over, Ainsley and I can get together."

"I'm sure she'd enjoy that too," Gabe said. "She's been here since the beginning of November, and between rehearsals and meetings with the artistic designers of the film, Ainsley's been putting in long hours."

"Well tonight will give us a chance to at least welcome her properly," Zack said. And with that, the four of us set off.

Our progress to the party was slow. It seemed all who were making their way to the sound stage wanted a word with either Gabe or Zack. I could tell from the set of my husband's jaw that he was eager to put some distance between Gabe Vickers and us, and when he spotted Nick Kovacs, his poker partner of close to three decades, Zack's face relaxed.

Nick was a rough-hewn, large-featured, burly man who had worked at his family's business, Kovacs Electric, after school and on weekends for as long as he could remember. He earned a diploma in electrical engineering from Saskatchewan Polytechnic, and during the halcyon days of the film indus-try, Nick had worked closely with lighting designers on films and TV shows. It was a first-rate apprenticeship, and even after the production companies left, Nick continued to learn. Kovacs Electric was now a large and successful company that provided lighting for film, theatre, rock and pop tours, corporate launches, TV, and industrial shows, and Nick was the lighting designer for *The Happiest Girl*.

Zack and Nick had spent the previous Wednesday night together with their usual cronies playing Texas Hold'em, but they greeted each other like long-lost brothers.

Nick had a transforming smile. He was a tough guy but when he smiled, he revealed an endearing sweetness. "I'm so glad the three of you are here to see this. We're doing the lighting for the show tonight, and you really are in for a terrific evening. Chloe and her aide are already in their seats waiting for the event to start."

"I take it Chloe is excited," I said.

"That's putting it mildly," Nick said. "A month ago, she drew a star around this date on her calendar, and the countdown was on. She had so much fun shopping for what to wear. There were two outfits she couldn't choose between, so we ended up buying them both."

Zack grinned. "You're setting the bar pretty high for the rest of us fathers."

"Chloe's the only child I have," Nick said. "I do whatever I can to make her as happy as she makes me."

"She is happy," Taylor said. "Every time I see Chloe, she gives me the loveliest smile."

"That smile of hers *is* something special, isn't it?" Nick said, and the pride in his voice was edged with pain. He glanced at his watch. "Time for me to make tracks. My crew will be wondering where I am."

"We'll pay special attention to the lighting," I said.

"Prepare to be impressed," Nick said. "An anonymous donor, who happens to be front and centre at tonight's event, poured some serious money into upgrading the equipment in this place. I'm like a kid in Toyland."

"The facilities *are* excellent. So are our crews," Gabe agreed. "Thanks to the anonymous donor and her extensive network of friends and former students, this production studio is equipped with the best of everything."

"Spread the word," Zack said. "Film companies are a boon for the city, and—"

Taylor had heard her father's spiel many times. As she finished his sentence, her expression was impish. "—they're good neighbours," she said.

We all laughed, but the camaraderie didn't last. A man, fit and well-dressed but clearly agitated, approached from behind us, grabbed Gabe's arm, and, oblivious to our presence, began blasting him. "You have to talk to your wife," he said. "My performance is on a par with that of anyone else in the company. Ainsley has replaced me in tonight's finale because she says I'm not projecting raw sexuality, that I'm grimacing. My ankle may be injured, but I'll do what it takes for the show."

Gabe's tone was caustic. "Has your contract been terminated, Shawn?"

Shawn appeared to be assessing whether Gabe's words were a threat. He narrowed his eyes and spat out a single-syllable response. "No," he said.

Gabe's lips formed a fraction of a smile. "Then you have no cause for complaint. You'll receive a paycheque, and as a model for a computer-generated image, there'll be no need for you to project raw sexuality. Face it, Shawn. You're getting old."

Gabe's assessment was unkind but accurate. Shawn was clearly a man who took meticulous care of himself, but age was making its inroads. His hair was thinning, and a delicate tracery of wrinkles fanned out from the corners of his mouth and eyes. He fought to control his voice. "I owe everything to Zephyr Winslow," he said. "Tonight is my chance to honour her."

"I doubt if watching you struggle to execute moves you're no longer capable of performing would make Zephyr's heart go pitter-pat," Gabe said. "The decision was Ainsley's, and I'm not going to ask her to change it."

Shawn's face was dark with anger. "You'd be smart to reconsider, Gabe. I know where you go when you need raw sexuality, and I'm in a sharing mood."

Gabe's features were impassive. He calmly formed his hand into a fist, drew back his arm, and punched, landing a solid blow on Shawn's nose. "Get out," he said quietly. "And think long and hard before you threaten me again." Blood was pouring from Shawn's nose, but he managed to turn. When he stumbled, Nick went after him, offered his arm for support, and led the injured man towards the door.

Stunned, Zack, Taylor, and I turned to watch the two men, but Gabe had no interest in denouement. He rubbed his fist with his palm. "No harm done," he said. When his phone rang, he glanced at the caller ID. "I have to take this," he said. "Have a pleasant evening." He took a pack of Camels from the inner pocket of his jacket and headed for the Exit sign on the east side of the hall. Apparently, it was time for a smoke break.

Zack began wheeling towards the entrance. "I'm going to check on Nick," he said. Zack had just reached the accessibility ramp when Nick came through the door.

The two of them returned together. Taylor saw the blood on Nick's shirt and took a tissue from her bag. She reached to wipe the blood off.

Nick took the tissue from her. "I'll take care of this," he said, "but thanks for offering."

Zack leaned forward in his chair. "Did you learn anything more about what just happened?"

Nick shook his head. "Shawn didn't say a word. When we got outside, a cab was dropping somebody off. He jumped in and that was it."

"What kind of guy is he?" Zack said.

"Shawn?" Nick shrugged. "Beats me. I've seen him at rehearsals, but I never even knew his name until just now."

"But when he was hurt, you went to him." Taylor said.

"And you reached out to rub the blood off my shirt," Nick said. "People help each other. It's what we do." He gave us one of his transforming smiles. "Now, I'd better get back to work."

A portion of Sound Stage 1 had been sectioned off for use as a rehearsal hall, and that night it was the site of the dance performances and party. When we arrived, the space was crowded with people enjoying a last drink before the dancing began. There were programs on a table by the door. I picked one up and Zack noticed my hands were shaking.

"Are you all right?" he said.

"I'm fine. It's been a long day, and that ugliness with Gabe Vickers got to me."

Taylor's face was pinched with concern. "You really are pale."

Zack narrowed his eyes to look at me more closely. "Taylor's right. You had to deal with some heavy news today; you don't need to be here tonight. Let's go home."

"You win," I said. "But, Taylor, you should stay. Roy wants you to see the performances, and Nick will be hurt if none of us can compliment him on his lighting. The program will only last about an hour and a half, and you can take a cab back to the house."

"If you're sure you're okay," Taylor said.

"I'm fine," I said. "So it's settled."

But as Robbie Burns said, "the best laid schemes o' mice an' men gang aft agley." Zephyr Winslow had spotted us. Her face alight with pleasure, she was gliding across the room towards us, graceful as a gazelle. Zack and I looked at each other. There was no way we could leave now. We were trapped.

In buttery leather flats, tailored tan silk slacks, and a draped champagne-coloured blouse the exact shade of her asymmetrical choppy bob, Zephyr was a head-turner. She held out her hands in greeting. "This is such a treat."

"It's our pleasure," Zack said, taking her hands in his. "Happy birthday, and happy anniversary of your dance studio. I'm glad the powers that be finally had the wit to acknowledge your incredible generosity to the arts community."

Zephyr's smile was sly. "And I'm glad that when you were mayor you kept the pressure on City Hall to acknowledge that the arts are an essential component of a civilized city."

"A recognition that was long overdue," Zack said smoothly, and with that we took our places in the first row of the two half moons of chairs that had been arranged for guests around the performance area.

I was delighted when Brock Poitras, the executive director of Zack's law firm and one of our closest friends, joined us. Brock had been a wide receiver for the Saskatchewan Roughriders before he earned his MBA, and Zack was clearly surprised to see the man with whom he most often talked sports at a celebration of dance. He held out his hand to Brock. "Hey, you're the last guy I expected to run into here."

"Margot handles Zephyr's legal affairs," Brock said, "and it's her sister's birthday, so she and the kids have gone to Wadena for the weekend."

Zephyr's hazel eyes danced. "And since Roy Brodnitz is going to be in town over the holidays, I thought he and

Brock might enjoy each other's company. Brock is single, and Roy has been alone long enough."

Zack guffawed. "You're being set up, Brock."

"Just doing what I can to make artists like Roy realize how much our city has to offer," Zephyr said primly, and then she laughed a dry, wicked laugh.

We chatted until the lights were dimmed, and Ainsley Blair and Roy, wearing the incomparably becoming clothing of the 1940s, walked hand in hand into the spotlight. Roy's style was Astaire breezy—white slacks, white sports jacket, bow tie, boutonnière, and white tap shoes. Ainsley was all sparkle—strawberry blond curls held in place by a sequined headband, sequined white pumps, a glittering bolero, and a filmy chiffon skirt.

She was riveting. It was hard to believe she was the same woman we'd met briefly in New York in June. She and Roy had been mulling over new projects, and Ainsley had been pleasant but preoccupied. Without makeup, wearing blue jeans, a faded Duran Duran T-shirt, and runners, her pony-tail pulled through the opening of a Mets baseball cap, Ainsley was unremarkable; but the spotlight seemed to draw something rare and lovely from her. It was as if she had become more brightly and beautifully alive.

Ainsley gave Roy an affectionate glance and stepped towards the audience. "As you can see, we are in the space we've been using as a rehearsal hall. Not much to look at: a wall of full-length mirroring, a sprung wood floor, a barre for exercises, lighting, and some AV equipment—just the bare bones. But add dancers, and this space becomes a window into other worlds.

"Tonight is a tribute to our amazing, unique, unforgettable, incredibly talented, and generous dance teacher, taskmaster, mentor, scold, and always faithful friend, Zephyr Winslow. Zephyr's life is about dance, not words, so you won't hear many words tonight, but you are going to see some amazing dancing.

"I'm Ainsley Blair and this is my dance partner of thirty years, Roy Brodnitz. We were fourteen when we met at Zephyr's studio, and we've been together ever since. Like every dancer you're about to see, we would not have been part of a single opening night if it weren't for Zephyr."

Roy joined Ainsley in the circle of light that surrounded her. "When we graduated from high school, Ainsley and I believed we were ready for New York. Zephyr didn't share our belief, and so for the next three months, we sat in her basement watching old musicals. When Ainsley and I thought we understood the steps to a number, we'd go to the studio and practise. The dance you're about to see was done first and better by Fred Astaire and Eleanor Powell in *Broadway Melody of 1940*, but when we finally went to New York, this number got us in the door, and once Ainsley and I passed through that door, we never looked back."

The rehearsal hall went dark, but in an instant, through Nick's inspired lighting, it became a starlit summer night filled with the brassy exuberance of a big band playing "Begin the Beguine." Roy and Ainsley began dancing, as nonchalant as if they were out for a stroll but with feet that, according to the program notes, were producing an astounding number of taps per minute. It was an illustration of extraordinary skill, but Roy and Ainsley's faces mirrored nothing but easy pleasure as they matched their partner's every clap, tap, and whirl. A smile played on Zephyr's lips as she watched their movements, her shoulders moving to the rhythm of their dance.

The program lasted fifteen numbers, each chosen to display dance's ability to reflect the deepest human emotions. Before each selection, a dancer explained the relationship between the number about to be performed and Zephyr's

presence in the performers' lives. As we watched the blending of biography and dance, Zack, Taylor, and I were rapt.

Most of the preambles combined light-hearted memories
with expressions of gratitude for Zephyr's steady support and
unshakable faith in her students. But three of the lead-ins
were deeply moving. Two men, who introduced themselves
as partners in both dance and life, spoke of their choice to
perform a contemporary routine created in homage to the
Pulse nightclub tragedy of 2016, in which forty-nine young
people, most of whom were gay, died. The men said that for
fifty years, Zephyr and her studio had stood guard between
the LGBTQ community and the hurting world, and they
were in her debt.

The dance they performed was an achingly beautiful story
of love and loss, and when it ended, I saw that Brock Poitras,
who as a gay, Cree player in the CFL had endured both hom-
ophobic and racist taunts, was fighting tears. He and I were
close, but when I caught his eye, he gave me a half smile and
turned away.

Before the next number, Ainsley took the stage in rehearsal
clothes and set the scene for the audience. "When I choreographed *The Happiest Girl*, I wanted movement to be simply
a continuation of the story. In the sequence you're about to
see, it's essential that the actor's words are integrated seam-
lessly into the dance. The scene is set in Churchill, Manitoba,
on the longest night of the year. The two figures you'll see
onstage are Ursula, a young girl whose beloved grandmother,
an anthropologist who spent her life studying the relationship
between humans and the bears of Churchill, has disappeared
into the tundra, and Callisto, an adult female bear who has
come to take Ursula to her grandmother."

Ainsley began reading from a script. "*There was a time
when we knew that bears had been sent to guide us. They
showed us patience, made us laugh, taught us to wonder. We*

learned from one another. Bears became people. People became bears. We honoured them. But now . . ."

Ainsley looked up from the script in her hand and addressed the audience directly. "In this scene, Ursula, knowing that if she is to discover her grandmother's final gift to her, she must transform from a human into a young female bear, reluctantly accepts the challenge."

The lights faded on Ainsley and came up on the actor who played Callisto and on Vale Frazier, playing Ursula. Both wore black tights and shirts.

Callisto: It's the only way, Ursula.
Ursula: I can't. I'm sorry.
Callisto: Your grandmother needs you.
Ursula: You said I wouldn't see her again.
Callisto: I said you wouldn't see her in the way you
          remember.
Ursula: What other way is there? I'm ready. What do you
          want me to do?
Callisto: Keep your mind open and your heart brave.

At that point, the action froze, and the light on Ainsley rose again. She spoke directly to the audience. "I'm going to read the stage directions for Ursula's transformation. The dancers will do the rest," she said. Vale Frazier began a series of movements that were otherworldly but seemed to emerge from a deeply primal place. The effect was utterly captivating and convincing. Although the artist playing Callisto was a respectable talent, at seventeen, Vale already had the lustrous presence of a true star.

"The transformation is choreographed as a kind of rebirth," Ainsley read. "The changes in Ursula come from within. Her sense of smell becomes more acute. She tilts her head so that the gland in her mouth that picks up scents is exposed. Her vision, particularly her peripheral vision, is diminished. She moves from the core of her body rather than solely through her limbs. She uses body language and basic verbal communications. The interlude during which Ursula tries out her 'new self' is filled with both joy and wonder.

"It is a perfect night for transformation. Long curtains of dancing light in pastel greens, reds, and purples illuminate the skies. We see that although Ursula is now a bear, the heart of a mischievous girl beats within her. She does flips in the snow, and then starts a snowball fight with Callisto. A snowball hits Callisto's nose, and she decides it's time to begin their trek. The sub-adult female tries to keep pace with the larger bear as they move playfully. Suddenly Callisto freezes. There is gunfire in the distance."

Throughout the scene, Nick Kovacs's lighting had created spellbinding luminescent veils around Callisto and Ursula that made what might have seemed impossible, believable. At the gunshot, the theatre went dark. The scene was over. There was silence, and then the audience began to applaud.

When the applause died down, Ainsley and Roy stepped out again. Ainsley was still in her rehearsal clothes; Roy was wearing tights and a loose-fitting top. Ainsley began. "This is the final number. It's a little over eight minutes long. It was originally choreographed by Bob Fosse, the brilliant and brilliantly self-destructive choreographer, director, and co-writer of the film *All That Jazz*."

Roy picked up the thread. "*All That Jazz* is a portrait of a man who knows he is killing himself but can't stop. Bob Fosse died of a heart attack at the age of sixty. Martha Graham once said, 'All that is important is this one moment in movement. Make the moment important, vital, and worth living. Do not let it slip away unnoticed and unused.' Those words were Bob Fosse's credo, and Zephyr Winslow imprinted them on the heart of every student she ever taught."

The lights were extinguished, and when they came back up, twelve dancers in various combinations of skin-tight bodysuits, half tops, and leg warmers were onstage, Roy Brodnitz included. All wore some variation of the headgear of commercial flight personnel. "Take Off with Us," the number they performed, began as a coyly provocative commercial for an airline. There were enticingly sexy double entendres and dance moves, and Taylor was clearly enjoying the sly humour.

Without warning, the mood and the stage lights darkened. The dancers began stripping off their clothes until the males wore only black leather thongs and the women, thongs and tiny bras. They invited the audience to join them for a flight that would take them to a place where they could make their desires and fantasies reality. The playful sexiness of the number's opening gave way to explicit encounters of simulated sexual encounters: male on male, female on female, male penetrating female vaginally, male penetrating male anally.

Zack gave me a sharp look and whispered, "Taylor."

"She's eighteen," I said. "She knows men wear underwear."

Zack harrumphed and leaned forward to continue monitoring the performance.

The erotic fantasy ended with a frenzied orgy and a stinging existential message from one of the male dancers. "Not once during any of our flights has there been evidence of any real human contact. We take you everywhere. We get you nowhere."

The finale was a showstopper and, not surprisingly, the dancers received a standing ovation. When Ainsley joined them, they reached out to Zephyr. The applause was sustained. When, finally, it subsided, Zephyr stepped forward. "Ainsley is correct," she said. "This is not a night about words. But my students know that the walls of my studio are filled with words about the passion we share. Their longing for something they can't articulate frightens every dancer who walks through the doors of my studio for the first time.

"Knowing that Tennessee Williams put that longing into words helps. 'I want to be seen, heard, felt,' he wrote. That's what all artists want. Art allows them to express what cannot be said. The advice I have is nuts and bolts: work hard, shine forth, be a total pro. Even then, there are no guarantees. As choreographer Susan Stroman once said, 'When you dance off the stage, you are always leaping into darkness.' For those who want to be seen, heard, felt, there is no choice. You must take the leap. But know always that I'm there in the darkness with my arms open."

Onstage the dancers beside Zephyr were wiping away tears, and many in the audience were crying too. As they gathered around the woman who had given them a community, their love was palpable.

Lydia Mah joined the dancers onstage to announce the renaming of the production studio and the arts festival that would be held in conjunction with it. Zack squeezed my hand. "This was worth sticking around for, wasn't it?"

I nodded. "It was. I'm glad we stayed."

When the knot of well-wishers onstage began to break apart, Roy Brodnitz approached us. He'd finished the finale wearing a black leather thong, but he'd pulled on the tights and shirt he'd been wearing during "Take Off with Us."

Brock stood, introduced himself, and extended his hand. "That was beautiful," he said. "I've never seen anything like it."

Roy took Brock's hand. He looked into Brock's eyes and the sexual charge between the two men was palpable. "Some of us are getting together for a drink and Chinese takeout," Roy said. "Would you be able to join us, Brock?"

"I would," Brock said.

Roy's gaze took in the rest of us. "Of course, you're invited too," he said. "Taylor, I promise you an entire order of almond prawns."

Taylor grinned. "You remembered."

"I did," Roy said. He turned to Zack and me. "Well?"

A crushing weariness had replaced the adrenaline rush I felt as I watched the dancers. The events of the day had caught up with me. I shook my head. "Thanks, but I think I'd better call it a night." I turned to our daughter. "The party does sound like fun. Why don't you stay?"

"I'll be happy to bring you home, Taylor," Brock said.

"It's settled then," Zack said. "Have fun."

As we were on our way out, we ran into Nick's daughter, Chloe, and her aide. When she spotted us, Chloe's face lit up. "Did you see the dancing?"

"We did," Zack said.

"My best was when the girl turned into the bear." Chloe turned to her aide. "Carly's best is the last one—the one where they take off their clothes. What was your best?"

"The same as yours," I said. "The bears. I liked the way the lights shimmered."

Chloe beamed. "My dad did the lights."

Delicate-featured with shoulder-length, silky raven hair, Chloe was a beauty. From afar, she appeared as would any healthy fourteen-year-old who had the latest fashionable clothes and haircut, but her too-guileless eyes revealed the heartbreaking truth behind her beauty. As a child, Chloe had been in a car accident and suffered a traumatic brain injury. Nick had been driving the car when they were hit. Krystal Kovacs started divorce proceedings while her daughter was still in the Alberta Children's Hospital, reputedly the best treatment centre in Canada for children with injuries like Chloe's. Zack said the alimony Krystal demanded was exorbitant, but Nick never questioned it, nor did he question his fate. He had a child to raise, and he believed she was his blessing.

As we said goodnight to Chloe and her caregiver, Nick's daughter beamed at us. "It's been a great time," she said.

Zack and I both smiled, but without the exuberance of youth on our side, we were ready to call it a night.

I was asleep as soon as my head hit the pillow, and I didn't awaken until Taylor kissed my forehead. "What time is it?" I said.

"A little after two."

I yawned. "When Broadway babies say goodnight. It's early in the morning."

"That reference blew right by me," Taylor said.

"It's a line from an old song," I said. "How was your evening?"

"Transcendent." Taylor snuggled in.

"Your hair smells like almond prawns," I said.

"It was that kind of night," Taylor said. I had no idea what she meant, but I was still smiling when I turned over and drifted back to sleep.

CHAPTER

4

I'm usually the first one up at our house, but Saturday morning when I padded barefoot into the kitchen, it was close to nine-thirty—four hours later than usual for me. Zack was already showered and dressed. "Good morning," he said. "I fed the dogs, gave them bones from Clancy's to comfort them for your absence, and they're out in the snow, burying their bones, digging them up, and burying them again. Taylor is having breakfast downtown with Vale Frazier, and as you can see, breakfast is ready when you are."

Zack has perfected the art of breakfast. That morning the coffee was made; the grapefruits were segmented; the porridge was bubbling, and the rye bread was in the toaster. I absorbed the scene. "Have I been declared redundant?" I said.

"Never." Zack's look was searching. "How are you doing?"

"Still a little off base, but I'm getting my bearings."

"Roy's news was a lot to process," Zack said.

"It was," I agreed. "And I can't stop thinking about Des. He was a terrific human being in every way. He lived with his arms open. It sounds like a cliché, but Des was always

ready to embrace new experiences, new people, new ideas.
He welcomed everyone into his life. I don't remember ever
hearing him say a cruel or dismissive word about another
person."

"A generous spirit like you."

"Thanks," I said. "But I'm not nearly as open as Des was.
I'm more like the father I grew up with—inner walls within
inner walls."

"Nurture versus nature?" Zack said, and his voice was
gentle.

"I don't know," I said. "But I imagine that particular
conundrum is going to be front and centre in my thinking
for a while."

Zack wheeled closer to me. "How can I help?"

"Just be there," I said. "And remind me of Taylor's twirl
in the parking lot last night. Zack, I never realized she was
troubled by the idea that there was no blood tie between us.
When she said, 'Knowing we're really family just makes
everything better,' she was so happy.

"Mieka, Peter, and Angus never knew either of my parents, so I don't imagine the disclosure that Desmond Love
was their biological grandfather will be a blow. They'll have
questions, of course, but I doubt the news will have much
effect on them."

"So we should make certain that Mieka, Peter, and Angus
realize how much it means for Taylor to know she's related
to them by blood," Zack said.

"I am so glad you're around," I said.

"So am I," Zack said. "So am I."

After we'd cleared off the breakfast things, we took our
coffee to the table overlooking the creek. It was snowing,
and the birdfeeder was doing a brisk business.

"More shovelling," I said. "But I love the snow."

"It *is* beautiful," Zack said, but I heard the note of resignation in his voice.

I touched his hand. "I know snow complicates your life."

Zack shrugged. "There are worse complications, and if need be, my Renegade chair is guaranteed to let me 'blaze my own trail.' So no more talk of that."

"Fair enough," I said. "Let's talk about our daughter's 'transcendent' evening. Did you get any details?"

Zack put down his mug. "A few," he said. "Incidentally, our daughter tells me details are now called 'deets.'"

"Good to know," I said.

"Anyway, the gathering took place at Ainsley and Gabe's condo. Living Skies has arranged accommodations for the main players in that new building on Broad Street, and Ainsley and Gabe are in a penthouse on the twenty-seventh floor. Apparently, it's mega cool—tons of floor-to-ceiling windows and a sweet view of the city."

"I wonder if Ainsley and Gabe are enjoying their sweet view," I said. "Did you notice there didn't seem to be any communication between them last night? That dance program Ainsley directed was brilliant, but Gabe didn't even watch it. He was over by the entrance talking to a group of other very rude people while the dancers were performing."

"Gabe hasn't exactly won your heart either, has he?" Zack said.

"He likes to pay for kinky sex, is quick with his fists, and is indifferent to his wife—not my kind of guy. And from what Shawn said last night, Gabe's sexual proclivities are not secret. I wonder if Ainsley knows."

Zack's sigh was weary. "My guess is that she probably does, but either way, it stinks. If Ainsley knows, that's a helluva thing to live with. If she doesn't, she's in for a nasty surprise sooner or later." Zack turned his chair so he was closer to the window. "Let's not waste this shining day on dark thoughts," he said. "I have more party deets to share. I know you've heard about the plethora of almond prawns, but I'll bet you didn't know that Roy and Brock's eyes were locked on each other all night."

"Score one for Zephyr," I said.

Zack raised an eyebrow. "What Zephyr wants, Zephyr gets."

"Did our daughter meet anyone fascinating?"

"As a matter of fact, she became reacquainted with Vale Frazier," Zack said. "She and Taylor bundled up and spent much of the evening on one of the balconies looking down at the Christmas lights and talking."

"Taylor's been missing her best friends," I said. "She and Isobel and Gracie text and Instagram all the time, but it's not the same."

"Apparently, Taylor and Vale really hit it off," Zack said. "And they got right down to essentials."

"Such as . . . ?"

A program from Zephyr's tribute was on the table, and Zack slid it across to me. Our daughter's handwriting was distinctive—vertical, with small letters so neatly formed they looked like printing. I read out loud the words she had written at the top of the page: *"We must be willing to let go of the life we planned so as to have the life that is waiting for us."—Joseph Campbell.*

"I take it Vale has recommended Joseph Campbell's work to our daughter."

"Indeed she has, and if you'd been awake, you too would have gained insights into what comparative mythologies can teach us about human existence."

"Good for Vale. I remember how exciting it was to talk about ideas when I was Taylor's age," I said. "If the Joseph Campbell recommendation came out of the young women's bundled-up-on-the-balcony time, Vale must be perceptive. Taylor is in a major transition. She knows where she's come from, but she doesn't know the shape her future's going to take."

"Right now," Zack said, "she needs this time to take a breath."

"She does," I said. "Last year was traumatic for us all, and it hit Taylor hard. Gracie and Isobel both lost parents, and Taylor lost a friend who'd been part of her life since I'd adopted her. But she handled it. She kept her grades up, she was always there for Gracie and Isobel, and she produced some impressive art."

"And now she's looking for answers," Zack said. "I'm supposed to ask you if we have any books by Joseph Campbell."

"We have *The Hero with a Thousand Faces*," I said. "I might as well get it while I'm thinking about it." I kissed the top of his head. "Thanks for breakfast. This was a very nice way to start the day."

Despite having moved back to our house over a year ago, there were still boxes to unpack, and the Joseph Campbell book was in one of them. Our garage is attached to the house, but it's never truly warm, so I threw a jacket on over my pyjamas and went out to search.

I'd just unearthed the book when I heard someone at the front door. Our caller was impatient and when the doorbell continued to ring, I sprinted back into the house to answer to a petite young woman holding a large and unwieldy package.

She was out of breath. "I apologize for leaning on the doorbell," she said. "But this was urgent. We do our best to wrap deliveries against the weather, but this plant is a showgirl and she doesn't like the cold."

I held out my arms. "Then by all means let me take her inside," I said.

The showgirl was not a lightweight, and when I got to the kitchen, I was relieved to see that the top of the butcher-block table was clear and I could put the plant down. Our gift was a poinsettia, the largest I'd seen outside a public space, and it was a beauty: bushy with dark green foliage and rich burgundy bracts. I opened the card. The note on it was puzzling: *"So a kingdom was lost—all for the want of a nail." Thanks for taking charge. Gabe.*

I was deliberating about where I could move the plant so it would get plenty of light and humidity when Zack wheeled in.

He eyed my bare feet, pyjamas, and ski jacket. "Damn," he said. "You had to answer the door. I heard the doorbell, and I tried to get off the phone, but my client just kept rattling away."

"Not a problem," I said. I gestured towards the poinsettia. "Look what we got."

Zack whistled. "Spectacular."

"It is," I said, handing him the gift card. "What do you make of this?"

Zack glanced at the card and laughed softly. "My God, it must be thirty years since I even thought of this, but I still remember every word. Listen and be amazed:

> "For want of a nail the shoe was lost,
> For want of a shoe the horse was lost,
> For want of a horse the knight was lost,
> For want of a knight the battle was lost,
> For want of a battle the kingdom was lost,
> So a kingdom was lost—all for the want of a nail."

Still smiling, Zack shook his head at the memory. "This was one of Fred C. Harney's favourites."

"Ah, the famous Fred C. Harney."

"Yep, the lawyer I articled with was right about many, many things, including this. He taught me that the failure to anticipate some initially small problem will lead to successively more critical problems and ultimately to an unpalatable outcome. The lesson for a lawyer is simple: "Never ignore what may appear to be an insignificant mistake, because if it's not caught and dealt with, it can cause you to lose your case."

"Well, I think there's been some kind of a mistake here. The name and address on the delivery were correct, but I'm guessing that Gabe ordered this poinsettia for someone else, and the card got switched with ours. I'll call the florist to figure out what's going on."

After I read the note on the card, the woman at Gale's thanked me, said she would phone the other person to whom their shop had delivered a poinsettia that morning, and call back.

When I stepped out of the shower, Zack met me with a towel. "Gale's called," he said. "Our card read, 'Hoping that unpleasantness didn't ruin your evening. Looking forward to the next time.' and it was signed 'Gabe.' So, mystery solved." He gave me a satyr's smile and wheeled closer. "Do we have time to fool around?"

"Why not?" I said. "Save me the trouble of getting dressed twice."

I've always found the sentence "Next year Christmas will be different" heartbreaking. In November the year before, reeling from three sudden deaths, we went through the motions of celebrating. We decorated the house, put up a tree, and exchanged gifts, but as Taylor said, it was as if everyone else's Christmas was in full colour and ours was in black and white.

Now it was next year, and I was determined that this Christmas would be merry. The outdoor lights were up and ready to blaze; the utility room closet was filling with gifts; and on a day worthy of Currier and Ives, Zack, Taylor, and I were about to drive out to the country to have lunch and choose Christmas trees.

It was a fine day for a drive. Pristine snow blanketed the fields and tree branches. The air was clear and the sky a sharp cobalt blue. We were having lunch at the farm seventy-five kilometres south of the city where our son Peter, his wife, Maisie, and their fourteen-month-old twin boys, Charlie and Colin, lived. Maisie had grown up on the property and she moved back there with Peter shortly after their wedding. Built before the First World War, the house was solid and beautifully maintained, but it had not been accessible, the rooms were small by twenty-first-century standards, and the only bathroom was on the second floor and had cranky plumbing.

Change was necessary. A new wing had been added, and with one exception, every room in the house was extensively renovated. Maisie had asked that only the parlour remain untouched. The room contained the twin desks where she and her late sister, Lee, had done homework and the twin pianos where they had practised forty-five minutes a day. So the old parlour, with its starched lace curtains and gleaming, dark formal furniture, sat like a revered dowager among the spacious bright new rooms that made the Crawford Kilbourn house warm, welcoming, and child- and wheelchair-friendly.

That Saturday as we gathered at the table to enjoy Peter's company dish, the Barefoot Contessa's macaroni and cheese, I was struck by how markedly the lives of everyone at the table had changed in the past year. For varying reasons, all of us had let go of the life we planned and accepted the life that waited for us. The deaths of three of Zack's law partners had been an incalculable personal loss, but the deaths had also created the need for major restructuring at his law firm.

Our younger son, Angus, had been moved from Regina to

the Calgary office of Falconer Shreve Altieri Hynd and Wainberg. His romance with Patsy Choi, a woman of whom we were all very fond, survived the separation. Angus and Patsy had both racked up a lot of frequent flyer points since Angus's relocation, and she would be joining us for the holidays. Maisie, whose twins were only a month old when the tragedy occurred, had been on maternity leave. Peter was a veterinarian committed to continuing his sister-in-law Lee's work with heritage poultry and livestock on the Crawford farm, and he and Maisie had planned to spend her maternity leave working out the logistics of their new life. Within two days of the deaths, Maisie was back full-time at Falconer Shreve.

At thirty-five, our daughter Mieka had settled well into the life she had made for herself as the single mother of two daughters—Madeleine, ten, and Lena, nine—and the owner of two small businesses. But Mieka's life, too, was about to change. She and a man named Charlie Dowhanuik had grown up together. As adults, their lives had, in Charlie's wry description, "bifurcated only to bifurcate again." Now the bifurcations had come to an end.

Charlie was still living in Toronto, but that would change when he came back to Regina in January, and he and Mieka were married. Charlie's late mother and I had laughingly plotted their marriage when the pair were weeks old and sharing a laundry-basket crib at a political event. I would give anything for Marnie to have lived to see their wedding day, but my happiness was big enough for us both.

Zack revelled in being a grandfather. When we ate with Peter and Maisie, Zack liked to position himself between the boys' high chairs so he could chat with them while they ate. That day, Peter and the Barefoot Contessa had not failed us. We all had second helpings of mac and cheese. When Colin and Charlie refused their steamed broccoli, Zack said,

"Mmm . . . my favourite" and dipped his fork in Colin's bowl and then Charlie's. The boys watched with interest as their grandfather put the cold, mushy green stuff in his mouth.

When Zack swallowed, they both laughed, and Charlie said, "Again." Zack obliged and miraculously the boys picked up their spoons and followed suit. It was clearly a triumph. They had earned dessert, and after Charlie and Colin had picked all the best fruit off the Pavlova Mieka brought, Maisie and I scooped the boys up to get them ready for their naps.

The twins' nursery was my favourite room in the house. Painted a warm, lemony yellow, it was spacious with a long, low, built-in window seat that the boys could climb up on to watch the heritage birds that strolled around their backyard and to see, past the fence, the Jersey cattle Peter had chosen to breed because each cow had a distinct personality.

Maisie had asked Taylor to paint portraits of the heritage birds her late sister had cherished, and the nursery walls were vibrant with the stately beauty of pink-billed Aylesbury ducks, Blue Andalusians, Ridley Bronze turkeys, Swedish Flower hens, and scarlet-combed Langshans. Charlie and Colin were already able to say "duck," "turkey," and "hen" and point to the appropriate pictures. That day, after Maisie and I had readied the boys for their naps, we carried them around the room so they could name the birds. The familiar litany lulled them, and by the time we placed Colin and Charlie in their cribs, they were both half asleep.

For a few minutes Maisie and I simply basked in the moment. "This room is so tranquil," I said.

My daughter-in-law nodded agreement. "Sometimes when I get home from work, I come in here just to watch them sleep. Pete and I have our schedule down to a science. I drop Colin and Charlie off by eight in the morning at Falconer

Shreve Childcare, and then Pete picks them up after lunch. Except for that crazy hour when Pete and I are trying to get Colin and Charlie cleaned up, dressed, and into their car seats so I can drive into the city, there are days when I don't spend any time at all with them."

"Zack's mentioned seeing you at the firm's daycare," I said.

"It's a rare sight," Maisie said. "Zack goes down to see the boys almost every morning. By the time I think about dropping by to visit, Colin and Charlie are usually on their way home."

"It's been a difficult year for all the lawyers at Falconer Shreve," I said. "According to Zack, you've worked harder than anybody. He believes that the firm is getting back on an even keel. You never took your maternity leave. I'm sure the other partners would understand if you worked part-time for a while."

Maisie's gaze shifted away from me to Charlie, who was murmuring in his sleep. "Here's the thing, Jo," she said. "I don't want to work part-time. I love what I do, and I wasn't cut out to be a stay-at-home mum." She turned back to me. "Do you think I'm making a mistake?"

"No," I said. "Charlie and Colin are thriving. Pete is as happy as I've ever seen him, and you're doing what you love."

"You were always there for your kids."

"Different time. Different circumstances," I said. "When it comes to parenting, one size does not fit all. As long as what you and Pete have chosen for your family works, carry on. If problems crop up, take stock."

Maisie gave me a one-armed hug. "I really lucked out when I got you and Zack for in-laws."

"We lucked out too," I said. "And don't forget to give me that recipe for the steamed broccoli you made for the boys. Zack couldn't get enough of it."

———

By the time Maisie and I left the twins, the table was clear, the dishwasher was chugging, and everybody had moved into the family room. When I joined them, Zack caught my eye and motioned to the chair next to him. Wordlessly, Taylor moved to my side. My husband never had a problem commanding a room. He took my hand. "Jo has news," he said. "Nothing terrible, just something you all need to know. Your mum has already talked to Angus."

Madeleine and Lena had pulled up hassocks inches from my knees. Pete, Maisie, and Mieka were seated on the couch facing me. For a long moment, I looked at my children and my granddaughters, searching for a trace of Des in them. There was none. Peter and Lena had the Kilbourn good looks: thick, dark, unruly hair, milk-pale skin, and finely chiselled features. Like me, Mieka and Madeleine were ash-blonds with green eyes and full lips. There was nothing in the appearance of my children or grandchildren that would suggest the connection with Des Love.

For the first time, it occurred to me how my parents must have felt about me bearing such a striking resemblance to my mother. People who saw me with her often remarked that I was "certainly Caroline's daughter." I had found the assessment chilling, but it must have been a relief to them.

I kept the explanation of how exactly Desmond Love had become my biological father to a minimum. When I'd finished, the room was silent. Finally, Lena piped up. "So what does that make Madeleine and me?"

"That's pretty much the same question I asked about myself when I heard the news," I said. "And the answer is that nothing has changed. We're still a family. We're still us."

The ice had been broken. There were questions. Peter was interested in the genetic factor, but no one seemed rocked by the revelation, and finally Mieka closed the discussion. "I think what we all feel that as long as you and Taylor are happy, Mum, we're fine." I shot Taylor a look and we both smiled.

Madeleine was pensive as she looked over at her mother. "This means that you and Peter and Angus and Taylor all have the same grandfather. And Charlie and Colin and Lena and me have the same great-grandfather. And if Angus ever gets married . . ."

Pete grinned at her. "Enough, already," he said. "Let's go get us some Christmas trees."

When the rest of started making motions to go, Maisie turned to Peter. "Babe, I know you were counting on getting some pictures of us all out being lumberjacks, but Colin and Charlie are still sleeping."

"I'll stay with the boys," I said. "Zack will want a tree that's far too big, but Taylor is always able to talk him down."

Maisie touched my arm. "Thanks, Jo, but I'll stay. I need some time with our sons." She brushed Pete's cheek with a kiss. "Be careful."

Pete grinned. "You do realize that Bobby Stevens is the only one allowed to actually turn on the chainsaw," he said. "The rest of us just get to hold it for the pictures."

Maisie's admonition to Pete to be careful was loving but unnecessary. The tree farm that was their neighbour Bobby Stevens's seasonal hobby was ten minutes away from Maisie and Peter's. Bobby had grown up with the Crawford twins. He was like a brother to Maisie and now to Peter. When he met us outside the lot to explain the process of selecting a tree, I knew we were in good hands.

It's hard to beat the good-to-be-alive vibe of walking through bracingly chilly air, breathing in the fragrance of several hundred evergreens, and marvelling at their beauty. We had a lot of fun. As always, there were moments that were less than Hallmark perfect. When Zack's trusty Renegade wheelchair found a trail it could not blaze, he muttered words that would have made the Grinch cheer. Lena, Master of the Impossible, managed to lose one of her UGGs in a snowbank, and it took us ten minutes to find the boot because she couldn't remember the exact snowbank where it went missing.

Mishaps aside, we finally all managed to make our choices. It was time for Bobby to fire up his chainsaw and explain the importance of making sure the cut is straight.

Pete and Mieka had just secured the last of the trees that would be returning to the city with us when Lena's eyes widened. "Here come the twins," she said and peeled down the driveway to greet them. Maisie was walking towards us, pulling the boys in their sled. Rowdy, the malamute-husky cross who'd wandered in off the road not long after Pete and Maisie moved to the farm, ran ahead. "This day just became perfect," Pete said, and to make certain there would be permanent proof that he was right, we all pulled out our phones and took pictures.

Taylor was riding back to Regina with Mieka and the girls. As Zack and I were leaving, Mieka took us aside and said that when she dropped Taylor off, she needed to talk to us about a problem at April's Place.

April's Place was important to Zack and me. Before Mieka's marriage ended, she owned and ran a successful catering business in Saskatoon. When she and her daughters moved back to Regina, Mieka had two priorities: spending time with Madeleine and Lena and continuing to share her love of good food with others. UpSlideDown, the combination café and play centre she opened in the Cathedral area of our city, met both criteria, and when it turned out to be a goldmine, Mieka decided to open a sister café and play centre in North Central Regina.

Zack and I shared Mieka's belief that North Central, characterized by a national magazine as Canada's worst neighbourhood because of its high rate of violence, addiction, prostitution, and abuse, was in need of a clean, well-lighted place where children and parents could gather. We were prepared to finance the undertaking, and Mieka and I spent days searching for a safe and appealing venue. We finally settled on a deconsecrated synagogue. The old building needed work, but it had good energy and was in the middle of a quiet block, so we went for it.

As soon as we were on the road, Zack raised the subject. "Have you heard anything about troubles at April's Place?" he said.

"As far as I know everything's running smoothly," I said. "Angela's a great manager."

"Maybe too great," Zack said. "I wonder if she's been offered a better job."

"If she were, I doubt she'd take it," I said. "She's committed to April's Place. She grew up in North Central, and she and her children still live there. She understands what the neighbourhood needs, and she's determined to provide it. There's no way she'd leave—especially not now. Tomorrow's the kickoff for 21 Days of Christmas, and she's been working on that event for weeks."

Zack sighed. "Well, we'll know soon enough," he said. "Until then, no use wasting our time together with 'what ifs.'" He leaned forward, pressed the CD button, and Bill Evans's evocative and soothing "Peace Piece" drifted from the speakers. "Good choice?" he said.

I leaned back and closed my eyes. "As our youngest daughter would say, 'transcendent.'"

The tree we chose for the family room was a gorgeous Scotch pine that had looked smaller in the field than it turned out to be, and I was grateful there were extra hands to get it into the house and fix it firmly in the tree stand.

Mieka had obviously spoken to Taylor about spiriting the girls away from our discussion. After the tree was in place, Mieka made hot chocolate, and without a nudge, Taylor and the girls picked up their mugs and headed for our daughter's room to assess some gifts with purchase Taylor had received with cosmetics.

Zack got straight to the point. "So what's up at April's Place?" he said. "I thought Angela had everything running smoothly."

"She does," Mieka said, checking to make sure the girls were out of earshot. "This is a new problem. Actually, it's an old problem—pedophiles. Wherever there are children, there are people who prey on them."

My blood pressure spiked. "Has there been an incident?"

Mieka bit her lower lip, a mark of tension that she'd had since she was a child. "Two weeks ago, when that cold snap started, unaccompanied kids began showing up at April's Place which sadly is not an uncommon event in this kind of weather. The kids get home from school and there's no one there to let them in. When it's cold, they either sit on their doorsteps, come to us, or wander the streets until someone gets home. We usually don't take kids in without an adult accompanying them, but in these cases Angela doesn't turn them away."

Zack's gaze was steady. "Sometimes rules have to be bent," he said.

"I agree," Mieka said. "The problem is that pedophiles have a way of sniffing out vulnerability, and they're trolling the area. A sex worker Angela knows from the old days told her that her boyfriend promised she could score big-time if she arranged to set up her nine-year-old daughter with a customer. Angela's friend said that she and some of the other sex workers are making sure parents in the neighourhood know to keep a close eye on their kids because the streets aren't safe."

"I assume Angela has talked to the police about this," Zack said.

"She has," Mieka said. "She asked for increased surveillance in the area. The police are cooperative, but they won't do much without any solid evidence or an incident. They say hot-spot policing ties up personnel and creates antagonism in the community."

Zack nodded. "As mayor, I was part of that discussion, and I get what the police are saying. Hot-spot policing is a last-ditch effort, and obviously, they feel the area isn't there yet."

"Meanwhile," Mieka said, "the parents Angela hoped would bring their kids to the 21 Days of Christmas have been turned off bringing them out at all."

For the next ten minutes, we floated ideas about how to deal with children's safety and the fear in the community, but there was little time to put anything meaningful into effect.

We ended up with a strategy based on something that was already in place. MediaNation's local station had agreed to broadcast the event's kickoff from April's Place live, starting at ten. The number of citizens watching the local station at that time on a Sunday morning rarely made it past three digits, but UpSlideDown and April's Place had a following on social media, and Mieka and Angela would urge followers from both centres to support the kickoff by coming to April's Place on Sunday at ten in the morning.

It was a start.

CHAPTER

5

Taylor, Zack, and I had an early dinner, and after a brief discussion about whether it was too early in the season to watch *Love Actually*, we strung the lights on the big tree in the family room, lit the fire, and settled in to watch that most romantic of holiday movies. As she always did, Taylor groaned at the flash mob wedding scene, and as he always did, Zack drew me close in the scene where Mark knocks on Julie's door and flips his homemade signs that read, "Without hope or agenda / just because it's Christmas— / (and at Christmas you tell the truth) / to me, you are perfect . . ."

The evening had been a gentle one, and despite the uncertainty about the event the next day, I slept well that night, and when Pantera and Esme and I returned from our morning run, I felt at peace and ready for what came next. Church was at 10:30, but we were able to watch the beginning of MediaNation's coverage of 21 Days of Christmas, and it seemed the last-minute social media push had worked. April's Place was filling up with parents and children with happy faces.

December 3 was the first Sunday in Advent. At the

cathedral, we would light the candle for hope, and the Service of Lessons and Carols, one of Zack's favourites, would begin. What my husband believed was a mystery to me. Then again, there was mystery in the fact that of all the women Zack had been with, the one he had been determined to marry was an Anglican widow five years older than him, with four kids, two dogs, a Ph.D. in political science, and leftist political leanings.

We had been seeing each other for a month when, one bright cool September morning, Zack showed up for the 10:30 service at our family's church, St. Paul's Cathedral. Until we were married five months later, Zack met with the dean of the cathedral once a week. I never found out what they discussed, but my husband had been a faithful congregant ever since.

Mieka and the girls were in our usual pew when we arrived. Mieka handed me her phone. There was a text from Angela Greyeyes that read, "So far, so good."

"Can't ask for more than that," I said.

Mieka raised an eyebrow. "No, but I'm leaving my phone on vibrate in case something goes amok."

Zack's voice was a booming bass and Madeleine and Lena's singing was spirited if unpredictable. As the girls and their grandfather sang "O Come O Come Emmanuel," the pleasure they took in their closeness and in the blending of their voices was a tonic. When the last verse of the recessional began, I noticed that, like me, Mieka had stopped singing and was simply appreciating the sight of her two young daughters sharing a hymnal with their grandfather.

As soon as church was over, our two families drove to April's Place. It was tough finding a parking place on Winnipeg Street—welcome news because that meant there was a crowd at the café/play centre. When we stepped into the warmth of April's Place and were met by the familiar

mingled scent of coffee percolating and muffins baking, I
felt my nerves completely unknot.

The place was festive. On Boxing Day the year before,
Mieka had asked local businesses that sold artificial trees
to donate their strays. The ten trees that had been donated
were placed artfully around the space, waiting for kids to decorate them. Garlands of snowflakes made from paper doilies
floated from the ceiling, and red and green patterned vinyl
tablecloths covered the café tables.

When Angela Greyeyes came out from the kitchen to
greet us, I felt the thrill of pleasure I always experienced
these days when I saw her. She was wearing bright green
overalls, a very white long-sleeved shirt, and green and
white high tops. Her shiny black hair was braided, her face
was innocent of makeup, and her smile was broad.

When I met Angela, she was a nineteen-year-old sex
worker and addict with three children and an abusive boyfriend. Now, three years later, the boyfriend was long gone.
Angela was clean and sober, and she and her children lived
in safe, decent, affordable housing. The children were thriving in a cooperative daycare, and after two and a half years
of upgrading her schooling and working at UpSlideDown,
Angela was managing April's Place. The changes in her life
were nothing short of miraculous, and their effect was far-
reaching. For every person who stepped through the doors
of the play centre, Angela was a reminder that there *are*
second chances.

"We're having a busy day," Angela said, gesturing to the
tables filled with neighbourhood kids and parents, mostly
First Nations, bent over projects. "I was just going to put
out more supplies for crafts." Plastic storage boxes of craft
materials, markers, glitter glue, and kids' safety scissors
lined the wall of the quiet-play area.

"We can help with that," I said.

"I'll take kitchen duty," Mieka said.

"Just in time," Angela said. "The oven just pinged—the muffins are ready."

After an hour, other volunteers had shown up. There were more than enough willing hands, and Zack, Taylor, and I said our goodbyes.

On the way to the car, our daughter texted Vale Frazier. When she dropped her phone back in her bag, she said, "Change of plans. Would you mind dropping me at the production studios. There's a dance rehearsal Vale thinks I'd be interested in."

"Fine with us," I said. "Taylor, do you think Vale might like to come to dinner? We've got that gorgeous rolled prime rib your dad bought. If she's vegan, we can change the menu."

"Vale is definitely not vegan," Taylor said. "Friday night, I watched her devour an entire order of Twice Cooked Pork. Usual time for dinner?"

"Yep," Zack said. "Six o'clock. I have been dreaming of that roast all day."

By three the table was set; the vegetables were prepared; the prime rib was rubbed with minced garlic and covered in bay leaves. We were ready to boogie, but I needed to check in one last time. I picked up my phone and called Mieka. "Are you still at April's Place?"

"I am. We're just about done with cleanup, and everything went off exactly as it was supposed to. Maddy and Lena had a blast doing crafts with the little kids, and Angela and I just enjoyed working together again and getting caught up."

"All is calm. All is bright?" I said.

"All is calm. All is bright," Mieka said. "Love you, Mum."

"Love you too," I said. As soon as I ended the call, Zack appeared and handed me a martini. "For getting through the day," he said.

"The day's not done yet," I said. "But I'll take that martini." We raised glasses, took a sip, and had thirty seconds
of bliss before Zack's phone rang. He glanced down at call
display. "Nick Kovacs," he said.

"Tell Nick 'hi' from me," I said, and then drink in hand,
I headed for the kitchen. I'd put the oven on to preheat and
mixed up cornstarch and water for the gravy when Zack
joined me. One look and I knew the news was bad. His
shoulders were tight and his face was strained.

"Trouble?" I said.

"Yeah," he said. "Exactly the trouble Angela warned the
police about. They believe a man picked up Chloe Kovacs
on Winnipeg Street."

My stomach began roiling. "But she's okay."

"No. Chloe was walking along Winnipeg Street crying,
with two fifties in her hand and her coat open, when the
squad car found her."

My voice was dead. "Was she raped?"

"She was sexually assaulted. There is no evidence of
penetration, but someone ejaculated between her breasts
and legs."

"Oh God. That poor child. Was she able to give the police
any information about what happened?"

Zack's laugh was short and harsh. "Nope. All the police
have is what I've told you, and the physical evidence. It was
that asshole's lucky day. He chose a victim whose cognitive
abilities were scrambled by a car accident when she was
seven years old."

"Zack, this doesn't make sense," I said. "Nick never lets
Chloe leave the house without an aide."

"There was a slip-up. Apparently, the girl on duty got a
call telling her there'd been a family emergency. She didn't
want to upset Chloe so she stepped into the kitchen and
started texting, trying to learn more about the situation

and find someone to take over her shift. While the aide was on her phone, Chloe walked out the door."

"How long did it take her to realize that Chloe was gone?"

"I don't know, but as soon as she understood what had happened, she called the police. Luckily, she was able to give the cops details that turned out to be useful. She and Chloe had been watching the telecast of April's Place. Chloe wanted to go down there and help. She and the aide were getting ready to leave when the call came."

"And Chloe didn't want to wait, so she set out on her own," I said.

"Yep." Zack sighed. "And you know the rest."

"Nick must be out of his mind."

Zack nodded. "He is. He's always blamed himself for the accident, and now this. You know what a big-hearted guy Nick is, but he's ready to tear apart the creep who did this limb by limb."

"I understand that," I said. "If it had been Taylor . . ."

Zack's face darkened. "Don't even go there," he said. "Anyway, Nick's on his way over. He's bringing Chloe. He won't let her out of his sight. And I'm not about to let Nick out of my sight until he's had a chance to get a hold of himself."

"I'll take Chloe so you can talk," I said. "We have dozens of pictures of the kids yesterday out at the farm, and Chloe loves children."

"She goes to UpSlideDown, doesn't she?" Zack said.

"She and one of her aides are there a couple of afternoons a week," I said. "It's a nice atmosphere for her, and Chloe enjoys being with kids who enjoy the same activities . . ." I let the sentence trail off.

"Who enjoy the same activities Chloe herself enjoys," Zack said. "Considering UpSlideDown is targeted at

preschool children and Chloe is fourteen, that's a tough
sentence to finish."

From the moment I met him, Nick struck me as a stoic who
accepted hard luck as his due, but the assault on Chloe had
shattered him. When he arrived at our door, I invited him
and Chloe in and took his jacket. "Zack and I are so glad you
knew you could come to us," I said.

Nick's voice was a whisper. "I need help," he said. His
eyes remained fixed on his daughter. At Christmas, I always
placed a dozen brass hand bells in varying sizes on a small
table in the hall. Chloe had discovered the bells and, like
every young child who visited, was ringing them carefully
and with obvious delight. "Look at her," Nick said. "What
kind of animal would use her like that?"

Nick always made certain Chloe was well groomed and
smartly dressed, but that day her hair was damp and she was
dressed haphazardly. My guess was that the police had taken
Chloe's own clothes as evidence and that, after she'd been
bathed at the hospital, the nurses had dressed her in whatever they had on hand.

I joined her at the table with the bells. "Hi, Chloe. It's
good to see you again."

Her face brightened. "Hi, Joanne. You and I had the same
best at the dancing—the one where the girl turns into a
bear."

I touched Nick's arm. "Why don't you and Zack go into
the living room? I have an idea about something Chloe and
I could do together."

Chloe tensed. "You're not taking me away from my
daddy, are you?"

"No," I said. "We're all staying right here, so let's get your
coat and boots off. Now here's my idea. We have two
Christmas trees: a big one for the family room and a small

one for the kitchen. After supper Zack and I are going to decorate the big one with our daughter, Taylor, but you and I could surprise Taylor by decorating the little one now. What do you think?"

"I think yes," Chloe said, then she looked at her father. "Do we have a tree, Daddy?"

"Not yet." Nick tried a smile. "We'll get one soon."

"Now?"

"In a while. Right now, I want to talk to Zack, but I promise we'll get a tree."

Chloe's smile was winsome. She held out her little finger to her father. "Pinky swear?" she said.

Nick hooked his little finger through hers. "Pinky swear," he said, and his voice was thick with emotion.

I had two reasons for suggesting that Chloe and I decorate the small tree in the kitchen. The first was pragmatic. Nick Kovacs was the rock in his daughter's life. He was crumbling, and for her sake and his own, he needed time to talk to Zack and pull himself together. The second was the human need to do something—anything—to alleviate another person's suffering. When I imagined the confusion and terror Chloe must have felt in the minutes after she slid into the passenger seat of the stranger's car, I wanted to weep. All I had to offer Chloe was a box of ornaments and a four-foot fir tree, and although she was showing no sign of either remembering or reacting to her ordeal, the offering turned out to be a gift for us both.

Chloe's delight in stringing the lights and deciding exactly where to hang each bauble was infectious. It took us over half an hour before Chloe stood back, cocked her head, looked at the tree critically, and said, "Now it's really pretty." I was still kneeling on the other side of the tree when Chloe turned abruptly and flew out to the hall. By the time I caught up with her, she'd already opened the living room door and seen her father. She whirled around, her blue eyes wide with shock. "My daddy's crying," she said.

I looked past her into the living room. Nick was sitting on the couch, his face buried in his hands, sobbing. Zack had pulled his wheelchair next to Nick and was leaning forward, stroking Nick's back. Chloe ran to her father. "Why are you crying, Daddy? Stop it! Stop it!" Her voice, sharp with hysteria, rose and grew louder. "Stop it! Stop it! Stop it! Stop it!"

Nick held his arms out, and Chloe threw herself into them. Nick held her tight. "It's all right," he said. "I'm fine now." He sat back so she could face him. "See. I've stopped crying." His daughter took a tissue from the box beside Nick on the couch and dabbed carefully at his eyes.

I looked at Nick. "Why don't Zack and I leave you and Chloe alone for a while?"

Nick looked at his daughter. "Okay with you?"

Chloe nodded and burrowed in closer. "We'll be fine," Nick said.

Zack and I closed the living room door behind us and went to the kitchen. When he saw the tree, Zack's shoulders slumped. "Chloe?"

"She wanted it to be pretty."

He wheeled over to the tree. "And it is." His voice broke. "Jo, did Chloe talk about what happened?"

"Not a word," I said. "If she hadn't run out of the room in a panic, you'd think nothing had happened."

"She hasn't said anything to Nick either. All he knows is what the authorities told him. He was working at the sound stage, and the police called and said his daughter was in Emergency at Regina General. When Nick got there, Chloe was off somewhere being examined, and he was sent to a waiting room. He had no idea what had occurred."

"And no one told him?"

"You know how it is. Finally, he buttonholed a cop who told him a patrol car had spotted Chloe walking along Winnipeg Street, crying. They picked her up. She wouldn't say anything, but her shirt was stained and she was terrified. The police suspected she'd been molested so they took her to the hospital. Chloe's only physical injury is a scraped knee. The assumption is that she got that either when she was pushed out of a car or when she fell running away. There were no marks on her that would suggest she put up a fight."

I felt light-headed. "Zack, do you think Chloe even understood . . . ?"

He closed his eyes against the image. "I don't know, and I wasn't about to ask Nick. We've been through a lot together, but no matter what I said, I couldn't get through to him. Finally, I told Nick he needed a doctor and I was going to call Henry."

"And Nick was all right with that?"

"He didn't say, but Henry's on his way, and I'm relieved. I have no idea how to help Nick. It's as if something inside him has broken."

"I don't get it," I said. "What happened to Chloe is beyond sickening, but Nick's endured a lot and he's always made it through. Was this just the last straw?"

Zack shrugged. "That makes as much sense as anything. Nick's had a tough life. His dad died the year Nick graduated from high school. They were close, but they'd quarrelled, and when his father died, they still weren't speaking. Nick never got over that. His mother died of septicemia two weeks later, and Nick blamed himself for not taking her into the hospital earlier. Anyway, at the age of eighteen, he was suddenly head of the household, making sure his brothers stayed in line and the family business didn't go under. When I met him, he had a problem with booze, but he joined AA, met the beautiful Krystal, and when Chloe was born, everybody thought Nick had found his happily ever after. Then the accident happened."

"But the accident wasn't his fault," I said. "You told me somebody blew a red light and hit the passenger side of Nick's car. Why would he blame himself?"

"Because Chloe wasn't wearing her seatbelt. She had complained that the belt was too tight. They were two blocks from home, so Nick unbuckled the belt. When the light changed, Nick started across the intersection."

"And the fairy tale ended," I said.

Zack brushed my cheek with his fingertips. "You know what Stephen King says. "'Life turns on a dime. Sometimes towards us, but more often it spins away, flirting and flashing as it goes: so long, honey, it was good while it lasted, wasn't it?'"

When Zack said that Henry Chan was on his way, I felt as if a burden had been lifted from my shoulders. Henry had been a godsend to me. At Zack's request, before he and I were married, Henry Chan sat down with me and explained in layman's terms exactly what paraplegia meant for Zack's life and mine. Henry had been factual, and I had been sobered but not daunted. We had talked for over an hour, and I had made copious notes, but everything Henry told me could be summed up in the words I circled in my notebook at the end of our interview: "Don't let anything slide."

I hadn't. I had not hovered, but I had been mindful, and twice when I felt I was out of my depth, I had called Henry. Both times, he had come as soon as he could, assessed the situation, and suggested the steps that were necessary to get Zack and me through the crisis.

When Henry arrived, Chloe was reluctant to leave her father's side, but Nick had promised his daughter he and

Henry wouldn't be long. They emerged from the living room in less than ten minutes, and Chloe immediately took her father to the kitchen to see the tree.

When they were out of earshot, Zack touched Henry's arm. "I'm not asking you to violate confidentiality," he said. "But as Nick's lawyer and his friend, I need reassurance. Right now, Nick is not the man you and I play poker with on Wednesday nights. He's out of control. He wants to kill the guy who did this, and I don't blame him."

"Neither do I," Henry said. "I guess that's why we have laws. Anyway, Gina's visiting her mother in Foam Lake, so I'm on my own. I've convinced Nick to let me stay overnight with Chloe and him. I've already given him something that will calm him. I'm optimistic that once Nick is able to gather his thoughts, he'll see that he has to pull himself together for Chloe."

"Would you and the Kovacs like to have supper here?" I said. "Taylor's invited a friend, but I can text her."

Henry gave me a quick smile. "Thanks, but right now, I think the best plan is just to get Nick and Chloe home and back in their routine."

"Fair enough," Zack said. "Call if you need me, and I'll be there."

After Henry and the Kovacs left, Zack turned his chair to face me. "So what now?"

"When I was in the kitchen with Chloe, I dumped our abandoned martinis, rinsed the glasses, and put them back in the freezer," I said. "Care to start again?"

"You're not just a pretty face, are you?"

I put the roast in the oven while Zack made the martinis. He handed me mine. "What shall we drink to?" I said.

Zack sighed. "Damned if I know."

"Works for me," I said. "Let's take our drinks into the family room, put on the Brandenburgs, and light a fire.

Taylor and Vale will be here for dinner at six, and everything is ready to go. I even uncorked the Shiraz."

The combination of Bach, a very dry martini, the warmth of a fire, and a moratorium on conversation was tonic. By the time Taylor and Vale arrived, Zack and I were able to be genuinely welcoming, and as it turned out, Vale was an easy person to welcome.

With her auburn hair pulled back in a mid-height ponytail, her face without makeup, and her grey-and-white J.Crew argyle sweater, she could easily have passed for the fourteen-year-old she was playing in *The Happiest Girl*. Vale was eager to see Taylor's art and to meet her cats. When they finally joined Zack and me in the family room, the young women were glowing. Clearly, each had found the friend she needed.

As we chatted in front of the fire before dinner, Vale was watchful, listening carefully, completely open to what was outside her but giving nothing of herself away. By the time we sat down for dinner, she seemed more assured, as if now that she knew us better, she could let down her guard.

The rolled prime rib was succulent—almost worth what Zack had paid for it—and at first the conversation at the table was limited to compliments to the chef and expressions of pleasure at the excellence of the meal, but it wasn't long before the pool of candlelight on the table drew the four of us together, and when Taylor said, "This is great—not just the food—all of it, but especially having Vale with us," Zack picked up on our daughter's comment. He turned his chair towards Vale. "Jo and I really are looking forward to spending more time with you," he said.

"I'd like that," Vale said, "but I promise I won't wreck your holiday by hanging around outside, pressing my nose against your window like the Little Match Girl."

"You're not going home for the holidays?" Zack said.

"No. My mother's in New York, but she's in rehearsal for

a play, and I'll be here working. Our cast and crew will get a couple of days off for Christmas, but not enough time to go anywhere."

"That's harsh," Taylor said.

Vale shook her head. "Not really, I've been an actor since I was six. My agent says any actor under the age of twelve who can't get a job at Christmas is either lazy or lousy."

"All those productions of *A Christmas Carol*," I said.

"I've been in three," Vale said. "Once as Cratchit Child #6, once as Cratchit Child #5, and once as Tiny Tim. That role turned out to be my lucky break."

"How so?" Zack said.

"Have you ever seen *A Christmas Carol*?" Vale asked.

"Joanne and I took Taylor to see it the week before we were married," he said.

"I remember," Taylor said. "Dad was a little teary at the end."

"I had something in my eye," Zack said.

Taylor and Vale exchanged knowing smiles. "Then you'll remember that at the end of the play Bob Cratchit comes back from church carrying Tiny Tim on his shoulders," Vale said. "That's when he delivers the line you probably heard when you got that something in your eye. Bob Cratchit says Tiny Tim told him coming home that he 'hoped the people saw him in the church, because he was a cripple, and it might be pleasant to them to remember upon Christmas Day who made lame beggars walk and blind men see.'

"Anyway, the actor playing Bob Cratchit in our production had a drinking problem. The last night of the run, he was drunk. He stumbled, and I fell off his shoulders. He was tall, and I came down hard on the stage. I knew I was hurt, but I also knew every eye in the house was on me, so I pushed myself to sitting position and said, 'And Jesus was loving to children because he knew how easily they break.' I was crying, but my words were clear and the audience started to applaud and ended up giving me a standing ovation."

Taylor cocked her head. "How did you know to say that about Jesus and children?"

Vale shrugged. "I knew that's what Tiny Tim would say. Even when I was eight, I was the kind of actor who had to inhabit the character I played. Onstage I have to become that person and play each moment the way they would." As she looked around the table, Vale's gaze was probing. "I know that sounds weird, but, Zack, your process when you're in court must be similar to mine."

Zack was clearly fascinated. "It is," he said. "I play every moment the way it needs to be played to get the outcome I want."

"Exactly," Vale said. "And my impromptu Tiny Tim line got me the outcome I wanted. While the audience was still applauding, the actor playing Mrs. Cratchit rushed me into the wings, and they took me to New York Presbyterian. The doctors said the elbow was badly sprained and for a while I'd have to use a sling to keep my arm and elbow from moving. But theatre is a small world, and it wasn't long before producers heard that I'd reacted quickly to the accident onstage. I started getting auditions for better roles in better productions, and I was on my way."

"What happened to the actor who dropped you?" Zack said.

"He was already on the downward slope when he was hired for that production," Vale said. "I imagine when word got out that he'd been so drunk he dropped a child actor during a performance, he was pretty well finished."

"No second chances," I said.

"He didn't deserve one." Vale's tone was flinty. "Gabe says the moment an actor walks onstage or in front of a camera, she enters into a covenant with the audience to deliver her best performance, and that anything less than her best is a breach of trust. Gabe's standards are high, and meeting them isn't easy, but everyone working on set or behind the scenes knows that he gets the best results, and that's good for everyone." She slapped her palm against her forehead and grinned. "I believe you have already heard more than you care to know about Vale Frazier. Zack, if I could please have another slice of that amazing roast beef, I promise I'll shut up."

It was clear from the outset that Vale and Taylor's enthusiasm for decorating the tree outstripped Zack's and mine, and we brought our coffee into the family room so we could watch the young women work their magic. Once Vale learned that we had a photo ornament for every year of Taylor's life, she wanted to hear the story behind each one. Our daughter was delighted to oblige, and Zack and I were even more delighted to fill in the details that Taylor chose to omit.

When the last bauble was hung and we turned off the lights so the tree could reveal its luminous, sparkling splendour, the four of us were silent, rapt in the wonder of it all, but as it always does, reality crept in. Vale mentioned she had an early call the next morning, and we turned the lights back on and said our goodbyes. I felt a pang when the taxi arrived to take Vale back to her condo on Broad Street. She seemed very young to be going back to an empty apartment in a strange city.

The taxi hadn't pulled away before Zack called the Kovacs to check on Nick and Chloe. I went to the kitchen to empty the dishwasher and I'd just finished when Zack came in to report that the news was good. Chloe had gone to bed seemingly without anxiety, and Nick had calmed enough to realize that seeking revenge was not an option.

His daughter needed him to be the father he had always been: strong and supportive, and that meant letting the police track down the man who had violated Chloe and bring him to justice.

CHAPTER

6

At seven-thirty Monday morning, I sat down to the rare experience of breakfast alone. Zack was at Falconer Shreve. He'd stopped by the Kovacs, and when he called he was upbeat. Nick decided his daughter needed a day or two off school, and Chloe was excited about the special morning her aide had planned for the two of them: a trip to the library for Story Time and fancy hot chocolate afterwards at Chloe's favourite downtown restaurant, Crave. Nick was finding it hard to keep his rage in check, but his daughter's high spirits had buoyed him sufficiently to hug her goodbye and then go to work at the sound stage.

Taylor was at the sound stage too. Rosamond Burke, the esteemed British actress, had arrived in Regina on Saturday. Casting her as the grandmother in *The Happiest Girl* had been a coup for Gabe Vickers. Burke was much in demand, and at eighty, she chose projects with care. She made it clear that she planned to be back in London for her birthday on February 1, and the shooting schedule had been arranged to accommodate her. Today would be her first day on the set, and Vale wanted Taylor to watch the legend in action.

As much as I loved my husband and daughter, I welcomed the solitude. It had been three days since Roy
revealed to me that Desmond Love was my biological
father, and with family activities, the concerns for April's
Place, and the terrible attack on Chloe, I hadn't had a lot
of time to let the new information about my identity
settle in. The morning presented some space just to be. I
was a retired professor who would be sixty-one on my next
birthday—still a young woman. There were a dozen things
I could do, and it was a luxury to have a quiet morning in
which to contemplate options. I poured myself a second
cup of coffee and took it to the table overlooking the creek
where three days earlier, as the pine siskins fed on the
fresh nyjer seeds in our feeder, Roy Brodnitz had given me
the news that I sensed would somehow change the course
of my life.

When my phone rang and I saw that Roy was my caller, I
smiled. Synchronicity was apparently becoming my constant companion. Besides, I was growing fond of Roy's gentle
gallantry.

"Is this a bad time?" he said.

"Not at all," I said. "I was just trying to figure out what to
do with the rest of my life."

He laughed quietly. "So nothing significant," he said. "Jo,
could I come by your house this morning? There's something I'd like to talk over with you."

"Another hidden branch on my family tree?"

"Nothing like that," he said. "I can be there in ten minutes. Is that too soon?"

"Not at all. Come ahead."

When Roy and I settled in with our tea, he sighed with
pleasure. "It feels so right to be here."

"It feels right to have you here," I said. "But I'm surprised.

I assumed the production would be all hands on deck now that Rosamond Burke has arrived."

"All the necessary hands *are* on deck," he said. "But my job is done. On the first day of principal photography, writers become the eunuchs in the harem."

I laughed. "That bad, huh?"

"Power's never been a big number for me," Roy said. "Ainsley's always been ambitious enough for both of us. We'd been dancing in New York for ten years when she decided it was time we make the transition to choreography."

"A wise decision," I said.

"It was, and so was Ainsley's choice to add directing to her portfolio. That move had consequences for me. When Ainsley encountered script problems, we'd talk them through together, and finally I started writing my own plays. We had a string of respectable successes—nothing monumental, but enough to build on—and then Lev-Aaron died, and you know the rest."

"I know you went through an incredibly painful time," I said.

"I work in narrative," Roy said. "I take experiences and shape them so they make sense. Without shape, life is chaos. There was no narrative to explain Lev-Aaron's death. He was a young, healthy man who came through the door one night the way he had hundreds of times, said "Hi," and died in my arms. Some genetic fault in his heart, the doctors said. For a long time, it seemed that the genetic fault in Lev-Aaron's heart had ended my life too."

"And then you discovered *Aurora*," I said.

"And it changed everything. I've never understood the creative process, but for me, the spark has always been a small thing that miraculously leads to a big thing. *The Happiest Girl* was a very big thing for both Ainsley and me.

"When it was such a huge hit, Ainsley and I felt this amazing reckless joy, and then Gabe approached us about making the movie. He promised the moon, and he has delivered. Rosamond Burke is solid gold, and Vale is going to be the next big thing . . ."

There was uncertainty in his voice. "You must be wondering where I'm going with all this," he said.

"Not at all," I said. "You're apprehensive about when your own next big thing is going to turn up."

Roy's smile was endearingly crooked. "Am I that transparent?"

"No, but I'm familiar with terror creeping in on the heels of success—it's a phenomenon in politics too."

"Because as soon as you succeed, the ante is raised," Roy said. "You've done something extraordinary, but it could have been a fluke. Maybe you'll never be that good again."

"And that's where you are now?"

"That's exactly where I am now. I've been working on a project about the period in the 1950s when the Emma Lake Artists' Workshops became the centre for modernist artists in North America."

"In retrospect, it is pretty remarkable," I said. "Some of the biggest stars of the New York art world meeting at a pretty lake in Northern Saskatchewan to challenge the old orthodoxies and embrace abstract expressionism."

"Did you know Des spent three summers there when he was very young?" Roy said.

"I didn't," I said. "I guess there's a lot I don't know about Des."

"That's what I want to talk to you about." Roy took a deep breath. "I've written a draft of *Emma Lake Summer*. My idea was a six-episode TV series about the passions that drive visual artists, willing them to sacrifice everything simply to make art."

"I'd watch that," I said.

"So would I," Roy said. "But not to put too fine a point on it, what I've written is shit."

"I know the feeling only too well," I said. "I wrote most of my first husband's speeches and most of Zack's. But I think you want more than my empathy."

"Not much gets by you, does it?" Roy said. He leaned forward. "On Friday, when you told me the story behind Sally's painting *Flying Blue Horses*, about Des giving her the magic and you the porcupine quill box, I knew I had what I needed."

"The small thing that miraculously leads to the big thing?" I said.

He nodded. "You, Sally, and Des. I haven't stopped thinking about the three of you, and how your story relates to the themes of art and sacrifice that I've been exploring with Emma Lake. The problem I've had with that script is that I couldn't get to something raw and human with it. You've seen the kind of work Ainsley and I can do when we have the right material, and, Joanne, the story of you, Sally, and Des *is* right, but I won't go ahead with it unless you agree."

"What am I agreeing to?"

"That's up to you. So far all I have is a weekend's worth of notes and a head full of ideas. If you say no, that's the end of it. I promise you that. But if you say yes, you and I can work on the early development together, and you'll have a say in everything that comes next. It's your decision." Roy paused, his gaze intent upon me. "Take as much time as you need."

I stood. "There's something you need to see," I said. I led him to the painting in the living room that Taylor had brought me to the night I told her that Des was my father. Roy was silent as he examined *Perfect Circles*. Finally, he pointed to Nina. "Sally's mother?"

"Yes," I said. "That's the only painting Sally ever made of her. Sally said Nina was so beautiful, she could almost forgive her."

Roy frowned. "Forgive her for taking Des's life?"

"That, and forgive her for destroying Sally's own life," I said. Suddenly, everything that had happened in the past three days coalesced into a single thought. I was being given the opportunity to recover something I never knew I'd lost: knowledge of Sally as a sister and of Des as a father. I was being offered a second chance. I turned to Roy. "I don't need time to consider collaborating with you," I said. "I'll do it."

Clearly elated, Roy took both my hands in his. "Do you have the feeling that this was meant to happen, Joanne?"

I laughed. "All of it?" I said. "Starting with you seeing Des's painting in the window of that gallery in New York?"

"It's possible," Roy said.

"If everything that's happened so far was fate bringing us to this point, Jerry Garcia was right about life being a 'long strange trip.'"

"Jerry Garcia was right about many things," Roy said. "So where do we start?"

"You saw that documentary on Sally, didn't you?"

"*The Poison Apple*? Yes, I've watched it."

"Ben Bendure, the filmmaker who made *The Poison Apple*, was a friend of Des and Nina's. Ben and Izaak Levin were both frequent guests at the Loves' cottage at MacLeod Lake. A couple of years ago, Ben sent Taylor two DVDs he'd made of the material he didn't use for the documentary. One of them covers Sally's last summer at the cottage, and the other focuses on her life during the year after Des died. Do you have some time to watch them this morning?"

"I'm free till lunch."

We went into the family room. I found the DVD, but after I slipped it in, I didn't press Play.

Roy noticed my hesitation. "Is something wrong?"

"Just second-guessing myself." I turned to look at him. "Roy, how do you feel about Sally?"

Roy drew a deep breath and exhaled slowly. "Honestly, I don't know—at least not yet. Before I met Lev-Aaron, I was in a relationship with an actor. I was certain it was the real thing, but in the middle of rehearsals for a new play, he told me we were finished. I was devastated. I pleaded with him to tell me what I'd done. He said living with me was interfering with his clarity of thought about the character he was playing, so he had to move out." Roy's laugh was short and angry. "That ended *my* clarity of thought for over a year."

"But you did get over the breakup."

"I did. I met Lev-Aaron. He was the least judgmental person I've ever known, and the most generous. He helped me realize that while people like my ex seemed ruthless, they were simply desperate. Lev-Aaron said they'd put all their eggs in one basket, and they had to do whatever it took to protect that basket."

"That's a very homely image," I said. "But it's true, isn't it? Sally made no secret of the fact that she would leave behind anyone or anything that got in the way of her making the art she had to make."

"The art she *had* to make," Roy said. "Making art was not a choice for Sally; it was a compulsion. Lev-Aaron said the key to understanding people like my ex was identifying the events from their past that made them believe the only thing they could trust was their talent. He said if I found that 'defining moment' in my ex's past, I could see him differently."

"That makes sense," I said. "When we watch Ben Bendure's DVDs, you won't have trouble identifying the defining moments in Sally's life," I said. "The first, of course, was Des's death, but after that the blows just kept coming."

"And she never recovered?" Roy said.

"She never had a chance to. A surgeon told me once that the worst situation he faces is when he has to operate on a patient who's had a number of botched surgeries. When it's clear the first surgery has failed, another surgeon tries to repair the damage, but by then scar tissue has grown over the incisions; if the second surgery fails, there's new scar tissue to deal with."

"And the wound still hasn't healed."

"No, it's still there buried beneath layer upon layer of scar tissue."

"You think that's what happened to Sally," Roy said.

"I do. She was fourteen when Des died. At that age, the body heals rapidly, but if the wound is psychological, it doesn't heal itself. All the injured person can do is grow protective layers." I began to choke up. "This is the first time I ever realized that's what must have happened to Sally. We were close. We talked about everything. If she and I had been together after Des died . . ." My voice broke.

Roy spoke in a whisper. "But you weren't . . ."

"No," I said. "Sally went to New York with Izaak Levin before I had a chance to see her. At some point, she discovered that making art was an antidote to pain, so until the day she died she created amazing art."

"I wonder if Sally felt it was a fair trade," Roy said. "I guess we'll never know. Meanwhile, you and I have work to do," He picked up the remote. "Ready?"

I nodded. "Ready as I'll ever be," I said.

I adjusted the throw pillows behind me and watched as the screen filled with images as familiar to me as the back of my own hand: Muskoka chairs, bright with fresh paint, facing a sun-splashed lake; a raft bobbing on the waves; a dark green rowboat with yellow life jackets folded neatly on the seats, waiting beside the dock.

"'That's MacLeod Lake in the Kawarthas," I said. "It's about a hundred miles north of Toronto. The Loves and my family, the Ellards, owned the only two cottages on an island there for generations. Nina renovated theirs, but ours was the same as it had always been. Squeaky screened doors, bookshelves filled with paperbacks that had long since lost their covers, mismatched sets of dishes, and faded crazy quilts on all the beds. I loved it."

Roy smiled. "Sounds idyllic," he said.

"It was for me," I said. "Of course, those memories ceased to be halcyon when the truth about Nina emerged. Ben told me that when he learned about Nina's role in the events that led up to Des's death, he wanted to edit her image out of every roll of film he'd shot, but he couldn't do it."

"Do you wish Ben had carried through with his plan?"

"No. I understood why he couldn't destroy his images of Nina. But see for yourself. Ben is about to zoom in on one of what Nina always called our 'al fresco' lunches."

Roy was silent as he took in the scene: the table, set for five, covered with a pale blue linen cloth that touched the grass; the individual bouquets of pansies in goblets set at each place. The pansies were the same shade of violet as Nina's eyes and of her sundress, cut to reveal just enough of the flawless ivory of her skin to enhance her mystery. "Every detail is perfect," Roy said finally.

"Nina never settled for less," I said. When I saw my face, glowing with love and gratitude as Nina greeted me, my stomach clenched. "Nina always said that Sally didn't want her, and my mother didn't want me, so fate had brought the two of us together."

"How did you feel about that?"

"Blessed," I said.

When the focus shifted to Des and Sally building a sand-castle, I leaned forward. I had watched this footage a dozen times but never with the knowledge that Des was my father and Sally was my sister. The sandcastle they were building was a complicated affair, with turrets, winding stairways, and secret doors. Both father and daughter were tanned, long-limbed, and blond, and the slope of their shoulders as they bent to do their work was identical. "They're so much alike," I said.

"Not just physically but so connected in what they're doing," Roy said. "You notice how Des hands Sally the tools she needs before she asks for them."

"There was always that special closeness between them."

"And that was a problem for Nina," Roy said.

"It was," I said. "You can see the darkness gathering in this next scene. Ben filmed it at a dinner party Nina and Des were hosting on their deck."

For a few minutes Roy watched in silence. Finally, he said, "It's a 1960s magazine cover: beautiful guests, beautifully attired, enjoying one another's company on a beautiful evening. And that table—vintage sand pails filled with pink roses, lavender, and delphinium—exquisite."

"And Nina is the most exquisite of them all," I said. "At least until Sally walks through the door."

When Sally, deeply tanned, without makeup, her hair tied in a loose ponytail, pulled a chair up to the table and began telling the guests about a Monet exhibit she and Des had seen the week before, the energy in the room changed. As she talked about the violent brushstrokes in Monet's haystacks, Sally's long arms cut through the air, unconsciously mimicking Monet's movements, and every eye was upon her.

When her hand knocked over a glass of red wine, staining Nina's pale blue tablecloth, Sally leapt up in mock horror. "Well, I guess I'm banished," she said, laughing. Des smiled at her fondly. "Nonsense. You're the best thing at this party.

Now sit back down and tell us about Monet's brushstrokes."
Ben Bendure's camera caught the easy camaraderie between
father and daughter. It also caught the pure loathing in
Nina's eyes as she gazed at the daughter who had ruined her
perfect party.

"That was chilling," Roy said. "I understand why Sally and
Des might not have picked up on Nina's reaction, but Ben
captured that moment on film. Why didn't he warn them?"

"I'm sure he just regarded it as a disturbing but isolated
event. It's easy for you and me to see the truth. We know
how the story ends, but Ben was living the story, and most
of that summer was like every summer we spent on the
island—an endless spool of hot sunny days, still moonlit
nights, and fun."

No matter how many times I watched the next scenes,
they still made me smile: Sally and I swimming out to the
raft with the indefatigable old yellow hound dog that had
followed Des home one day and never left; the two of us
waterskiing, showing off for the camera and taking some
spectacular falls; Ben trying to conduct an interview with
Sally about her art and Sally responding with monosyllabic
or totally off-the-wall answers until she and Ben were both
convulsed by laughter and he had to give up.

That interview was the final scene on the DVD that contained the footage of the last summer of Sally's life at the
lake. When it ended, Roy looked at me questioningly. "Are
you up for the next one?"

I shook my head. "No," I said. "But you need to see the
first scene. It encapsulates everything."

The next DVD opened with Sally sitting on a couch
beside Izaak Levin. Her hairstyle was boho; her makeup,
artful; and her outfit, chic. She was smoking a cigarette. At
the moment when Ben's camera moves in for a close-up,
Roy's intake of breath was audible. The Sally of the previous

DVD had been sparkling, effervescent; now, she seemed spiritless and her eyes were dead.

Roy hit Pause. "My God, what happened to her?" he said.

"Overnight, she became an adult," I said. "You saw the interview where Sally said that after she moved to New York, she painted, and she and Izaak went to galleries, and they fucked."

"Jesus," Roy said. "She was what, fourteen? Nina could have had Levin jailed."

"Nina didn't care," I said.

"Levin should have cared."

"That's what I told him."

"You talked to him about his relationship with Sally?"

"I did. It was just a few weeks before that terrible night at the Valentine's dinner where Sally and Izaak both died. I was angry about everything Sally had been through since her show opened at the Mendel and that anger spilled over into rage at everything that had happened to Sally since Des died. Izaak had been present for it all, so I confronted him. The story he told was appalling, but I believed him."

On the screen, fourteen-year-old Sally's lifeless eyes stared out at me. I turned away. "I can't look at that," I said. Roy picked up the remote, and the screen went black.

"Tell me when you're ready," he said softly.

When I'd gathered my thoughts, I began. "The night of Des's death, Nina and Sally were taken to Wellesley Hospital in Toronto. They were still there the night of his funeral. Izaak lived not far from the hospital. There was a vicious thunderstorm that night, and Izaak decided to stay home and get drunk. He was well on his way when someone started pounding at his door. It was Sally, soaked to the skin. She hadn't been discharged from the hospital. She'd just put her coat on over her gown and found an exit. Izaak asked who he should call, and Sally became hysterical. She was terrified that she was going to be forced to go back to the house on Russell Hill Road and live with Nina. She wouldn't let Izaak call anybody, so he went upstairs to run a hot bath for her.

"He'd left his bottle of rye on the table, and when he came downstairs, the bottle was almost empty. Luckily, Sally's stomach rebelled and she threw up most of the liquor. Izaak got her into the tub and sat outside the door until she called him. He handed her a pair of his pyjamas, and she slept in his guest room.

"The next day he went to the hospital to tell Nina what happened. According to Izaak, Nina was ready for him. She wept, said she was too weak and grief-stricken to care for Sally, and suggested he take Sally back to New York with him."

"So Nina just handed her daughter over to the trusted family friend who it turned out was not that trustworthy," Roy said.

"I'm sure Nina knew that it was just a matter of time before Sally ended up in Izaak's bed. She didn't care," I said. "She wanted Sally out of her life. And despite Nina's all-consuming grief at her husband's death, Izaak told me she did manage to summon a lawyer to her hospital bedside and have him draw up the documents Izaak would need to get Sally into the U.S."

"You must have had questions," Roy said.

"I did. I was frantic. I couldn't believe Sally would just leave without even saying goodbye to me, but Nina told me that Sally needed to cut all ties with her old life. She would be attending a special school for the arts in New York City, and she wanted to make a fresh start. She said Sally had asked her not to give me her new address. Not long before she died, Sally told me that during those first months with Izaak, she asked every day if I'd called or written, and after a while she simply stopped asking."

Roy winced. "God, Nina really was a piece of work, wasn't she?"

"She was that," I said.

"Jo, I'm not being prurient, but did you ever learn when Sally's sexual relationship with Izaak began?"

"I imagine it wasn't long after they went to New York. Why do you ask?"

"I guess because the change in Sally is characteristic of an ugly phenomenon. Vale Frazier is applying to Yale, and as part of her admission package, she wrote an essay about child actors being used by sexual predators. She asked me to read it and give her my opinion of the writing."

"And . . ." I said.

"It was a powerful piece, but it made me sick. I've heard things, of course, but Vale's essay really opened my eyes. These children live in a world where their bodies are the coin of the realm. They're lost. Often their parents are under the sway of the very people who prey on their children—producers, directors, agents, mentors, coaches, older actors—and they entrust their children to them completely. After that, these predators are safe to start making advances. The children have nowhere to go. Sometimes parents will even turn a blind eye to what's happening to their son or daughter because they believe these so-called mentors and benefactors will give their children the breaks or the skills they need to succeed in their careers."

"And the children have no way out."

"No more than Sally did," Roy said.

"So you think when Sally said that going to galleries and fucking Izaak was good preparation for life in the arts, it was just bravado?"

"When she gave that interview, Sally had thirty years to work through what happened to her," Roy said, "but in the clip we just saw, she was raw. In her essay, Vale explained she could always spot a child who was being molested because when they weren't onstage, it was as if they'd been hollowed out. Their eyes were dead. Vale wrote that to succeed at an audition, an actor has to have extra wattage, so managers of children who have lost their ability to sparkle often tell them that when they're auditioning they should imagine they're playing the role of a child auditioning for a part she or he wants more than anything in the world."

"And they learn to suppress what they're feeling, so they can sparkle," I said.

"But the emptiness is always there," Roy said. "And often they turn to drugs and alcohol to fill the void, and they bounce between rehab and relapse until one day their life ends in a tabloid headline."

"But Sally didn't let that happen to her," I said. "Despite everything that was done to her, she survived. She chose a life; she lived it on her terms and she left an incredible legacy. Most of what's written about Sally is lurid and misogynistic—the sexual swashbuckler who slept with anyone, male or female, who struck her fancy. Even the kindest assessments of her life are condescending."

"Forgive Sally her trespasses because she was an artist," Roy said.

My smile was thin. "That's pretty much it," I said. "But Sally didn't need to be forgiven—at least not more than the rest of us do. She was strong, determined, brave, funny, and very smart. She never stopped asking questions and seeking answers. After she died, I discovered that she'd been going to the weekday five o'clock mass at St. Thomas More chapel in Saskatoon on and off for months. She and one of the priests there had become close."

"That surprises me," Roy said. "Nothing I've read about Sally suggests that she was devout."

"Father Ariano said Sally would have called herself 'interested' rather than devout. He told me the first time he talked to Sally after mass, she said that as far as she knew, the only good things about the Catholic Church were its art collection and its funerals, but she was prepared to hear more."

"And she kept going back?"

"She did," I said.

"Did she find what she was looking for?"

"I don't know. I met Gary Ariano when I approached him for help planning Sally's funeral. He was as angry about her death as I was. We had a drink together in the priests' lounge, and then he took me downstairs to show me the college chapel. I wasn't in the mood for a tour, but Father Ariano said he was sure I would find the mural in the chapel worth seeing."

"And it was?"

"It was exactly what I needed. I didn't think so at first. I was fighting a losing battle with my rage and confusion, and the mural was sweetly pastoral: Christ in a prairie field performing the miracle of the loaves and fishes. When I said something politely dismissive to Father Ariano, he told me to move closer. I did, and I saw that the light in the sky was greenish-yellow—apocalyptic—and the earth beneath the crowds gathered to listen to Christ was cracking open. Arms were thrusting themselves through the broken soil, shaking their fists at God. It was incredible."

"An accurate reflection of your worldview after Sally's death?" Roy said.

I nodded. "That's why Gary Ariano took me to see the mural."

"He sounds like a remarkable man."

"He is, and I will never stop being grateful for him being there in the days before the funeral. Stuart Lachlan, Sally's ex-husband and Taylor's father, had broken down completely. The Irish have an expression—'he looked like a man who spent the night asleep in his own grave'—that's how Stu looked. Nina said she was too overcome with grief to deal with the arrangements, so she begged me to take charge."

"And you did."

"Yes, and I couldn't have done it without Father Ariano."

"Have you kept in touch with him?"

I laughed. "Zack always says I never leave anyone behind. Once someone's in my life, they're there forever. Gary Ariano certainly is. I'd like you to meet him, get his perspective on Sally. He's still at St. Thomas More. And, Roy, Ben Bendure's connection with Sally lasted until her death. He had a huge amount of material about her that none of us has seen."

"Do you think he'd talk to us about it?"

"I know he would, and Ben lives in Saskatoon too. I'll call him, and once I know when he can see us, I'll call Gary."

Roy took my hand. "I feel the way I did when I began *The Happiest Girl*—excited and terrified."

"That's about where I am too."

Roy grinned. "There's no better place to start than 'excited and terrified.' Anything I can do to help with the terror?"

"As a matter of fact, there is," I said. "Tell me your opinion of Gabe Vickers."

My request seemed to startle Roy. "Gabe?" he said. "He's the best producer I've ever worked with, and once he takes a project on, there's no one more committed to making the vision a reality. He's every writer and director's dream."

Gauging Roy's response, I chose my next words carefully. "I'm a little uneasy about him," I said.

Roy was thoughtful. "I heard that you were there when Gabe mixed it up with Shawn O'Day the night of Zephyr's fete. I'm not condoning the violence, but Shawn should never have told Gabe to reverse Ainsley's decision. It was Ainsley's call, and it was the right one."

"Shawn seemed to have a personal stake in honouring Zephyr," I said.

"Everyone on that stage had a personal stake, Joanne. They all love and revere Zephyr, and they didn't want their tribute to her to be shoddy. Ainsley made the only choice she could."

"I'm sure you're right," I said. I wondered if Roy knew that Gabe had punched Shawn after he threatened to expose Gabe's deviant sexual proclivities, but if he did, the subject was off limits. "Vale had dinner with us last night," I said. "She seems very impressed with Gabe," I said. "She feels that everyone working on *The Happiest Girl* knows it's a privilege to be part of his production."

"She's right," Roy said. As he waited for me to respond, Roy's gaze was intent. When I remained silent, his blue-grey eyes narrowed. "But you have another concern."

"I do," I said. "I'd like to know more about the kind of person Gabe Vickers is," I said. "You and Ainsley have been working with him on the movie for months, and she's married to him. You must have some insights into what matters to him, not just professionally but personally."

"I'll be honest with you, Joanne. I don't know much at all about Gabe's personal life. All I know is that he is a consummate professional, and if you agree, I'd like to pitch *Flying Blue Horses* to him as a six-part series. If Gabe buys into it, he'll produce a show that will honour your vision and be both beautiful and true. Millions of people will see your story and for some of them, it will be life-changing. I don't think we can ask for more than that."

I turned so I could watch the creek as I considered Roy's words. It didn't take long. I didn't know Roy well, but I trusted him. "Pitch the idea to Gabe," I said. "Let's see what happens."

Roy took my hand. "You won't be sorry," he said. "Now, let's get the legal papers drawn up so we both know exactly where we stand."

At that moment, my phone rang. When I saw Zack's caller ID, I felt it was a good omen. "Perfect timing," I said. "Roy and I just decided we needed a lawyer, and here you are."

"You may want to use another lawyer," Zack said. "Because I'm obviously *non compos mentis*. Pete called this morning. He and Maisie are taking the boys to see Santa. He wondered if we wanted to come, and I said we'd be there."

"Great. So what's the problem?"

"We're supposed to meet them at Falconer Shreve Childcare in twenty minutes."

"Roy and I just finished," I said. "I can do that."

"Are you angry that I've given you such short notice?"

"Nope. But you understand that Roy and I will be expecting to get the firm's discount on those papers you'll be drawing up for us."

"You've got it," he said. "I can't wait to hear all about it. See you in twenty."

I said goodbye to Roy, left Ben Bendure a message, and then headed out the door. Toyland was calling, and there were contracts to be drawn up and signed.

CHAPTER

7

The day Margot Wright became an equity partner at Falconer Shreve, she began pressing for on-site daycare. She was forty-one years old, drop-dead gorgeous, and, according to my husband, the second-best trial lawyer in the province. Margot had no interest in marrying or having children. Her reasons for advocating on-site childcare were philosophic and pragmatic. She believed working mothers and fathers made significant contributions to the companies that employed them and the employers should give them the support they needed. Closer to home, she had seen too many promising young lawyers leave the profession because the demands of a traditional law office made it impossible for them to raise a family while practising law.

Margot was persuasive, and within a year Falconer Shreve had a shiny new childcare centre on the second floor of the building that housed their offices. Time passed, and when Margot Wright Hunter, now a widowed mother of two very young children, returned to work, she knew her daughter and son would be well cared for. Best of all, she knew that Lexi and Kai were only a quick elevator ride away.

That day, when I walked into Falconer Shreve Childcare, Margot was the first person I saw. For two and a half years, her family and ours had lived across the hall from each other in the restored warehouse building she owned on Halifax Street. I had been with Margot on the day her husband died, and I was in the delivery room when both her children were born. We had been with each other through the best of times and the worst of times. Now it seemed we had both finally reached that most desirable and elusive of states, relative equilibrium.

Margot was back at Falconer Shreve, working part-time, which, as Margot was quick to point out, meant eight hours a day, five days a week, and as required on weekends. I'd grown accustomed to seeing her in what she ruefully referred to as the "wash-and-wear/who-gives-a-care" clothes of mums at home with very young children, but that afternoon she was in sleek, stylish, stiletto-wearing lawyer mode. Whatever Margot wore, her smile was always high wattage.

"How was your weekend with your family in Wadena?" I said.

She cocked her head. "I think I had a great time, but it was a blur. My sister kept trying to count all the kids—she has six, my four brothers have four each, and I have three although Declan's away at university. So there were twenty-four legit cousins, but a lot of the legit cousins brought friends, so the numbers fluctuated. Anyway, a good time was had by all, and bonus, Brock texted me just before I started the drive home and told me that he and his friend were making dinner for us and would help carry all our stuff in from the car and get the kids to bed."

"Another gold star for Brock," I said.

"And a big gold star for his friend. Roy Brodnitz actually knows how to cook. He made the best sliders and chopped salad I've ever eaten. The kids cleaned their plates, and after dinner Roy promised them that as soon as they had their baths and were in their PJs, he'd show them how to tap dance. Lexi just about leapt into the tub, and as you well know, my daughter has her own ideas about personal hygiene. That man is magic."

"So you liked Roy?"

"How can you not like a guy who teaches your kids how to do a shuffle? But to answer your question, I liked him very much." Margot's smile was mischievous. "Of course, not quite as much as Brock likes him. He is smitten, and Roy is smitten right back. Every time they looked at each other, they blushed."

"Zephyr Winslow will be pleased," I said. "She set them up."

"If Zephyr set them up, she'll make it happen," Margot said. "I handle her legal work. She's a whiz at deal-making."

"Why *do* you handle Zephyr's file?" I said. "You're a trial lawyer."

"I'm also a senior partner, and after the horrific event last year, there weren't many of us left. Zephyr's a blue-chip client who demands blue-chip representation, so I stepped in. I've already said more than I should. Your turn now. I saw Pete with the twins a few minutes ago, but I was running after Lexi, and he was headed to the bathroom to clean up the boys up for their Santa pictures, so we didn't have a chance to talk. He looked a little overwhelmed. He'll be glad to see you."

"Zack and I are backup for Pete and Maisie today. After the boys see Santa, we'll probably all have lunch."

Margot groaned. "A visit to Toyland. Yet another blow to Zack's reputation as the legal community's Prince of Darkness, and your daughter-in-law is already breathing down his neck."

I was incredulous. "Maisie? I don't believe it."

"Believe it. Maisie is not afraid to get blood on her hands. She has a high-stakes trial on right now. I wouldn't count on her for the Santa thing, but if she makes it, it'll be when court recesses for lunch. And I'll bet you a box of Timbits that when she goes back to the courthouse, Zack goes with her."

"Is he worried about her case?"

Margot chortled. "Hardly. Maisie's client may be a dick-wad, but he's smart enough to know he's got himself a dynamite lawyer. Zack will drop in on Maisie for the same reason other trial lawyers do—she's scary as hell, and she's fun to watch."

"I'd like to see her in action," I said.

"Let's find a time when our schedules mesh, and I'll go with you," Margot said. Her gaze shifted to a point past my shoulder. "The current Prince of Darkness approaches," she said.

Zack wheeled over to join us. "Am I interrupting?"

"Nope," Margot said. "I should get back upstairs. Have fun with Santa, you two. Jo, I'm home tonight. You can drop the Timbits by anytime."

Zack shot me a questioning look. "What was that about?"

"Predicting your behaviour," I said. "Now let's find Pete and our grandsons and hit the road."

Our excursion to Toyland was a flop. Maisie called while we were still at childcare to say she was running behind and she'd meet us at the mall. Charlie and Colin were dapper in their matching red corduroy overalls and green-and-white checked shirts, but they had resisted attempts to tame their springy copper curls and they looked as if they'd been caught in a wind tunnel. Maisie wasn't there when we arrived, so we joined the line of parents and kids and kept an anxious eye on the mall entrance.

Toyland was starting to show its age. The gingerbread on
the roof of Santa's Workshop needed a paint job, the giant
snowman guarding Santa's big green chair was wearing a
battered ball cap, and the lollipop garlands linking the giant
candy canes on Toyland's lawn had a forlorn droop. The line
wasn't long, and as it shortened, I grew tense. There was
only one child between us and Santa when Maisie, breathless and apologetic, arrived. "I made it," she said. "I am so
sorry. I just couldn't get out of there."

"Perfect timing," I said. "You didn't miss a thing."

Maisie ran her long, strong fingers through first Charlie's
and then Colin's hair, and their curls sprang into place.

"How did you know to do that?" I said.

Maisie raked her own copper curls. "Practice," she said.

The child on Santa's knee had whispered his list, had his
picture taken, been given his toy and candy cane, and was
on his way to join his mother, who was huddled with the
photographer. It was the turn of the little girl ahead of us, an
angelic blonde wearing a poufy, cotton-candy-pink dress.
She looked to be about two and half, a dangerous age. When
her mother took her by the hand to lead her to Santa, the
child shook her off and began to wail. The mother reached
for her again, but the child was wily. She threw herself down
on the Styrofoam snow and began to kick. The mother and
Santa's elves attempted to calm her, but the little girl had
youth and temper on her side, and she was clearly prepared
to go the distance.

The twins and I had made some preliminary forays into
etiquette. I had been teaching them the old standby I had
taught all the children in our family: "Two little magic words
that will open any door are these / One little word is 'Thanks'
and the other little word is 'Please.'" Charlie had been standing by his father, watching with interest as the little blonde's
writhing and keening reached epic proportions. Finally, he

decided it was time for action. He took a few steps towards the little girl, pointed at her, and shouted, "Please!" The little girl sat upright, gave Charlie a comradely smile, and bolted for the exit, with her weeping mother in tow.

It was our turn. When the elves helped them onto Santa's knee, Colin clouded up, Charlie looked grim, and Maisie's phone buzzed. "I have to go back," she said. She turned towards the photographer. "Please, just do what you can." She touched Peter's arm. "I'm sorry, babe."

"You were here," he said. "That's all that counts."

Zack gave Pete and me a quick glance. "It seems we're through with Santa," he said. "If you don't need me, I'm going to drop in on Maisie's trial for a few minutes."

"We're fine," Pete said.

"Absolutely," I said. "But I owe Margot a box of Timbits."

When the realization dawned, Zack's face fell. "Margot bet I'd go back to the courthouse, and you bet I'd stay with you," he said. "I am a selfish prick."

"Don't beat yourself up," I said. "Plans go awry. This one did. That's all. What do you want for dinner?"

"Captain Jack's is on the way home from Margot's," Zack said. "After I drop off the Timbits, I could get fish and chips."

"You're in luck," I said. "I'm grateful that you're covering my gambling debt and I'm in a grease-and-salt frame of mind. All is forgiven."

I'd just arrived home and curled up with the dogs, a cup of tea, and C.P. Snow's *The Masters* when Ben Bendure returned my call. His voice was deep and melodious, and he always spoke slowly, as if he had carefully considered every word he was about to say. The documentaries he made often raised uncomfortable questions that, even as the film ended, were not answered, but Ben himself was a comforting presence. Portly, bald, and bearded, he was partial to long-pocketed vests, well-worn Oxford cloth shirts, roomy slacks, and stout walking boots—a look more country squire than film-maker, but it suited him.

Ben and Izaak Levin had frequently occupied the Loves' guest cottage—separately or, on occasion, together—during our summers at MacLeod Lake. Ben and I had a shared history, and we were always delighted to have a chance to pick up where we left off. After I gave him a quick rundown on what everyone in our family was up to, I told him that Roy Brodnitz was interested in doing a project on the Love family, and I wondered if Roy and I could visit him on a day that worked for him.

Saskatoon is two hundred and sixty kilometres from Regina, but despite the distance, I could feel the chill in Ben's voice. "I'm not a vain man, Joanne, but I'm proud of *The Poison Apple*. I respect Roy Brodnitz's work, but I believe my film about Sally was scrupulous and just. Frankly, I don't see the point of making another film on a subject that many feel has already been dealt with competently."

I rushed to reassure him. "You and I both know that *The Poison Apple* goes well beyond competence. It's become the gold standard against which other documentaries on artists are measured. Roy's project is a TV series, and the approach would be fictional." I took a breath. "Ben, there's something else. I was hoping we could discuss it face to face, but I've gotten off to a bad start, and I don't want to leave you with the wrong impression. Last Friday, I learned that Des Love is my biological father."

He didn't respond. When the silence between us became uncomfortable, I said, "I'm sure this has been a shock for you too. If you have questions, I'll do my best to answer them."

"So much time has gone by," he said. "I'd hoped that particular painful chapter was behind us."

I felt as if I'd been kicked in the stomach. "You knew?"

"I knew," he said wearily. "So did Izaak. So did Nina."

"Why didn't anyone tell me?" I said.

I sounded like a petulant child, but Ben's response was gentle. "Des wanted to," he said. "When your father told Des he was sending you to Bishop Lambeth because he felt you'd be safer there than in the house with your mother, Des was adamant about taking you to live with Nina, Sally, and him."

"Why didn't he take me?"

"Because your mother convinced your father that giving you up would lead to questions that would destroy her reputation and harm your father professionally. Your father's refusal to do what was best for you was a bone of contention between Des and him that lasted until Des died. Your father suffered for that afterwards."

My mind was racing. I couldn't seem to form a coherent thought. Finally, I said, "I guess it really doesn't make any difference now."

"Maybe not," Ben said. "But I can tell from your voice that the news has hurt you. I'd like to see you, Joanne, and I have no plans for Thursday. Come, and bring Roy Brodnitz along. I'm interested in meeting him and in hearing what he has in mind."

After Ben and I had agreed on a meeting time and said our goodbyes, I texted Roy and told him Ben had agreed to see us Thursday morning at 10:30. Roy texted back a few minutes later to say he'd booked us on a flight to Saskatoon at eight in the morning and a return flight at four in the afternoon, and that our family was invited to a dinner Gabe and Ainsley were holding for Rosamond Burke on Saturday evening.

Father Gary Ariano said he would welcome a visit Thursday afternoon because he was always pleased to talk about Sally and he'd read the reviews of *The Happiest Girl* and was eager to meet the playwright. My dance card was filling rapidly.

———

When Taylor bounced in at half past four, I was back on the couch with a fresh pot of tea, *The Masters*, and the dogs on the floor beside me. Our daughter stepped carefully over Esme and then Pantera and perched at the end of the couch. As she always seemed to be these days, she was breathless. "Just going to change into something more artsy," she said. "Vale has an interview scheduled with this online arts magazine from New York, *Nexus*. They're doing a big piece on Rosamond Burke, and she suggested they talk to Vale and to me too."

"About Rosamond?"

Taylor shook her head. "About us."

"That makes sense," I said. "You and Vale both started your careers when you were young and you're both successful."

Taylor was thoughtful. "That's true," she said. "But there are differences. Theatre is collaborative. Vale's work has always been connected to what other people do—not just actors, but playwrights, directors, producers, set and costume designers, tech people, her own manager. She needs other people for her work."

I smiled. "And you don't need anybody," I said.

Taylor rubbed my foot. "I need all kinds of people, but you're right, not for my work. Darrell's gallery sells my paintings, and Dad and I oversee the business with Corydon, but apart from that it's just me in the studio."

"And you prefer working alone?"

"I've never thought about it," Taylor said. She stood and stretched. "But that question might come up in the *Nexus* interview, so I guess I'd better figure out an answer. Vale's been doing interviews all her life, but I haven't and I don't want to look like a dork. And something else . . . do you have any idea where that red coat of mine with the black belt is?"

"The one you loved so much you couldn't give away even after you outgrew it?"

"That's the one."

"It's in a garment bag on a clothing rack in the utility room. Every time I asked about giving it away, you said you were waiting until you found someone who would love it as much as you did."

Taylor grimaced. "Now that *is* dorky."

"I always thought it was kind of sweet," I said. "Like something in a fairy tale."

"Well, I've finally found someone I want to give it to. Her name is Lizzie. I met her through Vale, and at times Lizzie does seem like a girl from a fairy tale. I just hope I can convince her to keep the coat and wear it."

"It's a beautiful coat," I said. "Why wouldn't she wear it?"

Taylor frowned. "Lizzie has issues," she said. "Not bad ones. She's just . . . I don't know . . . she's just different. Anyway, she can't bear to see anyone unhappy."

"That's not a bad thing," I said. "You were like that when you were little. You'd start to cry if you saw someone else cry. You wanted everyone to be happy all the time."

"And you told me I couldn't kiss away every hurt and dry every tear," Taylor said. "You said I should always do my best to help, but I couldn't take care of the whole world. Lizzie doesn't understand that, but she's my age, Jo. She gives everything she has to other street people, and she doesn't take care of herself. She's still wearing a summer windbreaker. Vale tried giving her money to get something warmer, but of course, Lizzie gave the money away. We're hoping if I give her this coat, she might wear it."

"Fingers crossed," I said. "How did Vale come to know Lizzie?"

"It was just one of those things. When shooting's over for the day, craft services sends the food the cast and crew haven't eaten to a homeless shelter. Lizzie heard about the food and showed up at the studio one night to get a meal. The craft services people aren't authorized to give the food directly to needy people. Apparently, there are regulations. Vale was certain Lizzie wouldn't go to the shelter, so she filled a plate for herself, gave it to Lizzie, and stayed with her while she ate it.

"The next morning when Vale left her condo to go to the studio, Lizzie was curled up in the outer vestibule of her building. She followed Vale to the studio, ate something, and took off. Vale didn't see her for three days, and then one morning when Vale came down to go to work, Lizzie was back, asleep in the vestibule. That's been the pattern ever since. She comes and goes. Anyway, I'd better grab the coat and get moving. Vale and I are taking the woman doing the *Nexus* piece to Afghan Cuisine for dinner after the interview."

"Good choice," I said. "But I'll need to alert your dad. He's bringing home fish and chips and he always gets your order with extra halibut."

Taylor's head shake was vehement. "Don't call him. I'll have what's left over for breakfast."

When Zack came home, I met him at the front door with a martini. "Excellent," he said. "But aren't you supposed to be wearing Saran Wrap?"

"Don't push it," I said. "But I do have the fire going and the tree lights on."

Zack removed his scarf and jacket and handed me a file folder. "For you," he said. "Contracts."

I opened the envelope. "That was quick."

"I was making amends. As soon as I got back to the office, I called Roy. He said to make certain the contract specified that Gabe should be his and your surrogate for all production matters," Zack said.

"What?" I said. "Is that standard? I don't know if I like signing so much power over to Gabe."

"I thought you might feel that way," Zack said, "but I consulted with Falconer Shreve's entertainment lawyer, and she said this is all par for the course. However, she and I agreed that we should include a clause stating that as the owner of the material upon which the series would be based if, at any time, you were dissatisfied with the direction in which the project was developing and if, after reasonable consultation between Living Skies and you, agreement could not be reached, the option would be declared null and void."

"Well, I guess it's okay then . . ." I said.

Zack gave me a Cheshire cat grin. "Good, because Gabe Vickers has already signed the contract."

I flipped to the signing page of the top copy. "So he has," I said. "Zack, how did the contracts end up with Gabe?"

"Roy's contract for *The Happiest Girl* gave Gabe rights of first refusal on Roy's next project. As soon as you'd agreed to have him pitch *Flying Blue Horses* to Gabe, Roy spoke to him and Gabe got on board. When I called Gabe, I thought he was going to jump through the phone. He really wants this, Jo. My guess is he's on the phone right now starting to put together the financing."

"That's crazy," I said. "Not a word has been written."

"I mentioned that to Gabe. He said the pitch for the series *Weeds* was only four words: 'suburban,' 'widowed,' 'pot-dealing,' and 'mom,' and Roy had more than that."

Zack pointed his chair towards the family room. "Now that we have a contract in hand, let's settle down."

I put the fish and chips in the oven to stay warm and brought in our drinks.

"So how was your day?" Zack said.

"I'm still working that out," I said.

Zack's brow furrowed. "I thought you'd be happy about this."

"I am. The terms of the contract are generous. I'm not creative, but I've always enjoyed doing research. I like finding the pieces, putting them together, and seeing what I come up with."

"So what's the problem?"

"The first piece of information I've unearthed has rattled me. I talked to Ben Bendure this afternoon. I thought he might have memories or even old home movies that would shed light on the relationships between Des, Sally, and me." I took a large sip of my drink. "It turns out Ben knew I was Des's daughter. So did Nina and Izaak. Ben said that my father decided to put me in boarding at Bishop Lambeth because I'd be, quote, 'safer there than in the house with my mother.' Des wanted to tell me the truth and take me into their family, but my parents wouldn't allow it."

"Let me get this straight," Zack said, and his voice was coldly deliberate. "Your father felt you wouldn't be safe with your mother, so rather than let you grow up with people who cared for you, he sent you to a boarding school for thirteen years." Zack put down his drink. "I know you loved your father, so I'm not going to say a word."

"I appreciate that," I said. "I just hope there aren't too many other landmines out there."

"Jo, what would happen if you decide not to be part of this and don't return the signed contract to Gabe."

"Roy said he won't go ahead without me, so that would be the end of it."

"That might be the simplest solution," Zack said.

"The simplest, but not the best," I said. "The more I think about it, the more I'm convinced that I have to do this. And not just for my sake."

"For Sally's?"

"Among others," I said. "Zack, I have always felt bad about how Izaak Levin's life ended. He suffered the heart attack that killed him just seconds after Sally died at the Valentine's Day dinner. Nina planted evidence on Izaak that made it appear he had murdered Sally, and he wasn't there to defend himself. He never had a chance to clear his name.

"I went to his funeral. Hardly anyone else did. I met his sister. I was grateful that the truth about Nina's guilt came out while Izaak's sister was still alive, but by then the murder was an old story—page three news. Izaak Levin was a major figure in the art world, but the suspicion that somehow he was involved in Sally's death never lifted, and his accomplishments were eclipsed."

"Levin was also a major figure in the life of Taylor's mother," Zack said, and his eyes were full of concern. "Jo, are you really prepared to have what happened to Sally in the months after Des died dug up again?"

"The truth about her relationship with Izaak is complex," I said. "But Sally would want it known. She was honest and she was fair. She would want Izaak's contributions to be recognized, and she would want Des's significance as an artist and teacher acknowledged. Until Roy discovered *Aurora* in that gallery in New York, Desmond Love was an asterisk in Sally's biography. He deserves better, and *Flying Blue Horses* can show the kind of man he was."

Zack's gaze was steady. "You sound certain again."

"I am," I said. "Sure enough to take the next step, anyway." I picked up the folder with the contracts. "May I borrow your pen?" I signed the copies and handed the folder back to Zack. "Well, that's done," I said. "Tell me about your day."

"Maisie was sensational. When the judge gave her a tongue-lashing, Maisie waited him out and then turned back to the witness and kept pummelling until he handed her what she needed to move in for the kill. She's unstoppable."

"Remember the first time I met Maisie?" I said. "She'd just come from lacrosse. She'd chipped a tooth and her lower lip was bleeding, but her smile lit up the room."

"The first time she shook my hand, she crushed four of my fingers," Zack said. "Now, I don't know about you, but I'm ready to eat."

We were in the kitchen emptying the dishwasher when Taylor arrived, rosy-cheeked, eyes streaming from the cold, but exuberant. "I'm home," she said.

"I knew it," Zack said. "The house always feels off-kilter when you're not here."

Taylor kissed Zack on the head and gave me a quick hug. "Better?" she said.

"Infinitely," I said. "So how was the interview?"

"Stellar." After that, the words tumbled out. "Answering Siba Biyela's questions made me start to understand why I wasn't ready to go to OCAD last fall," Taylor said. "Siba asked Vale and me both how our work has changed in the last year. Vale answered first, which was lucky because it gave me a chance to think, and I actually came up with something, which I was glad for because Gabe Vickers walked in just as Vale was finishing up her answer."

Our daughter pulled off her toque, untied her scarf, removed her jacket, and piled everything on a chair. "I've read a ton of books about art and artists," she said. "I've taken classes. I've learned about technical stuff like plumb lines and how to structure space in a painting. I've made art and I've sold quite a few pieces. I figured that's the way it would always be, then a few weeks after we got back from New York, I had a kind of crisis, and I stopped painting."

"You never talked about it," I said.

"I wasn't unhappy," Taylor said. "But after I saw Des's paintings and looked at Sally's work again, I knew that before I made any more art, I had to decide what my work should be about. I made a lot of false starts, then I remembered the way the actors moved from human to bears and back again in *The Happiest Girl*, and I knew I wanted my work to have that . . . fluidity . . ." She narrowed her eyes. "Is that a word?"

I nodded. "Yes. *Fluidity* is definitely a word."

"Good, because that's what I want in my art. I want it to show how nothing is static, how everything is constantly flowing, transforming, and becoming something else." Taylor grimaced in frustration. "Does that even make sense?"

"Makes sense to me," Zack said.

"Do you know the term *painterly painting*?"

"I have an idea," I said. "But why don't you tell us."

"Painterly painting is when, instead of trying to hide the strokes you make with your brush or your knife, you use the strokes to be part of what you're doing. I've been noodling around with this, and I'm discovering that when I start out with an idea of what I want a piece to be and then let the brushstrokes and the knife strokes take it another way, I get that sense of movement I need to show that nothing is fixed, that everything is constantly transforming." Taylor laughed and threw up her hands. "I'm not good at explaining," she said. "Today when Siba asked Vale to explain her acting technique, Vale said, 'If I talk about it, I kill it.' I guess that's the way it is for me too."

"You and Vale really connect, don't you?" I said.

"We do. It's great being with her. We have so much in common, but we also seem to stretch each other. It's the best!" Taylor picked up her jacket and shrugged into it. "I'm going to go out to my studio awhile and check out my painterly painting."

"Come in and say goodnight to us when you're through," Zack said.

"I always do," Taylor said. "I know how you two count on having me tuck you in."

After Taylor crossed the backyard to her studio, Zack and I looked at each other. "Ready to call it day?" he said.

I took a deep breath and exhaled. "Am I ever."

Zack was already in bed, and I was on the way, when my phone rang.

I checked the caller ID. "Zephyr Winslow," I said.

My husband's lips twitched in a smile. "Her wish is our command."

Zephyr and I exchanged greetings, and then she got to the point. "Joanne, there's something I'd like to discuss with you. Would a meeting at my house at ten o'clock tomorrow morning be convenient?"

"I'm sure it can be arranged. Zephyr, could you give me an idea what this is about?"

"It involves Taylor."

"Our daughter is eighteen," I said. "She handles her own affairs, but I'd be happy to pass along a message to her."

"Thank you. However, we'll be able to speak more openly if Taylor's not there."

"In that case," I said, "I'll see you at ten tomorrow morning."

Zack peered at me questioningly over his reading classes. "What was on Zephyr's mind?"

"She has an idea that involves Taylor," I said.

"Shouldn't she be talking to Taylor?"

"That's what I said. But apparently Zephyr has another item on her agenda, and she wants to talk about it privately.

"Could be about Brock and Roy's relationship," Zack said. "Zephyr set them up, and she likes to keep an eye on her arrangements."

"According to Margot, Zephyr can rest easy on that score. Margot says every time Roy and Brock look at each other, they blush."

"How do you think Margot feels about that?" Zack said. "She made no secret of the fact that she was in love with Brock."

"And Brock made no secret of the fact that he's gay," I said. "From the moment Margot decided she wanted to have a second child, and Brock agreed to be her sperm donor, they became a family, but they both knew the day would come when one of them would meet someone with whom they wanted to have a romantic relationship. I guess that day has come for Brock."

"Let's hope it comes for Margot too," Zack said.

CHAPTER

8

Tuesday was a day of placid loveliness—still, blue-skied, and sunny. The weather was far too beautiful to miss, and I left early for Zephyr's to do something I had intended to do for years: explore Dieppe Place, the area on Regina's west side where Zephyr lived.

The neighbourhood had an interesting history. Named to commemorate the Second World War battle on the beach at Dieppe, in which Canadian forces suffered devastating casualties, the community offered half-acre lots at favourable rates to veterans, provided they built homes and lived there. Many who lived in Dieppe now were relatives of those veterans. Zephyr Winslow was one of them.

I pulled up in front of Zephyr's ten minutes early, and I was glad of the extra time because it gave me a chance to sit in the sunshine and admire her extraordinary home. Zephyr's father had been a money manager and he, and later Zephyr, had managed the family's money well. By all accounts, Edward Winslow was a practical man, but the house he built for his wife and daughter was a fanciful silver-grey clapboard affair with a many-windowed cupola, wraparound porch, and widow's walk. The house was as idiosyncratic as it was charming. My guess was that Edward Winslow had designed it himself and that the contractor charged with bringing the design to life had earned every penny of his fee.

I was wool-gathering, imagining summer parties spilling onto the wraparound porch, when a man bolted out Zephyr's front door, ran across the lawn, jumped into the car parked in front of me, gunned the engine, and peeled down the quiet street. He moved quickly, but not so quickly that I failed to recognize him. It was Shawn O'Day, the dancer with whom Gabe had quarrelled the night of Zephyr's fete. The car Shawn had jumped into was a silvery-grey BMW with a vanity plate that read, "DANCE." It wasn't much of a leap to believe the shiny new car belonged to the lady of the house.

At one minute to ten, I walked up the front path and rang the doorbell. Zephyr answered immediately, and with a graceful sweep of her arm invited me in.

"You arrived on lawyer time," she said, smiling. "That's what Father always said about people who were punctual to the minute. May I take your jacket?"

I handed her my coat and removed my boots. The entrance hall was large and welcoming, with pale yellow walls, warm wood floors, and an antique credenza of burnished mahogany. "That's a lovely piece," I said.

"It is," Zephyr agreed. "My parents had it in the dining room, but it takes up so much space, I always suspected guests felt crowded."

"It deserves a place of its own," I said. "And those watercolours on the wall behind it are the perfect balance. They're so filled with light."

"The paintings are of heritage buildings that my family owned," Zephyr said. "The Winslows have left their mark on Regina."

"You're certainly leaving your mark," I said. "The Zephyr Winslow Studios will bring some exciting projects to our city. I'm really looking forward to the official dedication and to the arts festival celebrating the renaming."

"So am I," Zephyr said. "And that's part of what I wanted to talk to you about. Let's go into the living room where we can be comfortable."

The living room was stunning, with walls of the same pale yellow as those in the entranceway, and mahogany furniture upholstered in pastel florals, but what drew my attention was the huge poinsettia in front of the room's bow window. With its bushy dark green foliage and rich burgundy bracts, it was indisputably the twin of the poinsettia sitting in front of the south-facing window in our living room. Seemingly, the card we received, with its curious inscription, *So a kingdom was lost—all for the want of a nail*," had been intended for Gabe's anonymous donor to *The Happiest Girl*, Regina's own Zephyr Winslow. Now the man whom Gabe had punched in the face and told to stay away from the production studios was driving her BMW.

Zephyr led me to matching settees flanking a table where tea had been set out. She gestured to one of the settees. "These look a little formal but they're surprisingly comfortable." We took our places facing each other, and Zephyr poured the tea. "I've been thinking about the celebrations in May, and I wonder if Taylor would be interested in curating an exhibition of works by young artists."

"I'm sure she'd be interested in talking with you about it, but as I said last night, Taylor makes her own decisions."

"And you trust her ability to make sound judgments."

I felt a tendril of irritation growing. "We do," I said. "Zephyr, if you have a specific concern about Taylor, let's talk about it."

Zephyr was dressed casually, in dove-grey slacks, flats, and a silk shirt the same vibrant pink as her lipstick. "I seemed to have raised your hackles," she said. "But I'm on Taylor's side, Joanne. I've talked to her at a number of gallery openings, and she's a lovely girl. I wouldn't want to see her hurt."

"Neither would I," I said and let the words hang in the air.

Zephyr poured the tea and handed me my cup. "I understand your daughter and Vale Frazier have become close," she said. "Gabe Vickers mentioned to me that he was at the studio yesterday and sat in on part of the interview they did for *Nexus*. He said Taylor and Vale appear to trust each other completely."

"And that's a problem?"

"It could be," she said. "I understand Vale is a complex young woman. She's been acting professionally since she was very young. Gabe feels that she sometimes blurs the line between truth and fantasy."

"She lies?"

Zephyr narrowed her eyes. "That's a little harsh."

"Yes, it is," I said. "Vale had dinner with our family Sunday night, and Zack and I liked her. We found her open and perceptive. I appreciate your concern about Taylor, but I think we'd like to make up our own minds about her new friend."

Zephyr stiffened. "I don't mean to offend, Joanne. According to Gabe, during the interview Vale said that Taylor was the first person with whom she could be fully truthful about her life without fear of being judged. But I don't believe Vale is a reliable narrator about the circumstances of her own life. Taylor is a fine young woman. I wouldn't want her to be taken in by Vale's *embellishments*."

My first impulse was to tell Zephyr that Taylor's relationship with Vale was none of her business, but I bit my tongue, in part because of what Zephyr's former students had said about her kindness and generosity, in part because she was a significant client of Falconer Shreve, but also because the seed of doubt she planted had found fertile ground. The night Vale had dinner with our family, she said that to get the outcome she wanted as an actor, she had to play each moment completely in character. When she pointed out to Zack that, as a lawyer, he knew the value of playing the moment to get what he wanted, Vale had found an ally. There was no mystery about the outcome Vale wanted with Taylor. She longed for our daughter's friendship. Given her history and training, it was entirely possible that Vale would present herself to Taylor in a guise that would ensure our daughter reached out to her.

The possibility was concerning, but it was by no means a certainty, and I was not about to act on it. I smiled at Zephyr. "I'll ask Taylor to get in touch with you about the project with the young artists," I said. "It really does sound like something she'd enjoy being involved in."

It was time for a change of topic, and the Winslow home with its high ceilings, spacious rooms, and spiral staircase offered one. "This house must be beautiful at Christmas," I said.

"It is," Zephyr said, "More accurately, it was. My parents believed in decking the halls. I'm always so busy with the studio, I never quite get around to doing everything that they did."

"That gorgeous poinsettia in your window is certainly welcoming," I said.

As Zephyr gazed at the plant, her lips curved into a small and private smile. "It is spectacular, isn't it?"

She turned back to me. "I imagine you and Zack have a busy holiday calendar."

"We do. Between friends, clients, and our granddaughters' endless December recitals, the days *are* full, but it's fun. We're looking forward to Gabe and Ainsley's dinner for Rosamond Burke. I understand you'll be there."

"It should be an evening to remember," Zephyr said.

"Have you met Rosamond?"

"I have," she said.

"And . . . ?"

Zephyr raised an eyebrow. "My father would say that Rosamond Burke, CBE, has panache."

We both laughed and moved on to other topics, but Zephyr and I didn't linger over our tea. We were both pre-occupied. I had not assured her that I would caution Taylor, and my time with Zephyr had raised questions that I knew would nag at me. She walked me to the door and I thanked her for her hospitality. Just as I was about to step into the brisk morning air, Zephyr took my elbow and spoke with a low urgency. "For everyone's sake, Joanne, give serious thought to what I said about Vale." The intensity of her gaze rattled me. I assured her I'd take it into consideration and then said goodbye and hurried down the front walk.

For Taylor's eighteenth birthday, her friend Gracie Falconer had sent her a handsome leather-covered journal. On the first page Gracie had written, "How people treat you is their karma. How you treat them is yours." As I slid into the driver's seat of our Volvo, I knew that neither Zephyr nor I had sent much positive energy into the universe during our time together. It was time to redress the balance.

I took out my phone and called April's Place. Angela Greyeyes answered. "It's Joanne," I said. "Could you use an extra pair of hands for the next couple of hours?"

"Come over," she said. "We're gearing up for soup and bannock time."

"I'll be there in fifteen minutes," I said.

I was just about to pull out when the silver BMW approached, slowed, and then sped off. The sequence piqued my curiosity, so I turned off the engine and waited. It wasn't long before the BMW reappeared, and the scene repeated itself.

I picked up my phone and hit speed-dial. Zack answered on the first ring. "Got a minute?" I said.

"For you, always," he said. "Luckily for us the jury's still out. Hey, I thought you were having tea with Zephyr."

"We didn't linger. At the moment, I'm parked outside Zephyr's, playing hide and seek with Shawn O'Day."

"Shawn the dancer that Gabe Vickers attempted to cold-cock?"

"That's the one," I said.

"I'll bite," Zack said. "What the hell's going on?"

"I wish I knew," I said.

After I sketched the events of the last half-hour, Zack whistled. "Weird," he said. "So are you planning to spend the rest of the morning spooking Shawn?"

"No. I just talked to Angela. I'm going to April's Place to give her a hand with lunch."

"Maybe you can help me out," Zack said. "I can't get Chloe out of my mind. I called Nick this morning. Chloe slept well, and she and her aide were planning to go to April's Place this morning to check out 21 Days of Christmas. Every time I think about how much Nick and Chloe were suffering on Sunday, I want to put my fist through a sheet of glass. When I talked to Nick, he sounded optimistic, but I'd welcome a first-hand report."

"I'll keep you posted."

"Gotta go," Zack said. "The jury's coming back."

"Are you going to win?"

"Not a hope in hell. But I get to come home to you, so all is not lost."

UpSlideDown serves light fare, and Mieka's comfortably well off clientele have always been happy to pay market price for freshly squeezed orange juice, quality tea and coffee, and baked goods still warm from the oven. April's Place is the twin of UpSlideDown, but when Angela Greyeyes took over the management she saw the need for a substantial lunchtime meal. The communal arrangement she came up with was working. Angela and her staff made a nourishing soup every day, and neighbourhood women volunteered to have their names placed on a daily duty roster for bringing bannock.

When I arrived, Chloe and her aide were sitting at a craft table by the front window, hard at work. Chloe spotted me, flashed me a smile of recognition, and returned to gluing cotton balls on a cardboard snowman. After introducing myself to the aide and admiring Chloe's handiwork, I joined Angela in the kitchen.

I checked the soup pot. "Hamburger stew," I said. "One of my favourites."

Angela's laugh was deep and infectious. "That's because it's never the same twice," she said. "Wash your hands and grab an apron."

"Got it," I said.

Angela and I loaded trays with dishes and cutlery and arranged condiments and butter and jam for the bannock on a low serving table. We'd just begun ladling out the soup when Chloe's aide, Bronwyn, peeked into the kitchen. "We'd like to stay for lunch, if that's okay," she said.

"Everybody is welcome here," Angela said.

Bronwyn slipped a twenty-dollar bill under the salt shaker on the serving table.

"You don't have to do that," Angela said.

"You're giving Chloe a happy morning, and we want to do our part," Bronwyn said.

Angela watched as Bronwyn walked back and joined Chloe at their craft table. When they were settled, she turned to me.

"I try not to stick my nose into other people's lives, but what's the story there?"

After I gave her the brief history of Chloe's life, Angela's obsidian eyes filled with tears. "Sometimes life really sucks," she said.

"It does," I agreed. "Angela, there's more. Chloe's father wants to keep this private, but I think you should know that last Sunday Chloe was assaulted on her way to April's Place. Her aide was on the phone dealing with an emergency, and Chloe left the house. The police picked her up on Winnipeg Street. She wasn't able to tell them much except that a man had given her a ride. She was gripping two $50s in her hand and there was physical evidence that the man who picked her up had ejaculated on her—there was semen between her breasts and near her genitals."

"Marking his territory," Angela said. "Sick bastard." Angela, her face grim, simply gazed at Chloe for a long time. Finally, in a voice harsh with anger, she said, "It's better if she doesn't understand what happened. That way, she'll have a chance of getting over it."

As we served the soup, Angela joked with the kids. When it was time to serve Chloe, she was tender. As she watched Chloe put butter and jam on her bannock and take her first taste of hamburger stew, Angela's eyes were anxious. "Everything okay?" she said.

Chloe looked up at her. "Everything's really nice," she said. "Can I come back?"

Angela bit her lip. "As often as you want to."

"That's really nice of you," Chloe said, and she went back to her hamburger stew.

CHAPTER

9

I hate flying. I've tried hypnotism, fearful flyer classes, three
fingers of bourbon, and a variety of pharmaceuticals that
guaranteed a carefree flight. Nothing worked. The flight
from Regina to Saskatoon lasts forty-five minutes. Thursday
morning, as I waited for the cab that would take Roy
Brodnitz and me to the airport, my anxiety level was spik-
ing. When the phone rang and Ben Bendure's name appeared
on the caller ID, I felt a stirring of hope. Ben was in his
eighties. He might have decided he wasn't up for a visit. But
when he greeted me, his voice was robust and his spirits
were high.

"Joanne, I've had a thought," he said. "Instead of coming
to my condo, why don't we meet at Izaak Levin's old house
on 9th Street. It's just around the corner from me."

"I haven't thought about the place in years," I said. "I just
assumed that after Izaak died, his sister cleared out all the
art and sold it."

"Then you're in for a surprise," Ben said. "That house is
exactly the way it was the day Izaak walked out the door
for the last time. Ellie Levin couldn't bring herself to sell it,

so an old colleague of Izaak's lived in it till he passed on six
months ago. Then Ellie died and left the place to me. I've
been trying to figure out what to do with it ever since. Shall
we meet there? I'm sure the contents of the place would
intrigue Mr. Brodnitz."

"I'm sure they would," I said.

I'd just written down the address and said goodbye to Ben
when the cab taking us to the airport pulled into my driveway. I patted Esme and Pantera, told them to behave, and
picked up my bag. It was too late to turn back. The meter
was ticking.

Roy had arranged for us to pick up a car at the Saskatoon
Airport, and after the papers were in order and we were settled in our mid-sized Hyundai, he turned to me. "So where
to?" he said.

"We have over an hour before we meet Ben, plenty of
time to go down to the river and see where Sally lived when
she and Stu were married, her studio on the riverbank, and
the old Mendel Gallery where she died at the banquet celebrating her retrospective. Everything's within a few blocks,
so it'll be an easy walk."

Roy's brow furrowed. "Could we grab something to eat
first? I haven't had breakfast."

"I wouldn't mind a cup of coffee," I said. "The Parktown
Hotel is on the west bank of the river, a stone's throw from
where we want to be, and they have a restaurant."

Roy and I sat at a booth overlooking the river. The sky
was a piercing December blue, the river was only partially
frozen, and the sun bounced off the flowing water and the
still-forming ice.

After we'd ordered, Roy looked out the window at the
river. "This really is beautiful," he said.

"I agree," I said. "To me, the South Saskatchewan River

valley has always seemed like the heart of Saskatoon, and the province was smart enough to create a conservation authority to preserve its natural beauty, and make it people-friendly. There are over sixty kilometres of trails winding through the valley—great hiking in any weather. When we lived here, the kids and I came down to the river almost every weekend."

Roy's breakfast arrived, and after he'd made a good start on his bacon and eggs, his attention returned to me. "How long did you and your family live in Saskatoon?"

"It was only for a year. I'd been teaching sessionally at the university, but after my husband died, I needed a permanent job, and that meant finishing my Ph.D. My dissertation was on Andy Boychuk, who'd been a bright light in Saskatchewan politics. He was from Saskatoon, and his papers are in the university archives here. The kids and I had finally adjusted to life without Ian, and we didn't want to be apart. We talked it over and through the university grapevine, I heard about a sabbatical house that was available July 1st. The owner was a Milton scholar who'd built the house himself. It was perfect for us. All the pieces just seemed to fall into place."

Roy's smile was wry. "Those words about pieces falling into place have a familiar ring," he said. "Fate seems to be pushing you and me into the Jungian camp, Joanne."

"I've been there for years," I said. "But in retrospect, my decision to spend a year in Saskatoon really did seem like kismet because that was the year Sally and I got back together."

"Were you able to pick up where you'd left off?"

"We made a start that summer, but we were both still wounded and feeling our way, and then Sally met a gorgeous, very young man and the two of them left for New Mexico. I didn't see her again until she returned for the opening of her retrospective at the Mendel in December.

"That night it was clear something had changed. As soon as she spotted me in the crowd, Sally took my arm, said there was a painting we had to see together, and led me to it. It was of Izaak Levin and us at the lake. That summer we'd had crushes on him and the painting brought back all the hours we spent writing steamy stories about Izaak's lips pressing themselves against our lips and his tortured body lowering itself onto ours." I laughed. "We were never quite sure what happened after that, but those memories of unrequited lust did the trick. Sally and I were close again. She died in February, so we didn't have long, but we made the most of our time together. After Christmas that year she made a trip to Vancouver, and she sent me a sweatshirt—bubble-gum pink with *"I LOVE JO"* written across the chest in sequins and bugle beads, and a note saying, '*Now you've got it in writing.*'"

Roy heard the pain in my voice. "Why don't we just stay here and talk until it's time to go to Ben's?"

"That's fine with me," I said. "The house Sally and Stu lived in has been renovated and is pretty well unrecognizable, and the Mendel has been closed and replaced by the Remai Modern Art Gallery, but sometime you should see Sally's studio. It's still part of her estate. The university has a program that allows visiting artists to live and work there for a semester. I didn't want to sell it until Taylor was old enough to decide whether she wanted to use it."

"Has Taylor expressed any interest in the studio?"

"She's never seen it." I said. "Her plan to go to OCAD was in place for so long, we never talked about Saskatoon as a possibility. But it's a great space. I haven't seen it since I was there with Sally, but it's worth checking out. I'll call the university and see if we can stop by this afternoon."

Roy motioned for the cheque. "Full day ahead," he said.

"Right, and before we go I should prepare you for Izaak Levin's house."

From the outside, Izaak Levin's was an unremarkable, well-maintained two-storey detached house with wood siding and a meandering front walk. Ben Bendure met us at the door. He wore his favoured gear: a long-pocketed khaki vest, a blue Oxford cloth shirt, comfortable slacks, and well-worn walking boots. His beard had always been neatly trimmed, but he'd let it grow full, and it was snowy and luxuriant. He remained physically fit, but I noticed that his ivory-handled cane was now a necessity, not an accessory.

"You're looking dapper," I said.

"In the pink," he said agreeably, "as are you, Joanne. Marriage continues to agree with you."

"It does," I said. When I introduced Roy, Ben shook his hand warmly. "Welcome," he said. "I hope Joanne warned you that you are about to enter a temple dedicated to Sally Love. Izaak Levin didn't just collect works by Sally. Most of the art in this house is work by other artists, with Sally as their subject."

Roy smiled. "I've been forewarned."

"Forewarned is forearmed," Ben said. "Follow along."

We hadn't made it out of the hall when Roy stopped in front of a felt portrait of Sally. The razor cuts the artist had made in the pressed wool fibre were stark, but she had managed to suggest both Sally's strength and her vulnerability. Roy was absorbed in the piece. "There's such tenderness here," he said. His expression was sheepish. "I have so much to learn about art."

"You've come to the right place," Ben said. "Every piece in this collection is first rate. Izaak would never have anything shabby connected with Sally."

"Did she ever see all this?" Roy said.

"Oh yes," Ben said. "She contributed the first piece. Izaak always called Sally 'an academy of one.' He had told her that artists admitted to the American Academy in New York must give the academy a self-portrait, so Sally gave Izaak one for his birthday."

Ben gestured to the art that spilled from the living room into the dining room and hall and up the staircase to the second floor. "What you can see here is less than half the art in this house."

Roy gazed around the room, taking it all in. Finally, he turned to Ben. "I don't need to tell you how powerful these rooms are, not just cinematically, but for storytelling. Why didn't you use them in *The Poison Apple*?"

"Loyalty," he said. He picked up a ceramic of a teenaged Sally sprawled on a rocker, holding a cat. "Izaak was my friend, and he had been a real power in art circles. This was his private world. I feared making it public would expose him to ridicule." Ben regarded the ceramic in his hands thoughtfully. "Over the years, I've wondered if I was mistaken."

"You'd agree to letting me include scenes of this house in *Flying Blue Horses*?"

"I would," Ben said. "I'm aware of the rumour that Izaak was a pederast. He was not. It's true that Sally was far too young for a sexual relationship when theirs began, but Izaak's obsession was not with children; it was with Sally. He loved her. There was never anyone else for him. He was her teacher. Her mentor. Her champion. Her agent. And throughout her life, whenever she welcomed him into her bed, he was her lover. Revealing the devotion evident in this house might put the lie to the ugly stories about Izaak's relationship with her. She wasn't his victim. She was his life.

"When I heard that Izaak suffered a fatal heart attack seconds after Sally died from an anaphylactic reaction to almonds she'd ingested, I was devastated. But I was also relieved. As Izaak's friend, I knew he wouldn't have wanted to live in a world where Sally Love no longer existed."

"That much, at least, is true," I said.

Ben smiled. "A poet whose name I no longer remember said, 'Poetry turns the cube of reality.' I'm beginning to think that living does that too. Our perspective is always shifting. Now, I can't offer you food or drink. The kitchen in this house is not stocked, but there are a number of very nice specialty shops in my neighbourhood. After we've explored the house together, there's a picnic lunch waiting for us at my condo."

Ben had done us proud: a small selection of very fine cheeses, a rustic baguette, and a plate of fruit that was surprisingly flavourful for a December day on the prairies. During lunch, Ben and Roy talked shop. I stayed quiet. I had nothing to contribute, and it was fun learning about movie making and watching these two men take each other's measure, and take pleasure in what they saw. After we cleared away the dishes, Ben led us to his home office. On the desk were neat piles of plastic DVD boxes with yellow labels.

"This is all the material I didn't use in *The Poison Apple*," Ben said. "Joanne, since we spoke on Monday, I've reviewed the DVDs of your summers at MacLeod Lake. To be frank, until this week I hadn't paid much attention to the material I shot before Sally was born, but there's much in these early tapes that will be meaningful to you." He picked up a DVD. "This one starts with the Thanksgiving weekend just after you were born and picks up months later with your first summer at the lake. You were a month shy of your first birthday, but in that very watchful child, I can see the woman you've become. Why don't you take that one home with you today? I think you'll be glad you did."

He turned to Roy. "Given the perspective of your project, I'm sure everything here will be of interest to you too. The content notes on the DVD labels might spark some ideas."

"I'm eager to look at them."

"Why don't you start right now?" Ben said. "If you don't mind, I'd like to speak with Joanne privately for a few minutes. We won't be long."

Roy's smile was easy. "Take your time. There's plenty to occupy me here."

Ben led me back to the kitchen. "These days I find sitting at the table best for serious conversation. My hearing is not what it once was. Besides, I like to watch people's faces."

Ben pulled out a chair for me and took his place across the table. "After we spoke the other day, it occurred to me that I might have left you with the impression that your father was indifferent to you," he said. "That's far from the truth. Your father wanted a child, and he loved you. Your mother did not want a child, and she resented the fact that he loved you. That's the crux of the matter. Everything else—the cruelties, the betrayals, the heartbreaks, the bitterness—springs from those not-so-simple facts."

"I know my father believed my mother would grow to love me after I was born and she didn't," I said. "That happens in families. If one parent discovers he or she wasn't cut out for raising a child, the couple works out a solution. They find middle ground. Why couldn't my parents work it out?"

Ben shook his head. "There was never any middle ground for your mother," he said. "As you know, she was brilliant."

"Actually, I didn't know that," I said. "I barely saw her."

"That's a pity," Ben said. "Because Caroline was impressive. Your father met her in medical school. She planned to become a psychiatrist."

"I'd forgotten that," I said. "She had a breakdown and never graduated."

"Yes, and it was a grave disappointment to her."

"Med school is brutal," I said. "There must have been other options."

"Not for Caroline," he said. "She tried again, but the result was the same. She had a history of mental illness. I always wondered if she chose psychiatry because she wanted to discover what was wrong with her."

"And she found her answer," I said. "She never hesitated to tell me that I had ruined her life."

"Caroline was her own worst enemy. She couldn't share your father's love with anybody. She loathed your Grandmother Ellard and Des and you equally. To keep her hold on your father, Caroline agreed to conceive a child she didn't want with a man she was jealous of. When she saw how much your father loved you, she froze you out of their lives. That's why you all but lived with your Grandmother Ellard until you were old enough to go to Bishop Lambeth."

"Why did my father let that happen?" I said. "They told people my mother was not strong enough emotionally to raise a child, but she was hardly a recluse. She had an active social life, and she travelled. My father could have hired a nanny and let me live at home. Why didn't he do that?"

"She threatened him. Having convinced your father that letting you live with Des would potentially ruin her and your father's medical practice, she shuttled you off to your grandmother's and then to boarding school. She promised your father that if he ever brought you home to stay, she would make the truth about your conception public. It was a grenade that would hurt everyone."

Ben took my hand. "I hope the truth will help more than it hurts."

"I hope that too," I said. "The motto of my old school was *Vincit omnia veritas*. Truth conquers all. The crest of the tunic I wore every day for thirteen years was embroidered with those words." I tried a smile. "Maybe they will have become part of me through osmosis."

"In that case," Ben said, "take the DVD I mentioned. It covers a time that you were far too young to remember, but seeing the life that went on around you at MacLeod Lake during those years may help you understand what happened later."

Ben was clearly tiring, so after I collected the DVD and Roy arranged to have the others shipped to Regina, we thanked Ben for his hospitality, and the three of us said goodbye. Before we pulled out of the parkade next to Ben's condo, Roy phoned Ainsley to fill her in on our meeting with Ben, and I called the university's Department of Art and Art History to see if Sally's old studio was occupied.

We were in luck. The outgoing artist in residence had left the previous weekend and the incoming artist wouldn't arrive until January. The place had been cleaned, and the heat had been turned on. The admin assistant to whom I spoke gave me the numerical code to the electronic door lock and asked me to get back to her if there were any problems.

When Roy rejoined me, he was buoyant. "Ainsley's as excited about *Flying Blue Horses* as we are," he said. "She's already asking when she can read the script."

"Did you tell Ainsley she can read the script as soon as you write it?"

"I said I thought I could have something to show her by the first week in the new year. That may be overly optimistic, but I feel good about this, Joanne. The scenes seem to be forming themselves. Our time with Ben at that remarkable house made me quiver."

"Well, prepare to quiver again," I said. "Sally's studio is available. No one's living there, so we can take as much time as we need to look around before we're scheduled to meet Father Ariano."

"Everything's going our way," Roy said. "Now, do you have an address I can plug into the GPS?"

"I'll do it." I punched in the address on Spadina Crescent. "Set to go," I said. "Depending on traffic, it's only about ten minutes from here."

Roy pulled out of the parkade. "How did Sally end up having her studio in Saskatoon anyway?" he said.

"Happenstance. By the time Sally was in her early twenties, she'd made a lot of money. The art world was abuzz with rumours that Sally Love's work was a smart investment, so people were paying highly inflated prices for her work. Izaak was her agent so he was raking it in too. Sally said they were both getting tired of travel, and Izaak suggested they use their money to put down roots somewhere."

"And out of all the places in the world, they chose Saskatoon," Roy said.

"Over the years, I've wondered about that too," I said. "But when you told me that when Des was young, he'd spent time spent at Emma Lake, I saw the connection. The Artists' Workshops were affiliated with the University of Saskatchewan Kenderdine Campus. Des left the U of S a sizable bequest in his will and asked that his papers go to the university archives.

"Most importantly, Sally had fallen in love with the river valley in the centre of the city. The area was central and it was close to everything Sally wanted to be close to. She bought a one-storey bungalow a stone's throw from the Mendel Gallery and converted it into a studio with a work area overlooking the river."

"And Izaak bought the house we were in today, so he could be close to her," Roy said.

"Sally was glad Izaak was there," I said. "Suddenly there was a great deal of money floating around her, and according to Sally, when the sharks started circling, Izaak protected her."

Roy sighed. "That is one complex relationship," he said.

"It is, and the only two people who will ever fully understand it died an arm's length from each other fourteen years ago on Valentine's Day."

The wind off the river was cold, and I welcomed the warmth of Sally's studio. The cleaners had done yeoman's duty. The place was spotless, and the sun pouring in through the skylight and the window overlooking the river pooled invitingly on the hardwood floor.

Roy looked around appreciatively. "This is a great space for an artist."

"It is," I said. "I was only here once before, and I was too angry and frightened to take anything in."

Roy's look was quizzical. "Do you want to talk about it?"

"Not much," I said. "But it's part of the story, and as awful as everything was, that day Sally and I were together in a way we hadn't been for a very long time. Her life had been hell since *Erotobiography* opened. I'd never felt the kind of hatred that was in the air that night. People weren't just protesting Sally's work; they were protesting her right to exist."

"And that continued?" Roy said.

"It intensified. Sally's phone never stopped ringing, and the threats were bloodcurdling. The morning before Christmas, Sally called to tell me that during the night womanswork, an art gallery she owned on Fourteenth Street, had burned to the ground, and the fire department suspected arson."

Roy's eyes widened. "Arson? My God, that certainly crosses the line."

"Sally asked me to meet her at the gallery to assess the extent of the damage," I said. "It was a nightmare. All that was left of that graceful showcase for women's art was a charred skeleton."

"Sally must have been devastated."

"She was. I thought she was on the verge of shock, and I knew we had to get out of there. When we started towards our cars, a young fireman ran up and handed Sally an antique porcelain doll. He said he thought it might have sentimental value. Sally tucked the doll inside her coat and we came back here. The doll's hair and clothes had been burned off and she was covered in soot. Sally set to work with solvents and creams to restore her. When she was finished, the doll was still battered but her eyes shone through, bright blue and defiant. Sally handed me the doll and said it was my souvenir of our morning."

"What did Taylor think of that story?" Roy said.

"I've never told her. I didn't want her to know about all the vitriol that was aimed at Sally that winter. But the doll Sally gave me is in one of the packing cases in our garage. When I get back I'll give it to Taylor and tell her about this place. She was talking the other day about wanting to make art that showed that nothing is static, that everything is constantly transforming." I walked to the window and beckoned Roy to join me. "From here it seems as if the river is flowing both ways, and look at how the ice and water on the river are dappled by the light. I think this studio might be a good fit for Taylor."

I called ahead to let Father Gary Ariano know we were on our way. The college bells were chiming three o'clock when Roy and I walked through the main entrance and Gary Ariano, wearing blue jeans and a Gonzaga University sweatshirt, greeted us with a grin and an outstretched hand.

After I introduced Roy, I turned to Gary and raised an eyebrow at his sweatshirt. "I thought you graduated from St. Michael's," I said.

"I did," he replied. "My brother, Lou, went to Gonzaga, and I lost a bet. I don't want to talk about it."

"I imagine Lou does," I said.

Gary's lips twitched towards a smile. "Time to move along," he said. Roy and I followed him up two flights of stairs through a door marked "Private" into the priests' common room. Nothing had changed in the fourteen years since I'd last been there. The ambience was still 1960s recreation room: worn but comfortable furniture, a TV, a well-stocked wet bar, and an outsized aquarium.

Gary gestured to the bar fridge. "Too early for beer?"

Roy raised his hand in a halt sign. "I'm driving."

"And I had wine with lunch," I said. "But thanks."

"I'd better pass too," Gary said. "I still have students to see."

"Aren't they in the middle of exams?" I said.

"You'd be surprised at how many students decide to seek God the night before a final," Gary said.

Roy had gravitated towards the aquarium. When Gary joined him, Roy was apologetic. "Sorry. I've never been able to resist the allure of tropical fish."

"Please don't apologize," Gary said. "Our lives are busy, and that silent, timeless world is very compelling. Sally never tired of watching life in the watery kingdom."

"That surprises me," I said. I stepped closer to the aquarium. "But maybe it shouldn't. Look at that gold and lapis lazuli on that angelfish gliding through the coral reef— absolutely breathtaking—and the spines on that pair of lionfish look like sunbursts radiating off their bodies. Miracles."

"Maybe," Gary said. "But what intrigued Sally was the thought that those exquisite creatures lived out their lives not realizing that no matter how gracefully they swam they would never get anywhere and that their sole reason for existing was to please us. She said when it came right down to it, they were just pretty little fish swimming in an artificial environment. When one of the pretty little fish died, it was scooped up, flushed down the toilet, replaced by another pretty little fish, and the universe rolled on."

My throat tightened. "Did Sally see herself as one of the pretty little fish?" I said.

Gary shrugged. "I don't know. She was still grappling with the big questions when she died. Sally had a very fine mind and she was knowledgeable about a surprising array of subjects. Izaak Levin made certain she received a first-rate education."

I shot him a sharp look. "Sally paid in hard coin for that education," I said.

"She didn't entirely see it that way, you know. She thought of her relationship with Izaak as a fair exchange."

I was stunned. "She was fourteen years old, Gary."

"Joanne, I'm not giving Izaak Levin a free pass on this. I'm just telling you that at least a part of Sally believed Izaak saved her. They travelled the world together; he took her to the great galleries and to lectures that awakened her mind. They read books together. Most importantly, he made it possible for her create art." Gary's dark eyes bore into me. "Sally's alternative was to live with a mother who wanted her dead and who ultimately did kill her. It wasn't right for Izaak to sleep with Sally when she was a fourteen-year-old girl, but I find it difficult to be unequivocal about his influence on her life."

Roy had been listening intently. "I hear what you're saying, Gary, but Joanne and I were watching old footage of Sally as a kid and I saw a profound change in her, a devastating loss of innocence, the year she became involved with Izaak Levin. She may have benefitted from him, but she suffered too."

"I'm sure you're right, Roy," Gary said. "I didn't know Sally for long, and I only know what she told me. Sadly for us all, she's not here now to share more of how she experienced life."

"If all goes according to plan, Joanne and I will have twelve hours to tell our story," Roy said.

"Time enough to turn the cube of reality and show that no single truth explains any of us," I said. "Certainly, there is no single truth that explains Sally."

The college bells struck the half-hour. Reflexively, Gary checked his watch. "I'm going to have to cut this short. I'm meeting that student in my office and I don't want to keep him waiting, but I would really like to help you in any way I can. Sally deserves that."

"She does," I said. "Gary, I'm glad she had you in her life."

"The pleasure was mine," he said softly. "Joanne, there's something you should know. The last time Sally and I talked was less than a week before she died. She was in a strange mood. It was almost as if she knew what was ahead. She was more at peace than I'd ever seen her. She said that now you and Taylor were part of her life again, she was complete. And then, Sally being Sally, she gave me that wicked smile and said, 'Well, as complete as I'll ever be.'"

Neither Roy nor I spoke until we were in the car and on our way to the airport.

"That was quite a day," he said.

"It was," I agreed. "Zack would say it doesn't take many days like this to make a dozen."

Roy reached over and touched my arm. "But you're okay?"

"I am." I took a deep breath. "I can't believe I'm saying this, but I'll be glad to get on that plane."

CHAPTER

10

Brock picked us up at the airport. As always, he was warm and considerate with me, and after we arrived at my place he and Roy walked me to the door. When I was inside, I turned to say goodnight and saw that they were walking hand in hand towards Brock's car. On the drive back, they'd decided they would go to Roy's apartment, order the Pikillia Platter for two from the Copper Kettle, and watch *Die Hard*, which they agreed was the ultimate holiday movie and contained the ultimate holiday song, Run-D.M.C.'s "Christmas in Hollis." Love was in the air.

Our family's evening plans were less action-packed but not without appeal. The casserole of lasagna I'd earmarked for nights like this was already out of the freezer and in the oven; the table was set. Zack had changed out of his lawyer clothes, and he and Taylor were chopping vegetables.

When I bent to kiss the top of Zack's head, he said, "There are martinis in the fridge. Why don't I pour them, and you can pull up a chair and tell us about your day while our daughter and I finish what promises to be a salad to remember."

"Hold that thought," I said. "There's something I want to get for Taylor, and if I have a martini, I'll lose my initiative." I headed for the garage. It took a while to find the doll Sally had given me. As always, it was in the last place I looked, still in its packing box.

When I came back, Zack exhaled with mock relief. "I was just about to send a search party out for you."

"I would have welcomed them and asked them to help me unpack the boxes I never seem to get around to."

"Do you want me to call somebody?" Zack said.

Taylor raised her hand. "Hello. I'm here," she said. "You don't have to call anybody, Dad. Jo and I can do it."

"In that case," Zack said, "let me get us all the beverage of our choice, and we'll see what's in the mystery box your mother brought in."

We settled around the kitchen table and sipped our drinks. "It was a full day and there's plenty to report," I said. "But after lunch, Roy and I went to Sally's studio on the riverbank. Taylor, when I was there, it suddenly hit me that we've never really talked about that studio." ·

"I think we did," Taylor said. "It was a long time ago, though. It's cool to know that it's still there."

I pulled out my phone and handed it to Taylor. "I took some pictures," I said. "The university has a year-round artist in residence program, but no one's using the space again until mid-January, so Roy and I were able to take our time. The studio is on Spadina Crescent—a great location on the west side of the river. The university's just across the bridge, the old Mendel Gallery is down the road, and the Remai Modern Art Gallery is a ten-minute bike ride away."

Taylor and Zack were looking at the photos. "Wow, that studio is huge!" Taylor said.

"That's because it used to be a house," I said. "Sally had the living room, dining room, and two of the bedrooms ripped out. All that's left of the original bungalow is one bedroom, one bathroom, and the kitchen. The rest is studio space."

As she looked at the photos, Taylor's brow wrinkled in concentration. "Those windows overlook the river, right?"

"I took a video of the view," I said. "My photography is not great, but you can see the ice is still forming and the water's flowing. A river is never static. It reminded me about you wanting your paintings to be more fluid, with more air and light in them so people can *feel* what you painted instead of just looking at the canvas."

Taylor's expression was pensive. "So you think I should go to Saskatoon and check out the studio?"

"That's up to you," I said. "You're exploring options, and that seems like a good one, and not just because of the proximity to the river, but because your mother made art there for so many years."

"Were you there often, Jo?" Zack said.

"No. Until today, the only other time I was in that studio was the morning after a gallery Sally owned burned to the ground. I'd gone with her to see what was left of it. It was snowing hard. Sally wore a brilliantly coloured blanket coat she'd brought back from New Mexico—the only splash of colour in that white, white world. One of the firemen brought Sally what was once a lovely porcelain doll. It had been ravaged by the fire.

"That day, Sally agreed to come stay with us, but she said she needed to check her messages first, and as Sally listened to her messages—most of them obscene, threatening, or both—she worked on the doll, cleaning the soot off with solvent, using some sort of cream on its face and hair. When she was satisfied, she cut a piece off an old scarf, wrapped it around the doll, and gave the doll to me." I handed the box to Taylor. "That moment encapsulated Sally," I said. "No matter what was done to her, she never stopped making art. Taylor, I know she'd want you to have this."

Taylor removed the doll from the box. The sarong had come loose. Her hair was just a singed frizz and a small patch of paint had flaked off her cheek, but her brilliant blue eyes were still bold. Taylor tightened the sarong and then held the doll at arm's length so she could look at her again. "Thank you, Jo," she said. "I'm going to put this in my studio to remind me never to give up on my vision." Taylor kissed me on the cheek. "Something I've learned from my two mothers."

The lasagna, salad, and garlic bread were on the table and we'd just begun to eat when our landline rang. Only family or close friends ever called it any more, so I answered.

When I returned to the dining room, Zack looked at me questioningly. "That was our oldest granddaughter," I said. "Madeleine reminded me very politely that tomorrow is a teacher prep day at St. Pius X, and I had promised that she and Lena and I would go to April's Place and help with crafts in the morning and then the three of us would go skate shopping and try out the rink in Victoria Park."

"That rink is great, especially at night when all the office buildings have their Christmas lights on," Taylor said. "I think I'll buy new skates this year."

"Have you outgrown your old skates?" Zack said.

"No. My feet haven't grown since I was fourteen," Taylor said, "which was when I chose the fluorescent purple figure skates with hot pink laces that are the only pair I own. I'm eighteen now. I think it's time I left fluorescent purple and hot pink behind."

Zack sipped his wine. "Are your purple skates comforta-ble, Taylor?"

Taylor knew her father well, and she smelled a rat. "They're comfortable," she said carefully.

"Do they still offer everything that you want from a skate?"

"They still offer everything I want from a skate," she said. "Dad, I know where this is going."

Zack nodded sagely. "Good, because this is what is called 'a teachable moment.' The purple skates are comfortable. They offer everything you want from a skate. You've heard the old adage: 'Better the skate you know than the skate you don't know.' Forget about new skates that may cause you untold grief. Stick with the skate you know."

"And by extension," Taylor said, "since I'm comfortable living here, and since living here gives me everything I want from a home, I should forget about Saskatoon or Toronto or New York and stay with you and Jo forever."

Zack beamed. "Exactly. I knew the skate analogy would make it clear. So that's settled. Now, could you please pass the garlic bread?"

On the label of the DVD I brought home with me, Ben Bendure had written the dates and description of the events he filmed. The three words on that label called forth a rush of images. *Thanksgiving: MacLeod Lake.* Autumn is often kind to Ontario cottage country: the skies are vibrantly blue; the lakes are clear; the leaves on the deciduous trees are a riot of gold, orange, and crimson; and cottagers are given a final chance to savour a spectacular dazzle of colour and light before winter, with its monochromatic palette, sets in.

Ben was big on establishing shots, and the footage with which he opened this home movie quickened my pulse. The camera was focused on our boathouse and dock. The point of view was that of someone arriving in the motorboat that ferried our family and the Loves back and forth from the mainland to the island. As the boat moved nearer to the shore, the driver cut the motor; the thrum of the outboard gave way to the slap of waves against the boat, and I could almost smell the fishy-weedy tang of the lake.

My father was standing at the boathouse door, and as the boat docked, he came to meet it. He was holding a baby, and I knew from what Ben had told me that the child in his arms was me. By the second Monday in October, I would have been almost two weeks old. There was a break as Ben climbed out of the boat. The next frames were of my father holding me out to the camera and, in an uncharacteristically tremulous voice, introducing me. "Here she is, Ben— Joanne Farlinger Ellard."

The camera zoomed in for a close-up of a pretty baby with a thatch of black hair, nestled in a blue crocheted blanket.

Zack hit Pause. "Look at you," he said softly. "The baby who would change my life."

"That goes both ways," I said.

Taylor was leaning towards the screen to look more closely. "So perfect," she said.

Zack pulled me closer. "Beautiful then. Beautiful now," he said. "Now, let's get back to the action."

Des Love had joined the group. His hair was windblown, and he ran a hand through it. "Choppy water today," he said. "Ben and I had a bumpy ride. He held out his arms. "My turn to hold Joanne," he said. My father handed me over. It was an image that had a powerfully ironic resonance: my two fathers and me in the middle, oblivious.

Most of the Thanksgiving footage Ben shot that year was an unbroken stream of pleasant moments shared by friends blessed by good health and good fortune. At the lake, Des began every day with a run around the island that finished when he dove from our shared dock into the water and swam for twenty minutes. Ben's shots of Des pulling himself out of the cold water after his swim, stretching and beaming at the sheer physical joy of being alive, brought a lump to my throat.

The rhythm of day-to-day life on the island captured by Ben's camera was remarkably like that of all the summers I would come to know. Life was quiet. Once a day, the radio was turned on to hear the CBC news, but there was no television and no one listened to music. People took walks. Des painted; my father worked on a biography of Dr. Norman Bethune that he seemed to begin anew every summer; and my Grandmother Ellard, Nina, and my mother read. Their reading tastes were diverse. My grandmother was fond of family sagas, my mother read psychology texts, and Nina read books about art and architecture. The three women were not close, and I can't remember ever hearing them discuss what they read.

Food was a preoccupation. The early 1960s were the days of hostess skirts, six-course meals based on menus from *Gourmet* magazine, and mandatory liqueurs after dinner. Nina, my mother, and my grandmother were all competitive, and they were excellent cooks, so we ate well. I loved watching them prepare food: Nina painting violets with egg wash before she twirled them by their stems in powdered sugar to create candied violets to set off her crème brûlée; my grandmother chiffonading sage for the herb butter she slid beneath the skin of the Thanksgiving turkey; or my mother, Caroline, preparing her acclaimed smoked salmon mousse. When I was three months old, a guest who had drunk well but not wisely at my parents' New Year's party fed me a spoonful. Smoked salmon mousse was my first solid food, and it's still one of my favourites.

That year, guests had been invited to share the Ellard/Love harvest celebration, and Ben's camera caught a revealing moment. When she was in the mood, my mother was a witty and compelling storyteller. She'd had an easy childbirth, and

she was relaxed and glowing as she chatted with the dinner
guests. Sitting in our family room with my husband and
daughter, I was mesmerized by how lovely Caroline had been
when she was young and sober.

She had just started telling a story about coming out of
the anaesthetic after my birth and seeing a nun in full habit
walking down the hall with a case of O'Keefe's ale under
each arm. When the mewing cry of a newborn pierced the
room, the camera stayed on Caroline as, ignoring the crying,
she continued her story. The cry was insistent, and my
father stood to go to me, but when my mother touched his
arm he sat down. Des sprang up from across the table. "I'll
take care of this," he said. When my grandmother started to
follow him, Des waved her off. "Stay and hear the end of
Caroline's story," he said. "I want to get to know Joanne."

At first, Ben's film of the following year's Thanksgiving
seemed much the same as the one we had just watched. The
foliage on the mainland surrounding MacLeod Lake was
as vibrantly hued; the blue of the sky was still intense; Des's
enthusiasm for his Thanksgiving swim was undiminished;
my father continued to write his biography of Dr. Bethune; my
grandmother, Nina, and my mother continued to read and to
create extraordinary meals. The Thanksgiving table was still
beautifully set and the turkey was perfection.

But there were signs that all was not well. There were no
guests for Thanksgiving dinner. Nina was pregnant and
plagued with morning sickness that lasted well into the
day. My mother, withdrawn and sallow, seemed to be never
without a drink or a cigarette. Ben kept the camera off both
Nina and Caroline, but there was plenty of footage of me
walking tentatively but with great determination, leafing
through storybooks with my grandmother, or being pushed
in my stroller by my father or Des as they ambled along
the shore.

My Grandmother Ellard had planned a barbecue on the beach for our two families, to celebrate my birthday, which had been on September 29. The party was not a success. Nina had brought a beautifully wrapped doll. When I began to tear at the toy's packaging, Nina took it and the doll away, explaining that the doll was a collector's item and worthless without the box. She and Des had a tense exchange, and Nina stalked off and didn't return. My mother sat with her drink and cigarette, present but absent, lost in her private world. My grandmother, my father, and Des sang "Happy Birthday," but despite their best efforts, the result was thin and without spirit.

In mid-October the sun sets at around six-thirty, so after dinner and the cake cutting, there was a bonfire. The flames appeared to mesmerize me, and Ben kept the camera on me as I sat on my grandmother's lap, a watchful child whose face was alternately lit by the flickering flames or lost in the shadows.

The film ended with that image.

When Taylor turned on the lights, her face was concerned. "Jo, you didn't smile once in that film—not even when they brought out the cake at your party, and you didn't cry when Nina grabbed your present. You just took it all in."

"I guess even then, I had learned to read the signs," I said.

Zack frowned. "It shouldn't have been that way."

"Maybe not, but that's the way it was," I said. "Let's talk about something else."

Taylor had never been easily deflected. "I understand why Ben kept his camera on you when you were watching the bonfire—the way the light and shadows played on your face said all the things you didn't have words for."

I took her hand. "But, Taylor, now I do have words, so I can tell you that I'm a happy woman."

———

That night as I lay in bed beside Zack, listening to his regu-
lar breathing and watching the branches of the trees along
the creek shiver in the wind, I knew that in telling Taylor I
was a happy woman, I had been truthful. But the image of
that watchful child whose face was sometimes lit by flickering flames, sometimes lost in the shadows, stayed with
me, and my mind gravitated towards the question that I had
asked myself many times over the years. How did I get here
from there?

I had come up with a thousand answers. Bishop Lambeth
school had been a good place to grow up: structured, with
female teachers who without exception were passionate
about their subjects and about encouraging girls to excel at
whatever field they chose. Many of the students were day
girls, but my closest friends were all, like me, boarders, and
as children do, we accepted our lives as the norm. When we
graduated, we had been together thirteen years, having spent
far more time with one another than with our families.

At the University of Toronto, I met my first and second
loves and married my third. Ian and I wed, moved to
Saskatchewan, had kids, accepted the price for Ian's meteoric
rise in provincial politics, and lived our lives, until the day
Ian was killed and my old, safe world shattered.

Rebuilding our family's life had been a slow and painful
process, but it never occurred to me that we wouldn't
succeed. There had been other losses, other blows, but I had
always felt in my bones that somehow everything would
work out, and over years the source of that unshakable faith
in the future had puzzled me. The watchful child in Ben's
film had not been born into a family that believed in silver
linings. As it turned out, the child did, and even in the dark-
est times of my life, there have been moments when, in the
shining phrase C.S. Lewis used as the title for his memoir, I
had been "surprised by joy."

That night, remembering the man who every morning after his swim had pulled himself up on the dock and stretched his arms heavenwards because it felt so good simply to be alive, I wondered if the capacity for joy had been his gift to me.

Zack was dressed and waiting for me when the dogs and I got back from our run the next morning. "You're getting an early start," I said.

"I've got a meeting about a new case."

"What kind of case?"

"The kind that involves a rich man, a used condom, and a woman with a plan that blew up in her face. Lawyer-client confidentiality prevents me from revealing anything more."

"Three cheers for lawyer-client privilege," I said. "It's too early in the day to hear about the adventures of a used condom."

I'd showered, dressed, and was ladling porridge when Taylor joined me. I handed her the bowl.

"I love porridge when it's cold outside."

"Me too," I said. I filled a second bowl. "What's your plan for the day."

"They're shooting that scene where Ursula's mother, Ruth, tells Ursula how much she hated growing up in Churchill, where everybody in town knew she was the daughter of 'the crazy bear lady.'"

"That's a powerful moment," I said. "It was the first time I felt sympathy for Ruth."

Taylor nodded. "The dynamic between Ruth and Ursula has to be right to make it work, and Vale's been having trouble with it. She said the mother-daughter relationship is 'an emotional gap' for her, and until she came here for dinner she couldn't get her head around Ruth's feelings about her mother."

I poured cream on my porridge. "I'm not making the connection."

"When Vale saw how close we are, she imagined how it would be for both us if we became estranged and believed we'd never have a chance to make things right again."

"I don't even want to think about that," I said.

"Neither do I," Taylor said. "But somehow imagining how we'd feel gave Vale a path into understanding how Ursula would react to her mother's experience. Anyway, she wants my opinion about whether the scene is working now."

"Vale's a perfectionist," I said.

"She is," Taylor agreed. "And she needs to prove to Ainsley that she can pull it off."

"Why?" I said. "Vale's brilliant."

"Ainsley doesn't think Vale Frazier is 'a name' that will draw audiences to the box office. She had someone better known in mind, but Gabe wanted Vale, and he won out."

"Is Ainsley making the shooting difficult for Vale?"

Taylor's headshake was vehement. "No. Vale says Ainsley's the best director she's ever worked with. Even I can see how good she is. She's quiet, but there's no doubt about who's in charge. When an actor nails a scene, she gives them a smile and a little pat on the arm, but if they're struggling, she's gentle about suggesting options. If something goes wrong on the set, there's no drama. Ainsley takes care of the problem and carries on. She listens to other people's ideas, but she never loses sight of her vision of what the movie should be. Vale is totally blown away by her."

"But Ainsley is not totally blown away by Vale?"

"Well, there *is* a problem," Taylor said. "I'm just not sure what it is. Vale's doing a great job, and everyone on the set knows it. Rosamond Burke has told Vale how much she values acting with her. The production manager and the crew are all veterans, but there's a lot of mopping of eyes and clearing of throats after one of Vale's scenes. The only one who holds back is Ainsley."

"Is it possible she's still smarting about Gabe overriding her on the casting?"

"She doesn't seem to be that kind of person, but who knows? Nick Kovacs told me Gabe's far more involved with the day-to-day business of production than an executive producer would normally be."

"He certainly has a tight hold on the reins," I said. "His wife is the director, her long-time collaborator wrote the script, and he insisted on his choice for the lead."

Taylor's smile was impish. "And I think *you're* a control freak." She checked her watch. "I'd better get going, but, Jo, there's something else. Would it be okay if I invited Vale to have Christmas with us?"

"Of course. Taylor, does Vale ever talk about her parents?"

"Just the bare minimum. Her father lives in Los Angeles. He's an actor on a soap opera, and he has a new wife, new kids, and a new life. Vale's mother lives in New York. She's an actor too. She and Vale share an apartment there, but they don't seem to share much else." Taylor's face clouded. "Vale started taking the subway to auditions by herself when she was nine years old."

"That is just so wrong," I said.

"It is," Taylor said. "But Vale survived, and she's a success."

The memory of Vale taking a cab back to her empty apartment the evening she and Taylor decorated our tree flashed through my mind. That would not have been the first night she'd turned the key in a lock knowing there was no one waiting for her on the other side of the door. Little wonder she was reaching out to Taylor.

Driving to Western Cycle on 8th Avenue in the Old Warehouse District for new ice skates has been part of my winter routine since my children were little. On a bad day, the only skates that fit were the ones the child hated. More than once, dashed expectations, tears, and tantrums have driven us to leave Western Cycle empty-handed, but that afternoon we were lucky. Within half an hour Madeleine and Lena found skates they loved and had them sharpened. Taylor had texted to say that she and Vale were heading over and she wondered if the girls were interested in meeting Taylor's new friend. They were, and the three of us were sitting on a bench waiting when Taylor, Vale, and Gabe Vickers walked in. The two young women flanked Gabe, and he had draped a heavy arm around the shoulders of both Taylor and Vale. As the three approached us, Taylor shook off Gabe's arm to give me, Madeleine, and Lena hugs. Vale held back, looking small as she lingered next to the older man. When he whispered something in her ear, she gave him a quick, stiff smile, and my nerves tightened.

Taylor made introductions, and the moment passed. Everyone admired the girls' purchases, and our granddaughters went off with Taylor and Vale to help them with skate selection. Gabe, however, stayed behind. I was sitting at the end of the bench and there was plenty of space free, but Gabe sat down so close to me that our bodies touched.

When I inched away, Gabe noticed. "Joanne, you and I are just beginning a relationship that I hope will continue well into the future, so let's wipe the slate clean and start again."

"All right," I said. "Let's start with you telling me what brings you here with the girls."

"Two days ago, Ainsley and Roy approached me about executive-producing *Flying Blue Horses*. You and I have a signed contract, but I thought before we moved forward, we needed to clear the air."

"So you tagged along with Vale and Taylor because you knew they were meeting me here."

Gabe's grey eyes, contrite and unblinking, met mine. "Meeting in person is always preferable to a call."

"You're right." I said. "And we're both here now, so go for it."

"I never heard back from you after I sent the poinsettia. Given what everyone says about your welcoming nature, that omission suggested you had lingering concerns about me. I know you witnessed my nasty encounter with Shawn O'Day the night of the party honouring Zephyr Winslow, and you've likely heard things about my personal life." The half smile Gabe gave me was chilling. "Now that you're working in our industry, Joanne, you and Zack should know, it's rare to find a closet in which there isn't a skeleton that can be shaken loose.

"I can't erase what you saw that night, and I'm sorry about losing my temper, but I had my reasons. I want you to know that I can make *Flying Blue Horses* a wild success. And I want you to know that to make this work, you don't have to be my friend. You just have to trust my professional judgment."

When I didn't respond, Gabe proceeded. "*The Happiest Girl* is going to be a classic. It's a great family film. All families have to deal with death. Roy told me your family found comfort in the play's message that death is not the end. Other families will too. At the moment, *Flying Blue Horses* is nothing but notes and ideas, but Roy and Ainsley's vision for the story of Sally and Desmond Love and you is extraordinary. Like *The Happiest Girl*, it carries a message about the power and the limitations of love that will have universal appeal. I can find the right people and arrange the right financing to bring that message to audiences that hunger to hear it. All I need is your approval."

"You already have it," I said. "Gabe, I respect professionalism. Roy tells me you're the best there is, and that if *Flying Blue Horses* takes shape as we hope it will, you should be at the helm."

In a gesture that I suspected he often used, Gabe raked his hand through his tousled hair and gave me a boyish smile. "You won't regret a decision to work with me, Joanne. You have my word on that."

When he offered his hand, reluctantly I took it. "Now Taylor tells me the second floor of this place houses the largest bicycle showroom in the province," he said. "The others won't be back for a while. Care to join me in checking them out?"

"You go ahead," I said. "That bike showroom really is impressive, but I promised Madeleine and Lena they could go skating when we were through here, so I'm taking advantage of the lull in the action to recharge my batteries."

Not long after Gabe returned from exploring the bikes on the second floor, Taylor, Vale, and the girls joined us. Vale held up the box containing her new skates and announced that plans were afoot. "Taylor and I are going skating with Maddy and Lena." she said. "I texted Ainsley and I'm not needed on the set for another ninety minutes. She said if it was okay with you, Gabe, it was okay with her. So, is it okay?"

Gabe saw that I was perplexed. "This isn't as paternalistic as it sounds, Joanne. It's an insurance issue."

"I understand," I said. "Lena suffered a nasty break skating on our rink at the lake a couple of years ago."

"She shattered her olecranon," Madeleine said quietly.

Lena rolled her eyes at the memory. "My arm was in a cast for six weeks," she said.

Gabe shuddered theatrically. "That's exactly what the insurance company doesn't need to know." He turned back to Vale. "Just be careful," he said, putting his hand on her arm.

Vale leaned into his side. "Your investment is safe," she said.

The rink in Victoria Park in our city's centre is a great place for a skate in winter. The park has plenty of trees, meandering walks, inviting benches, and a children's playground. Its cenotaph and statue of Sir John A. Macdonald are graceful reminders of part of our city's past, and Joe Fafard's multi-layered buffalo titled *oskana ka-asasteki*, which translates from the Cree into "bones that are piled together," is a stark reminder of Regina's beginnings as Pile O' Bones.

Depending on the weather, the school schedule, and the time of day, the number of skaters on the rink varies. That day, only a handful had braved the cold, so the girls had the rink practically to themselves. Madeleine and Lena were both solid skaters. Lena's injury had come when she tried the salchow after seeing it demonstrated on television.

Gabe had driven Vale and Taylor downtown and had stayed to watch the skating. He and I stood side by side waiting for the girls to emerge from the Warm Up Hut, where they were putting on their skates. Madeleine and Lena were the first to hit the ice, and as they circled the rink in their matching cranberry ski jackets, they were an exuberantly confident image of winter pleasures.

From the moment they hobbled out of the Warm Up Hut laughing, it was obvious Taylor and Vale were neither exuberant nor confident. Taylor was a decent skater, but at most she laced up her skates a half-dozen times during the season. Vale looked determined but dubious. I turned to Gabe. "This is Vale's first time on skates, isn't it?"

He sighed. "Looks like it," he said. "I'd better get her off the ice."

"She wanted to do this," I said. "Let her have a few minutes to at least give it a try."

Vale and Taylor were giggling as they clung to each other and circled the rink together. I could feel Gabe's tension. "She'll be all right," I said. "Taylor won't let her fall."

"I should be the one out there," he said, and his voice was surprisingly wistful. We watched as Taylor and Vale took another turn around the ice. Vale was improving, but after a quick confab, she and Taylor apparently decided to call it a day and headed back to the Warm Up Hut. Gabe and I joined them, and Madeleine and Lena skated over.

"Are we leaving already?" Madeleine said.

"No, we can stay a while," I said. "Vale has to get back to work and Taylor's going with her."

"But you'll miss the hot chocolate," Lena said.

Vale smiled at her. "Where I work, there's a thing called craft services. They have anything you want to eat or drink whenever you want it."

Lena's eyes were huge. "You are so lucky," she said.

A fleeting shadow crossed Vale's face. "Not always," she said.

Taylor still had her arm around Vale's shoulder. When Taylor drew her close, the sadness vanished from Vale's face. "But I'm getting luckier," she said, and with that the two young women disappeared into the hut.

CHAPTER

11

Facing a weekend that held two client holiday parties Friday night and the dinner for Rosamond Burke on Saturday evening, Zack and I had promised ourselves a lazy Saturday, but seemingly the word *lazy* was no longer in the Shreve family lexicon.

When Margot, Brock, and Roy had arrived at the first of the holiday parties on Friday, they made the rounds, then Margot, Brock, and Zack retired to a corner to discuss Falconer Shreve business while I introduced Roy to Regina's crème de la crème. At the second holiday party, the pattern repeated itself until, in the swell and surge of guests, Roy and I became separated. When I finally found my friend, he had been cornered by Roddy Dewar, a Falconer Shreve client who was rich, litigious, and a walking compendium of conspiracy theories. I joined them just as Mr. Dewar was explaining how two astronauts had been placed in a secret CIA Mars program, with the then nineteen-year-old Barack Obama, and trained to teleport to Mars in order to survey alien life. As he spotted me, Roy's eyes were beseeching. Luckily, I was able to throw him a lifeline. Roddy Dewar's food lust was legendary.

I leaned close to him and whispered, "The servers just brought in a tray of Fanny Bay oysters—they came here straight from the airport."

"Fanny Bay oysters straight from the airport," Roddy Dewar said, and his tone was reverential. Then, without so much as a by-your-leave, he was gone.

Roy shook his head in disbelief. "I don't know how you did that, but I am forever in your debt."

"I'll put it on your tab," I said. "Right now, let's see if we can score some Fanny Bay oysters before Roddy empties the tray."

Zack was in a meditative mood on our way home. Finally, he turned to me. "How would you feel about driving out to the farm and seeing the grandsons tomorrow?"

"I'm always eager to spend time with Charlie and Colin," I said. "Did something special come up?"

"Just business," Zack said. "This new case is going to need a female second chair. Margot and I have agreed it should be Maisie."

"And we're going to the farm so you can ask her?" I said.

"No, Maisie already said yes. I called from the party. She suggested Margot, Brock, and I go out there tomorrow to strategize."

"Brock's not a lawyer."

"No, but he manages the firm, and this case is going to be labour-intensive. We're going to have to figure out who goes where, and I want to cut down on the time I spend away from you."

My nerves pricked with anxiety. "You *are* feeling all right?"

He gave me a quick, reassuring smile. "Physically, I'm fine, but last year left its mark. It made me realize how quickly it can all end, and I don't want to spend every waking hour on this case."

———

The forecast had mentioned the possibility of strong winds, but Saturday morning the air was chilly and still—a good day to bundle small children up in snowsuits, grab sleds, and visit the animals and poultry on the Crawford Kilbourn farm.

Peter's breeding programs of heritage poultry and animals meant there was plenty to see. In addition to the heritage turkeys, ducks, geese, and chickens, there were goats, sheep, cows, and riding horses. Margot was a farm girl, but Roy, Brock, and Zack had always been city boys, and they were as fascinated by the sights, sounds, and smells of the barns as were Margot's soon-to-be three-year-old daughter, Lexi; her twenty-two-month-old brother, Kai; and the Crawford Kilbourn twins. It was a happy morning, but trudging takes its toll on small people, and after lunch all the kids, including Lexi, who was still insisting she was not tired when she fell asleep in Brock's arms, went down for naps.

When the children were settled, Pete headed off to do chores. Maisie, Margot, Zack, and Brock went to Peter's office on the main floor to talk strategy, and Roy and I sat down at the kitchen table and shared a pot of tea.

"Alone at last," Roy said. "And none too soon, because you and I have things to talk about."

"That sounds ominous," I said.

"Not at all," Roy said. "But I wanted to check in about our contracts, to make certain you didn't feel pressured because I went to Gabe as soon as you agreed to a collaboration."

"I didn't feel pressured, but I was surprised that the contracts gave Gabe Vickers so much power in making decisions for us."

"Well, we have exactly the same terms as Ainsley and I had with Gabe on *The Happiest Girl*. Zack and I talked about the rationale for giving Gabe the power to act for us in dealings with possible backers. That particular surrogacy is just part of the executive producer's job."

When I didn't respond immediately, Roy frowned. "Jo, are you still concerned about Gabe being a part of our project?"

"I am," I said. "You've assured me that Gabe is the right choice, and Gabe has given me his word that he'll create a series that will be revered worldwide, but I'm still uneasy. I guess I just wish I knew more about him."

Roy's smile was crooked. "So do I," he said. "Ainsley and I are as close as two people can be, but her marriage to Gabe Vickers came out of nowhere, and sitting here with you in an eminently sane world looking out at the fields of snow, I can't believe I didn't question her decision."

"Surely the subject must have come up," I said.

"It didn't," Roy said. "At least not directly. My only rationalization is that the time after *The Happiest Girl* opened was surreal. Ainsley and I had had successes before. Broadway shows have run as long as they're profitable, but when the house percentages start to drop, they close." Roy's laugh was rueful. "Sometimes very quickly. All our previous productions had a decent run, usually around 325 shows, but none made it to a year."

"And *The Happiest Girl* changed that."

"*The Happiest Girl* changed everything," Roy said firmly. "It put us in the stratosphere. The reviews and the buzz were incredible. Suddenly our musical was the hottest ticket on Broadway. Within a week, we were sold out for a year, and second-year sales were running at 100 per cent. Ainsley and I were in a daze. The phones never stopped ringing—everybody wanted to interview us, hire us, or just get a piece of us. Our agent was inundated with offers to option the movie rights. I was overwhelmed, but Ainsley told me to relax and let her handle it."

"She protects you," I said. "That's a gift."

"It is," Roy said. "Luckily for us both, she makes the decisions. She was determined to get a deal that gave us what we needed. She wanted to direct the movie and for me to write the screenplay. It was a lot to ask. We were unknown quantities in the film industry, and making a movie, especially one with computer graphics, takes serious money. We'd seen projects flounder for years because the financing never came together. But my collaborator has always been willing to roll the dice."

"And Gabe Vickers made an offer that met her demands," I said.

"Not immediately," Roy said. "Gabe had approached our agent the day after the opening. Our agent was ecstatic, but Gabe was reluctant to accept Ainsley's terms. Finally, Ainsley bypassed our agent, called Gabe, and said she wasn't going to walk away without a deal. She suggested the two of them hammer out a contract face to face."

"And they did," I said.

"Gabe agreed to our terms: Ainsley would direct, I would write the screenplay, and Gabe would guarantee financing within a year. It was as if the genie had emerged from the bottle and granted us all three wishes at once. That was on a Friday. Ainsley went away for the weekend and when she came back, she told me she and Gabe were married."

"And that was it?"

"That was it. I had questions, but Ainsley refused to answer. And since that day, she's carried on as if nothing has changed. We've always worked well together. We still do, but it's like Bluebeard's Castle. We still share everything, but now there's one room I'm not allowed to enter."

"Ainsley and Gabe's marriage," I said.

"Yeah. And I've read enough fairy tales to know what happens to people who unlock the doors to forbidden rooms."

"So you're not searching for the secret key."

"Not any more, although every so often I do get a glimpse inside the room. One day last summer, Ainsley and I went out for a sandwich. It was hot, and not far from our office. Ainsley just crumpled onto the sidewalk. A woman helped me get her inside the nearest building. I found Ainsley a chair, somebody brought a glass of water, and within a few minutes, she was fine. The woman who'd helped us asked if Ainsley was pregnant. Ainsley shook her head. When we got to the diner and ordered, I asked Ainsley if she was certain she wasn't pregnant. Ainsley was dumbfounded. She said, 'I thought you understood that it's not that kind of marriage.'"

"What kind of marriage is it?" I said.

"I wish I knew. The only answer that makes sense is that Gabe and Ainsley have what used to be called 'a marriage of convenience.'"

"An arrangement for a strategic purpose," I said. "So what's the purpose?"

"To make a movie that will become a classic."

"Is any movie worth that?"

"Only if it will save someone you care about deeply. Jo, you never saw me at my worst. For the two years after Lev-Aaron died, I was a seeping wound. During the period when I was writing *The Happiest Girl* I was obsessed and when it opened, I was euphoric, but I was also fragile. That play meant everything to me. Ainsley knew that if the producer who optioned the script made a movie that was shoddy, saccharine, or simply not true to the spirit of the play, I'd have been crushed. By marrying Gabe and ensuring that the film not only would get made but that she and I would shape it, Ainsley was giving me a safety net."

"She must love you very much," I said.

"She does, and I love her. We've been partners for thirty years. There's nothing I wouldn't do for her, and I don't say that lightly. Ainsley wants Gabe to produce *Flying Blue Horses*, Jo. So do I—for all the reasons you and I have already talked about. Gabe can arrange the financing, and he'll be hands off about the choices we make."

"But he isn't always," I said. "When Ainsley wanted another actor to play Ursula, Gabe insisted that Vale Frazier be cast."

"And we're lucky Gabe was insistent," Roy said. "Before she joined the New York production of *The Happiest Girl*, Vale was in an indie film that's just been released. It's attracting a lot of interest, and Vale is suddenly a very hot property. Gabe has already talked to Vale about playing the young Sally Love. She's keen, and with Gabe as executive producer, she'll sign. I know you have doubts, but *Flying Blue Horses* has the potential to be extraordinary, and Gabe is our best chance to realize that potential." Roy's eyes shone with hope. "So what do you say?"

I tried a smile. "We'll keep moving ahead," I said.

Lexi and Kai had awakened by the time the Falconer Shreve meeting ended. Brock, Roy, and Zack volunteered to take the little ones sledding, and Maisie asked if I'd mind listening for the twins so she could help Pete with chores.

Margot joined me when I took up my old place at the kitchen table, and together we watched the men as they set out for the sledding hill with the kids and Rowdy in tow. When Brock put his arm around Roy's shoulder, Roy looked up at Brock and their joy was palpable.

"I think Brock may have found Mr. Right," Margot said.

"And you're okay with that?"

"It's not as if I have a choice," Margot said softly. "But I want that for Brock. He and I have talked about it. We love each other, and we love the kids—that won't change. But I remember what physical passion is like. Sliding into bed with Leland and knowing that bliss was within easy reach was pretty cool."

"I remember when you and Leland invited Zack and me to dinner at your condo the night you got engaged," I said. "The electricity between you and Leland could have powered a small city."

Margot laughed softly at the memory. "Zack said, 'The faster you feed us, the faster Jo and I will get out of here.' That *was* a very quick meal." She sighed deeply. "But that was then, and this is now. I really am glad for Brock. What he and I have together is wonderful, but he deserves the whole package."

"So do you," I said. "Is that why you decided not to second chair?"

"So I can spend my nights cruising for a man who makes my loins twitch instead of curled up with my laptop? No, it's not that. It's a question of time. I've been practising criminal law for twenty years, and I love it, but it's no longer my all-consuming passion. I used to share Eddie Greenspan's hope that I'd die in a courtroom immediately after hearing a jury return with the words *Not guilty*. But not any more. I'm still a senior partner at Falconer Shreve and I'm still deeply committed to the work I do there. I'm not slacking off; I'm not cutting back. I'm simply going to have a life."

"But Maisie will be lawyering 24/7."

"Pretty much, but that's what she wants, and that's what she should be doing. Jo, if you repeat what I'm about to say, I'll tie your shoelaces together, but Maisie has the potential to be a better lawyer than either Zack or me. Her instinct for what works in the courtroom is extraordinary. She doesn't need tutoring there, but 95 per cent of trial law takes place outside the courtroom, and Zack's ability in that area is second to none. He has an uncanny ability to find common ground for mediation, and among other skills, he knows how to edit a case. He can shape a line of reasoning so that the details that matter are there from beginning to end, no

digressions, no showboating—just a case that unfolds powerfully and gracefully and carries the jury to the point where
they believe there's only one possible verdict they can reach."

"And Maisie can learn that from second chairing."

"Oh, she'll learn. I've seen what Zack can do to a lawyer's
trial notes. It's brutal. He scribbles all over them and then at
the end he writes a comment. I remember one real zinger:
'mediocre argument; flawed summation.'"

"Ouch. Was that directed at you?"

"Nope. That was Zack critiquing his own work." We
both laughed and then Margot's expression grew serious.
"You're worried about the effect Maisie's new workload will
have on the twins, aren't you?"

"I'm concerned about the effect it will have on all of
them, but my late husband's mother had a motto: Mouth
shut, arms open."

"Smart woman," Margot said.

"She was, and I'm doing my best to follow her example,"
I said.

Zack seemed preoccupied as we drove back to the city.

"Revisiting the idea of having a second chair?" I said finally.

"Nope. Actually, I was thinking about how great it's going
to be sitting in front of the fire with you on stormy days
listening to Bill Evans."

"The Prince of Darkness grows mellow." I squeezed
Zack's arm. "Taylor's right. Everything is constantly transforming. Speaking of . . ."

When I'd finished filling Zack in on the latest with the
Flying Blue Horses project, he whistled. "Gabe Vickers may
be a sleaze, but he knows how to get things done."

"That's what I keep telling myself. Zack, I know you didn't
ask about the particulars when Gabe asked you to hook him
up, so to speak, but what do you think he was after?"

"I don't know, and I don't want to know. Jo, are Gabe's sexual peccadilloes going to make it difficult for you to work with him?"

I sighed. "No, as long as the sex is consensual, and he's not breaking any laws, it's none of my business."

CHAPTER

12

Vale and Taylor had decided to go to the downtown library's Saturday afternoon showing of François Truffaut's *The 400 Blows* and come back to our place to get ready for the dinner party together. They were still discussing the final freeze frame of the boy hero at the ocean when they arrived. As I listened to their young voices arguing passionately about the meaning of the film's ending, I felt a frisson of delight. Prodigious talent was a gift but it was also a burden, and it was good to hear Taylor and Vale talking with youthful bravado about Life with a capital *L*.

I am not a woman who anticipates parties with pleasure, but as we drove downtown, the evening was looking more and more promising. According to Vale, Rosamond Burke had declared that since the party was in her honour, she would make her preferences known to the planners. By the time we pulled up in front of the glass condo tower where Gabe and Ainsley were subletting, Zack and I had learned that we would be dining on rack of lamb, that the flowers perfuming the air would be Rosamond's favourite Michelangelo roses, and that the help hired for the evening would all be young, attractive male actors who were between engagements.

A silvery-grey BMW with the vanity plate DANCE was stopped ahead of us at the entrance. I nudged Zack. "Zephyr's here," I said. As we watched, the driver got out, walked behind the car to the passenger side, opened the door, and when Zephyr emerged, escorted her into the lobby. With Zephyr safely inside, the man returned to the BMW and drove away.

"Shawn O'Day," Zack said. "Looks like dance's loss is Zephyr's gain. Shawn appears to be her new gentleman companion."

"I'll bet there's a tantalizing story there," I said. "I wonder if we'll ever know it."

"Of course we will," Taylor said. "This is Regina. Sooner or later, everybody knows everything."

Pointing to their short life spans, water leaks, and skyrocketing energy and maintenance costs, naysayers may call condominium towers that have floor-to-ceiling glass walls throwaway constructions, but on a December night when the snow is falling and the buildings rise up sparkling and shiny against the winter sky, they offer appealing sites for holiday parties.

Gabe had arranged for valet parking. As soon we'd handed over the keys to the Volvo, the four of us started towards the entrance. We'd just reached it when a girl with very short, hacked black hair appeared out of the shadows. She was bone thin with huge, darkly shadowed black eyes. The wind was sharp but despite her bare legs, the girl looked cozy in her cherry red princess line wool coat with its wide leather belt. She went straight to Vale. "Look at you, pretty girl," she said in a high breathy voice. "Where's your man?"

Ignoring the question, Vale stepped closer to the girl.

"Forget about me," she said. "Look at you, Lizzie. That coat's the perfect colour for you, isn't it, Taylor?"

"It is," Taylor agreed, "and it's a perfect fit. Promise you won't give it away, Lizzie. The days are getting shorter and colder, and it makes Vale and me happy to know you're warm."

"I want you to be happy," the girl said.

"We want that for you too, Lizzie, and we've been worried about you," Vale said. "When was the last time you ate?"

Lizzie shrugged. "I'm fine. I can go for days without eating. I'm like a camel."

"Camels can go without water for six or seven months," Vale said. "But they need the nourishment stored in their hump to keep going. You don't have a hump, Lizzie. There's food in my condo. Come up in the elevator with us, get off at my floor, and go to my place for something to eat."

"I don't like to go there alone," the girl said.

Vale took a twenty-dollar bill from her evening bag and tucked it in the pocket of the red coat. "Then go across the street to the café and get something," she said. "You won't be alone there."

The girl moved with the jerky rhythms of a marionette. "I'm not hungry," she said.

Vale's smile was fond but resigned. "Have coffee."

Lizzie laughed and shook her head. "Gives me jitters." She held up her hands. "Look." She was gloveless. Her fingers were skeletal, and they were indeed shaking.

Vale took off her own gloves. "Put these on. Now, go to the café, order some herbal tea, and warm up."

Docile as a child, Lizzie started down the semicircular driveway. We all watched as the girl crossed the street and walked towards the restaurant.

"Every time we see her, I wonder if it's for the last time," Taylor said.

Vale put her arm through Taylor's. "I wonder that too,"
she said. "But until Lizzie decides it's time to change course,
all we can do is give her a coat and money for herbal tea."

Once inside, Zack and I stopped at the first elevator, but
Vale pointed to the one at the end. "This goes to the penthouse," she said. When the elevator doors opened on the
twenty-seventh floor, we stepped into the entrance hall of
Gabe and Ainsley's condo. Two handsome young men in
black turtlenecks and tight jeans took our coats, and a third
handsome young man in the same uniform appeared and led
us into the party. As soon as they were out of earshot, Taylor
turned to Vale. "Those guys are hot."

Vale's smile was puckish. "Rosamond 'adores the sight of
nice, firm male buttocks.'"

We were still smiling at the image when Gabe approached
us. Like Zack, he was wearing a tux, and like Zack he wore
a tux well. Gabe complimented Taylor, Vale, and me on our
outfits. I'd deliberated about the gown I'd chosen to wear. It
was Vera Wang, a sleeveless, full-length black-velvet classic
with a very deep V back, the bottom of which was at eye
level and easy reach for a man in a wheelchair. Zack loved
it. I liked the dress too, but the first and only time I'd worn
it, the evening had turned out disastrously. For me, the dress
carried the memory of that evening, and I was returning it
to my closet when Taylor bounced in and convinced me to
wear it. As I looked around the penthouse with its crystal
bowls of buttery yellow Michelangelo roses and skillfully
arranged glowing candles, I was glad Taylor had insisted
that I pull out all the stops.

Gabe was the consummate host, making certain our drinks
were to our liking, encouraging us to sample the curried
prawns and the ploughman's pate, joking and cajoling, a
charmer determined to please.

Rosamond Burke had arrived before us and was chatting with Zephyr and Ainsley in the living room. Standing by the wall of windows, her tall, lean figure thrown into sharp relief by the background of night and falling snow, Rosamond was a formidable presence. The outfit she wore—a pale grey, high-necked jacket with a fitted bodice and silvery-grey chiffon slacks—showcased her tall, slender figure. Her white hair, silky and abundant, was looped into a chignon and she held her handsome head high.

Gabe ushered us over to greet Rosamond, patted his tux pocket to make certain his Camels were handy, and headed to the balcony for a smoke. Nature abhors a vacuum and after Gabe disappeared, Rosamond was quick to take charge of the situation, exchanging air kisses with Vale and Taylor and giving Zephyr and Ainsley a look of sincere dismay. "I'm anticipating our dinner together with pleasure," she said. Her voice was full-timbred, rich, and strong. "But I know you'll understand that Sally Love and I were once friends, and I have been longing to meet her sister ever since Taylor told me of the connection, so if you'll excuse us . . ." She waved a graceful, dismissive arm at Zephyr, Ainsley, and Zack. Zephyr and Ainsley had obviously been forewarned and when Zack, clearly amused, shot me a quick grin and wheeled off with our daughter and Vale in tow, Rosamond turned her clear, penetrating gaze on me.

"Let's find a place where we can talk about you and Sally without interruption. She looked at my half-filled glass. "What are you drinking?"

"Soda water with a twist."

"Do you like single malt?"

"Very much."

"In that case," she said, beckoning to one of the beautiful boys, "a bottle of Old Pulteney, a large platter of curried prawns, two whiskey glasses, and two small plates." She watched with an appreciative smile as the boy walked away. "Delicious," she said. "Now let's find a place to talk."

Rosamond and I settled on two sleek white leather chairs in a corner of the living room made private by a pretty four-panel Chinese screen. For the next half-hour, the legend of British theatre and I sat next to each other, looking out at the cityscape and talking about Sally Love.

Rosamond began by saying that she and Sally met one autumn when Izaak brought Sally to London to see a show at the Tate. Sally had been twenty-one and Rosamond in her early forties. They were separated by a generation, but in Rosamond's words, they were alike in their gifts as artists and their flaws as human beings, and they felt a kinship that they continued to nurture by spending time together when Sally was in Europe or Rosamond was working in America. Neither woman lived a conventional life. Neither felt the need to make permanent connections with other people. Both had many lovers, male and female. Rosamond said the last time she and Sally talked had been when Sally was working on *Erotobiography* and had called Rosamond in London.

"She was excited about the show," Rosamond said. "I promised I would call and hear how the fresco was received. To my regret, I never did. I had a play opening in the West End. It didn't go well, and I was too knotted up in myself to think of others. A friend who is a great fan of Sally's work flew to Saskatoon and gave me a detailed report on *Erotobiography*." She rubbed her hands together gleefully. "All those images of penises and clitorises sunk into the wall of a publicly owned art gallery in a small Canadian city—it must have caused quite the brouhaha."

"It did." We both laughed as I described the endless line-ups and the lip-smacking lasciviousness that greeted the "Penis Paintings," but Rosamond's face grew grave when I told her about the ugliness, the threats, and the violence that confronted Sally after the opening.

"Appalling," Rosamond said. "But having you beside her must have made it easier for Sally to withstand the slings and arrows."

"I hope it did."

Rosamond cocked her head. "What did you make of *Erotobiography*, Joanne?"

"I thought it was brilliant," I said. "Funny, smart, and provocative in the best sense. That fresco made people think. It was huge, you know: three metres by nine. And Sally had played with scale—some of the genitals were so large they looked like lunar landscapes and some were as tiny and carefully rendered as a Fabergé egg. But big or small, those clitorises and penises floating in the blue celestial sky delivered a message, and Sally and I talked about it. People had been made miserable yearning for those little dangling or hidden parts of us. Lives had been warped or enriched by them. They had made dreams come true, and solitudes join, but isolated that way against a sky that existed before they came into being and would be there long after they'd returned to dust brought perspective."

"You and Sally arrived at that interpretation together?"

"We did," I said. "And we agreed on something else: hanging out there in space, all those little fleshly clouds looked totally fucking ridiculous."

Rosamond's eyes widened with surprise, then she flashed me a brilliant smile. "That was pure Sally," she said. "She never cared what people thought of her. She was naked to life. You don't strike me that way, Joanne."

"That's because I'm not. Sally always made me feel brave."

"And you made her feel safe," Rosamond said. "Sally spoke of you often and always with gratitude. She said she knew that, despite the distance between you, if she needed you, you'd be there."

"But for years I wasn't there," I said. "I was too proud and hurt and confused to get close to Sally until her life was nearly over."

Rosamond saw that her words had wounded me, and her voice was firm. "But Sally knew if her need for you was deep, you'd feel that need and you'd respond. And you did. I've been watching Taylor as she's been sketching the cast and crew of *The Happiest Girl*. She has an extraordinary talent, and she is, as the French say, *bien dans sa peau*, comfortable in her own skin. That's because when Sally needed you most, you were there to draw Taylor into your life.

"Now, we should probably join the others," Rosamond said, rising from her chair. I followed suit and we stood facing each other. "Given the shooting schedule, this may have been our only chance to talk, Joanne, but I'm grateful we were able to say what needed to be said."

"So am I," I said. Rosamond opened her arms to me. Ours was not a casual social hug. It was the firm embrace of two women sealing a bond.

As soon as Zephyr Winslow saw that Rosamond had emerged from our hideaway behind the Chinese screen, she made a beeline for her. The outfit Zephyr had chosen was dramatic: an iridescent coppery toned V-necked taffeta jacket trimmed in stiff double ruffles over a simple black silk shirt and tailored black trousers.

Few women could have carried off the boldness of the jacket's cut and shimmer, but Zephyr's ageless vitality graced any design, and the iridescent copper of her jacket drew out the bronze flecks of her tawny eyes. In the brief glimpse I had of her before Rosamond spirited me away, I thought Zephyr looked terrific, but now I saw that her face was drawn and her expression, strained. Clearly there was something on her mind, and she was determined to share whatever it was with Rosamond.

She had moved in close and begun to speak when I started past them, and Rosamond beckoned to me. "Joanne will be interested in this," she said. "She's as partial to Vale Frazier as am I. Joanne, Zephyr has just asked me if I find Vale 'fanciful.' A teller of tales? A spinner of romances? A girl who transmogrifies truth? Have you ever suspected Vale of telling *fibs*?" Rosamond asked, and her tone was mocking.

"Never," I said.

Zephyr's eyes met mine with a ferocity that surprised me. It was an awkward moment, but when one of the lovely boys appeared and offered Rosamond his arm, and another appeared and offered his arm to Zephyr, the tension broke. Mercifully, dinner was about to be served.

Roy Brodnitz was the last to arrive at the table. He had a light, quick stride, and he slid into his chair with such grace and ease that the simple action was a pleasure to watch. That afternoon Burgandy Code, who played Ursula's mother, Ruth, and Kenneth LaBonte, the choreographer, had both come down with a nasty flu that was making the rounds, so there were ten of us at dinner, and Rosamond had dictated the seating order to suit her fancy. Rosamond herself sat at the head of the table with Roy to her right and Gabe to her left; Zephyr sat at the foot of the table with Zack to her left and Brock, attending as Roy's date, to her right. Vale and I sat between Roy and Zack, and Taylor and Ainsley sat between Gabe and Brock.

When we were all seated, one of the servers approached the table with a bottle of a wine Gabe described as a "top-quality Bordeaux that had a few years' bottle age." The server poured a sample into Rosamond's glass and when she pronounced it satisfactory, more bottles were opened and all

our glasses were filled. Gabe deferred to Rosamond to offer
the toast. Logically, the first glass would be raised to Roy,
Ainsley, and Gabe, the three principals bringing *The Happiest
Girl* to film, but Rosamond liked to surprise.

Spinning the stem of the wineglass between her fingers,
she turned to Vale. "I've seen videos of you in a number of
roles, including the one for which you earned a Tony nomi-
nation, but you've always lacked either a great script or a
great director. You've never had the support you needed to
do your best work, but now you have that support and
you're brilliant. So I raise this glass to everyone at the table
who is giving you the chance to truly shine. To Roy Brodnitz
for a superb script; to Ainsley for intelligent and sensitive
direction; to Zephyr Winslow for her generous support of
the project; to Zachary Shreve, who, I am told, did yeoman's
service as mayor working to bring movie production back to
Saskatchewan." She twinkled. "To Brock Poitras for glad-
dening my heart every time I catch a glimpse of him; to
Taylor and Joanne for giving Vale insight into the relationships between mothers and daughters; to Gabe Vickers for
bringing this project and the people at this table together,
but . . ." As Rosamond's splendid voice rose for the perora-
tion, everyone at the table was rapt. "But most of all to you,
Vale Frazier. Your knowledge of the heights and depths to
which the heart can drive us is deepening and enriching
every aspect of *The Happiest Girl*."

Zephyr's face tightened with anger at Rosamond's toast
praising the young woman whom she had so recently sought
to discredit, but Vale accepted the generous words with
poise, and when we'd all chorused, "To Vale," she simply
said thank you and took a sip from her own glass. The evening was underway.

Rosamond had chosen a fine menu: consommé madrilène;
potatoes, onions, and carrots done round roast lamb; savoy

cabbage; and for dessert, sticky toffee pudding. The food was cooked to perfection. The pairing of wines with the dishes was excellent, and the conversation flowed.

Rosamond was a staunch socialist and the pronouncements uttered in her beautifully modulated voice were reasoned and passionate. Zack's politics were progressive but pragmatic. Years in the courtroom had taught him how to use his voice, and he loved to play devil's advocate. Listening to Rosamond and Zack debate was a master class in the fine arts of both political discourse and theatre.

Taylor and Vale had a spirited discussion about the respective lives of visual artists and actors—the visual artist's freedom to make art on her own terms versus the actor's need to depend on the abilities and opinions of others. Roy repeated the comment he had made to me about writers universally being regarded as eunuchs in the harem of the truly creative people of theatre, and his rueful, self-mocking humour lightened our mood. Ainsley's explanation of the work of the director was thoughtful and poetic. Gabe's encomium to his delight in finding the best talents and bringing them together to create something greater than the sum of its parts was surprisingly moving, and his tribute to Zephyr as a person whose support of the arts gave it its lifeblood was warm enough to melt the ice that had surrounded her since we sat down to eat.

As she sat at the head of the table bathed in the gentle glow of candlelight, enjoying a superior meal with people who were as bright and passionate as she herself was, Rosamond was clearly in her element. But as an actor, she knew that timing is key. The evening had reached its high point, and Rosamond knew the moment for the coda had arrived.

"I believe in joy," she said. "Find the person within yourself who will bring you joy." Her eyes swept the table and settled finally on our daughter. "Taylor, I knew your birth mother, and I'm coming to know the mother who raised you. Both women took immense joy in how they chose to lead their lives. All of us have had to weigh options. It's never an easy process. Every choice between options cuts off possibilities, and loss is always unpalatable. "Choose joy," she said. "Choose joy, and the rest will fall into place."

CHAPTER

13

My husband is prodigiously gifted in many ways. He's a brilliant tactician in the courtroom: he calculates, he adapts to the unexpected, he understands his opponent's point of view, he has an uncanny ability to come up with the one move that will stymie the opposition, and he has an eye for error—his own or that of opposing counsel. The fairy godmother doling out gifts at Zack's birth was generous, but she withheld the gift of spatial sense. Their grandfather's inability to do the most basic jigsaw puzzle baffles our granddaughters. His determination to help them finish a puzzle they've been working on for two hours terrifies them. Sunday afternoon as Zack and I discussed how best to use the space in our soon-to-be-shared home office, I knew how Madeleine and Lena felt when their grandfather tried to jam a chunky piece of blue sky into a space clearly intended for a horse's eye.

The idea of creating a place where we could work side by side was Zack's. He said a home office would prove that he was serious about spending more time at home. I had suggested as tactfully as I could that I was happy to sketch a plan for arranging our office furniture, but Zack insisted that since we were both going to use the space, he should do his part in making our dream a reality.

My spirits rose when the landline rang and Zack picked up. It was possible a file at Falconer Shreve needed his immediate attention, and I would be left to my own devices. But the reality was even better.

"Chloe Kovacs wants us to come over and see her Christmas tree," Zack said.

Opportunity had knocked, and I was not about to dally. "I'll get our coats," I said.

When we went to Taylor's room to tell her we were headed for the Kovacs, she jumped up from her desk. "Wait a sec. I have something I think Chloe will like." She reached up to the top shelf of her closet and took down a box of coloured pencils and *The Secret Garden* colouring book for adults that our next-door neighbours had given her for her birthday. She handed them to me. "These are lovely," she said. "But right now, I'm kind of into my own work."

"I'm sure Chloe will be pleased," I said.

The Kovacs' comfortable two-storey brick house in an old inner-city neighbourhood had been built by Nick's father. A large and fragrant holiday wreath hung on the front door, but Zack and I barely had time to admire it before Nick and Chloe were welcoming us to their home.

Father and daughter were both wearing blue jeans, but Nick's were well worn and Chloe's were designer. Nick was in a green Roughriders sweatshirt that had seen better days, and Chloe was wearing a red cashmere turtleneck. Their colour coordination was festive, but Chloe's face was fresh and her father's features held the weariness of a man who had always ridden himself hard. Nick once had said to Zack that every morning he awakened to the memory of Chloe's accident and prayed that this was the day when he could make amends for ruining her life.

The Kovacs' living room must have looked much the way it had during the decades when Nick and his brothers were growing up. The furniture was comfortable, upholstered in fabric that would withstand the rough and tumble of adolescent boys. The walls were hung with holy pictures and candid shots of family. Pride of place over the mantel was shared by a studio portrait of a young woman with dark eyes and a heart-shaped face who must have been Nick's mother and a framed, enlarged colour photograph of Nick's father and his four sons standing in front of a shiny red truck with the words *Kovacs Electric* painted on the side.

As she led us towards the front window of the living room, Chloe was fizzing with excitement. "Here it is," she said. The Kovacs' tree, a tall, full plantation pine, was hung with fabric ornaments: hearts, roosters, sleighs, trees, and candy canes, each embroidered with tiny pink, blue, yellow, and white flowers. "These are from the Old Country," Chloe said softly. "My great-grandmother and her sisters made them." She pointed to the red and green ceramic hearts dotting the tree. Each was painted with the words *Boldog Karácsony*.

"That's Merry Christmas in Hungarian," she said. Among the fabric and ceramic hearts from the Old Country were a dozen or more Disney princesses. "These are mine," Chloe said. "Everything looks nice together, doesn't it?"

"It does," I said. "Your tree is absolutely beautiful, Chloe, and before I forget, Taylor sent something for you." When I gave her the colouring book and the pencils, Chloe's face lit with pleasure, but it fell quickly. "I don't have a present for her," she said.

"You don't need one. This is a regift. Taylor has plenty of paints and brushes and canvases so when our neighbours gave her these, she thought you might enjoy them."

"Thank you," she said. She showed *The Secret Garden* book and pencils to Nick and then carried everything to the dining room, arranged the pencils carefully on the table, and began.

As he watched his daughter, Nick's face relaxed. "I never know what to get her for Christmas," he said. "She loves to colour, but when I look at all the colouring books they're always meant for younger kids and I don't want to insult her."

"From what I've heard, the colouring books for adults are very absorbing," I said. "People say working on the patterns helps them de-stress, calm down, focus, and just have fun."

Nick turned to Zack. "You've been losing pretty steadily at poker, lately," he said. "Maybe you'd have more luck if we started colouring."

Zack's laugh was rueful. "You could be right," he said. "But Joanne's giving me the evil eye, so it's time to change the subject."

"Gotcha," Nick said. "How was the dinner party?"

"Actually, it was fun," Zack said. "Great food, and Rosamond Burke was worth wearing a tux for. She really is something."

Nick nodded. "She is. My guys were a little nervous about dealing with theatre royalty, but Rosie's great."

Zack was taken aback. "You call her 'Rosie'?"

"She asked us to," Nick said. "She talks to everybody—actors, grips, stagehands, the craft services people—and she actually listens. It's a happy set. Everybody gets along. And we're doing good work. It's a privilege to watch Rosie and Vale together. Vale's young but uncommonly talented and the camera loves her. Lighting her face is a dream. Everything is going our way." Nick leaned in to rap his knuckles on the coffee table. "Touch wood."

Chloe had appeared to be totally absorbed in her work, but she turned and looked at her dad. "What does that mean?"

"Touch wood?" Nick said. "It's just a way of saying you hope nothing bad happens."

Chloe nodded thoughtfully. "I hope that all the time," she said. "Maybe it hasn't worked because I didn't say 'touch wood.'"

Nick recoiled as if he'd been punched in the stomach. Zack wheeled closer and put his arm around his old friend's shoulders. For a few moments neither of them moved. Finally, Nick took a deep breath and tried a smile. "I'm all right," he said.

We carried on. Zack and I gave animated accounts of the dinner party and Chloe reminded her father that their live-in housekeeper, Mrs. Szabo, had baked special cookies and she'd left some on a plate for us. Chloe and her father made tea, and we sat around the dining room table and chatted about holiday plans.

When I said we were going to the cottage between Christmas and the New Year, Chloe was puzzled. "But cottages are for summer," she said.

"We fixed up our cottage so we can use it year-round," I said. "We have a skating rink and a place to toboggan. Why don't you and your dad come out to the lake and spend some time with us?"

As we made plans to get together between Christmas and the New Year, Chloe was in high spirits, but the effect of her words about knocking on wood lingered, and when the Kovacs walked us to the door to say goodbye, Nick's face was ravaged.

Chloe had wrapped some of Mrs. Szabo's cookies for Taylor, and when she ran back to the kitchen to get them, Nick was clearly stricken. "It's so hard to think of her future," he said simply.

His bleakness struck a chord with me. "Nick, if there's anything I can do, just call. Short-term, long-term—there's not much on my schedule that can't be rearranged."

———

It was snowing hard the next morning. On three memorable occasions during the previous winter, Zack and the Volvo had been trapped in a snowbank, and he had finally agreed that having me drive him on unploughed streets made a certain amount of sense. Taylor, too, was nervous about winter driving, and after I'd dropped Zack at the courthouse, I planned to come home, pick her up, and drive her to the sound stage.

We were on our way out our front door when the phone rang. It was Nick Kovacs. "Joanne, I didn't think I'd be taking you up on your offer so quickly, but I need a hand . . ."

"And here I am," I said. "How can I help?"

"I'm at work, and Mrs. Szabo just brought Chloe by. Mrs. S. has come down with that flu. She looked like death. She tried our roster of aides but between finals at the university and the flu, no one's available. I know it's a lot to ask, but could you come and get Chloe and take her home with you until I figure this out? I can't leave here. We're working on a cave scene and the lighting is tricky. Chloe won't go with someone she doesn't know. It'll take at least an hour before a cab shows up, so I'm not sure when we'll get to your place."

"Don't worry about a cab. I was just on my way to drop Taylor off at the sound stage. I'll be there in ten minutes."

I could hear the relief in his voice. "Chloe will be just down the hall with whoever I can get to sit with her while I set up. I'm already running late. Jo, I can't thank you enough."

"Maybe next time Zack decides to scoop all his chips into the middle of the table, let him win."

Nick laughed. "That can be arranged."

When Taylor and I arrived at the studio, the snow was still heavy, and the wind had picked up. I parked in the accessible zone by the front door, pulled the accessibility sign out of the glove compartment, and hung it on the mirror. Zack never used accessible parking, and Taylor raised her eyebrows. "Desperate times call for desperate measures," I said.

"I'm not complaining," Taylor said, and together we ran up the stairs into the building.

The classrooms off the long hallway in what had once been the main building of the old campus were now used for hair and makeup, costumes, props, and special effects. Chloe was sitting at a table halfway down the hall, just outside the door to one of the hair and makeup rooms. To my surprise, Lizzie was beside her, totally absorbed in watching Chloe colour, and one of the PAs was perched on a nearby bench checking her phone.

When Taylor called her name, Chloe held up her *Secret Garden* book. "See how many pages I've done," she said.

Taylor examined the drawings carefully. "The colours you've chosen are perfect."

"And look how she never draws over the lines," Lizzie said.

"I noticed," Taylor said. She shifted her focus to Lizzie. "It's good of you to keep Chloe company."

"It was fun," Lizzie said. "Vale made me come here with her this morning because of all the snow." Lizzie stuck her feet out. "She gave me these boots."

"It's certainly boot weather," I said. "And those boots match the belt of your coat."

"They look nice," Chloe said, but her attention had already drifted to arranging her coloured pencils back in their box.

The PA had been watching us. "Okay if I take off?" she said.

"Absolutely," I said. When the young woman left, I gave Taylor a quick hug. "And you carry on with your day. We're fine, but stay in touch. Lizzie, can I drive you somewhere?"

"No, thanks. I'm going to stay here for a bit, but I can help Chloe put away her things."

Taylor left for the set while Chloe and Lizzie began packing up. They had finished stowing the colouring book and pencils in Chloe's backpack and Lizzie was shrugging on her coat when Gabe, Ainsley, and, of all people, Shawn O'Day came down the hall from the north end of the building where the Living Skies offices were located. Seemingly, Gabe and Shawn O'Day had patched things up. Engrossed in their conversation, they walked by without noticing us. Lizzie flicked a glance their way, but Chloe seemed oblivious. They were near the exit when Chloe suddenly cowered and began screaming, "No, don't, don't, no." They all startled and looked back. Glaring down the hall, Gabe shook his head, grabbed Ainsley's hand, and pulled her towards the set. Shawn quickly turned and followed.

Lizzie took Chloe's hand. "What's the matter?"

Chloe's face was white with terror. She pointed towards the double doors through which the trio had already disappeared and sobbed. "That man . . ."

"What man?" Lizzie said.

Chloe just kept pointing and sobbing.

"Lizzie, help me get Chloe out of here," I said. "Could you bring her backpack to the car?"

Lizzie followed, waited inside the doorway till we were in the car, and then ran down the stairs and handed me the backpack. "What happened?" she said.

"I'm not sure. Chloe was assaulted recently and something about Ainsley, Gabe, and Shawn seemed to trigger her memory."

Lizzie froze. Her black eyes were wide but focused on something far beyond the scene she'd just witnessed. After a few moments, she returned to the situation at hand. "Vale told me about the attack. She wondered if I'd heard anything on the street that might help the police, but I hadn't." Lizzie wiped the snow from her eyes, smearing her mascara.

I reached in my purse and handed her a tissue. "You'd better get back inside," I said.

Lizzie nodded. "Don't leave Chloe alone," she said. "I know all about what it's like to be attacked." Lizzie held out her arms and pulled back her sleeves. Her wrists were crisscrossed with scars.

Chloe was still shaking and her breathing was hiccupy when we arrived back at our house. After I helped her out of her coat and boots, I put my arm around her shoulder, guided her into the family room, turned on the fireplace, and picked up an afghan Mieka had made for me. My heart was clenched in sadness for Lizzie, and for Chloe.

"When she was younger, if Taylor was upset, I wrapped her in this afghan, and we sat together and watched *Bear in the Big Blue House*," I said. "Want to try?"

Chloe's nod was dubious, but as we settled in to watch the DVD, her breathing calmed and her body relaxed. By the time Luna sang the goodbye song, Chloe was smiling. "Can we watch another one?" she said.

"Absolutely, you heard what Bear and Luna said. Whenever we want, they're waiting for us to come and play. While you get started on the next show, I'm going to go to the hall and phone Zack."

"And tell him what we're doing."

"Right," I said.

Zack picked up immediately. "I'll have to keep my voice down," I said. "Chloe's in the next room."

"What's going on?"

"Here's the short version. Nick called a little over an hour ago and asked me to take care of Chloe this morning. She was at the sound stage and I was driving Taylor there, so I picked her up. When Chloe and I were getting ready to leave, there was an incident."

"What kind of incident?"

I gave Zack a brief account of the episode in the hallway. "Obviously something about Ainsley, Gabe, and Shawn O'Day triggered a memory of the assault for Chloe."

"Did she see their faces?"

"No. I don't think she even heard their voices—maybe a murmur. I was right beside her, and I don't remember hearing distinct words. Zack, it all happened so quickly. The three of them were already down the hall when Chloe reacted."

"We'll have to tell Nick."

"I agree, but I think we have to hang tight for a while. Nick's lighting a complicated scene, and he has to be there. Right now, Chloe's fine."

I could hear the frustration in Zack's voice. "You're right," he said. "But if Chloe has remembered something and will talk about it, there might be a chance to catch the creep who hurt her."

"Nick needs to be handled with care too," I said. "Just multiply what you're feeling by a thousand, and you'll have an approximation of the kind of anger he's trying to control. He's holding on, but barely. We should talk to him about what happened when we can be there to support him."

Nick phoned at eleven. He said he'd had no luck getting an aide. I told him there was no hurry, that Chloe and I were curled up together on the couch watching a DVD, and she was fine. I'd just hung up and put Pantera and Esme in the backyard for a run when the doorbell rang.

Ainsley Blair would not have made the top ten list of people I expected to see on my doorstep that morning, but there she was, snug in a black quilted trench jacket with the hood up. "May I come in?" she said.

I stepped aside. "Of course," I said. "But we'll have to keep our voices down. Chloe Kovacs is in the next room."

Ainsley's dark, intelligent eyes remained steady. "I saw Chloe Kovacs having some kind of breakdown this morning," she said. "What was wrong?"

My hackles rose. Ainsley hadn't left her film crew twiddling their thumbs out of concern for Chloe Kovacs. She was after something, and I wasn't in the mood for sharing. "Chloe hasn't talked about what upset her, but when she's ready to talk, I'm here, so we're covered. She just needs peace and quiet, so unless there's something specific . . ."

Ainsley hesitated, clearly weighing her options. When she raised her chin, I knew she'd decided to press on. "After Chloe was assaulted, Nick Kovacs was so concerned about her that he asked to be replaced as lighting director," she said. "We didn't want Nick to be alone, brooding about that terrible incident. So, out of concern for Nick's well-being, Gabe convinced him to stay."

"That was probably the best thing for Nick," I said, "though I'm in no position to judge. But what does that have to do with what happened today?"

Ainsley looked at me pointedly. Her tone was firm. "*The Happiest Girl* is going to be a brilliant family film. We don't need a traumatized fourteen-year-old girl with impaired brain function on set stirring up conflict and controversy."

I kept my voice low. "That fourteen-year-old with impaired brain function is now a guest in my home, Ainsley." I moved towards the door. "And it's time for me to get back to her."

Ainsley was frowning as she stepped towards the threshold. Before leaving, she paused, calculating her words. "You know, Joanne, creating *The Happiest Girl* brought Roy Brodnitz back from the dead. He's the best person I've ever known, but he's not strong. If this movie were to blow up in his face, I doubt there'd be another project for him. It would definitely signal the end of *Flying Blue Horses*. I'm sure you can understand why it's important for all of us to make sure

The Happiest Girl is a success." She steadily held my gaze.
"I would be very discreet about what happened with Chloe
this morning. And for everyone's sake, don't tell Nick."

I was so taken aback that I didn't respond. I simply stood
at the open door with my hand on the doorknob while
snow blew into the front hall. As Ainsley stepped outside,
she said, "I hope Chloe feels better."

When I closed the door after her, my nerves were frayed.
As disturbing as Chloe's reaction that morning had been,
Ainsley's visit, with its strange innuendos and veiled warn-
ings, was more unsettling. I was turning several disturbing
questions over in my mind when I realized the dogs were
barking to be let in.

Pantera and Esme were big fans of the outdoors, but five
minutes in the blowing snow had been enough. Further proof
if, I needed it, that the barometer was falling. When she heard
the ruckus, Chloe joined me, and together we went to the
kitchen to bring the dogs inside. Both were snow-covered.
Both waited until they'd positioned themselves close to
Chloe and me before they gave themselves a vigorous shake.
When the snow hit her, Chloe squealed with delight. I threw
her a towel. "Want to give me a hand drying these guys off?"

Chloe knelt on the floor beside Esme and went to work.
When she was through, she buried her face in Esme's sodden
fur and sniffed deeply.

I grimaced. "Don't tell me you like the smell of wet dog,"
I said.

"It makes me feel happy," Chloe said, then her face darkened. "Not like . . ."

I waited. When she didn't finish her thought, I pressed
her. "Not like what, Chloe?"

She flinched, but tightening her hold on Esme, she whispered, "Not the way that man smelled."

"The man who hurt you?"

She nodded.

"Is that what bothered you this morning?" I asked. "Did those people who walked by us have the same smell?"

When Chloe gave another small nod, I felt my marrow freeze. I took her hand and we brought the dogs into the family room so they could get dry in front of the fire. Sitting on the floor with Pantera and Esme, watching the flames, Chloe seemed at peace, but my insides were roiling.

Chloe had given me tangible information that might well be evidence about her assault. I just didn't know what to do with it.

Chloe and I had lunch, then she napped, and I fretted. I knew I should call Zack. I also knew that once Zack was aware of the connection Chloe had made this morning, he would feel honour-bound to tell Nick. Contemplating what Nick might do after he learned about Chloe's discovery shook me to the core. Ainsley had said, "For everyone's sake, don't tell Nick," and I was sorely tempted to heed her advice.

Nick arrived at around two-thirty, and he'd brought Zack with him. Chloe ran to hug her father and I embraced Zack. "I am so glad you're home," I said.

Nick grinned. "I figured picking Zack up and delivering him was the least I could do after what you did for Chloe and me today."

Safe in her father's arms, Chloe's face was glowing. "We had a really good time, didn't we, Jo?"

"We did indeed," I said.

Nick was anxious to get home before the roads worsened, so after we said our goodbyes, the Kovacs left.

Zack took off his jacket, hung it on the hall tree, and then turned to me. "As soon as I saw your face when we came in, I knew something was wrong. What's happened?"

We went into the family room, and I told Zack about the connection Chloe had made between the man who assaulted her and her reaction that morning to Gabe, Ainsley, and Shawn. Zack was frowning when I'd finished. "We could tell the police, Jo, and they'll question them. But there were two men there this morning, and all Chloe has is the memory of a scent. I'm guessing what she smelled was one of the men's aftershave, but that's hardly solid evidence. Thousands of men must use the same brand."

"That's what I thought too. But something else happened this morning."

When I told Zack about Ainsley's visit, he leaned forward. "Now we have a problem," he said.

"And the waters are even more muddied," I said. "We have our suspicions about Gabe, but what's Shawn O'Day's story? The night of Zephyr's fête, Shawn said he knew where Gabe went for 'raw sexuality' and he threatened to share what he knew. If Shawn knows about Gabe's secrets, he might well travel in the same circles."

"So it could be either of them," Zack said.

"It could be," I said. "But I don't think it is. Zack, I don't like the way Gabe Vickers looks at Vale. And Roy told me Gabe and Ainsley don't have a sexual relationship."

"A fact that in and of itself is not conclusive." Zack sighed. "Let's think about this. What are the facts? Chloe had a bad reaction to someone's smell this morning, and Ainsley doesn't want you to tell Nick about it." Zack paused, deliberating. "It could get Gabe, Ainsley, and Shawn called in for questioning. I'm going to make a call to the investigations unit and let them decide if it's enough evidence to pursue it further." Zack pulled out his phone and began to dial, then he stopped to look at me searchingly. "If you're okay with this, Jo. It might unleash a world of hurt."

"I'm more than okay with it," I said. "Just the possibility

that whoever did this to Chloe has one more minute of freedom to hurt another child means we have to pursue every
lead." For a split second I thought of what Ainsley said
about Roy and *Flying Blue Horses*, and then I put my hand
on Zack's knee. "Make the call," I said.

Zack reached the detective in charge of Chloe's case. He
recounted the events of the day and told him our suspicions.
When he hung up, Zack turned to me. "The detective said
they've got a lot of cases on their desk, but they'll look into
it as soon as possible."

"So we've done what we can do," I said.

"For now," Zack said. Then we settled back in our chairs
and were silent as we looked out at the snow on the stark
branches of the trees in front of the creek.

Taylor arrived home around four-thirty. When she said that
Gabe had insisted on driving her home, Zack and I managed
not to cringe. Our daughter was uncharacteristically quiet,
and after hugging us, she went to her room and stayed there
till I called her to say dinner was ready.

It was a sombre meal. We had a shrimp and orzo dish that
Taylor usually devoured, but that night she picked at her
food. Finally, she put her barely touched plate in the refrigerator and said she'd eat it later.

Zack was concerned. "Do you think you're coming down
with that flu?"

She shook her head. "It's not that. Jo, when you're through
eating I need to talk to you about something." When she
saw the concern in her father's eyes, Taylor went to him
and kissed the top of the head. "I really am okay, Dad. It's
something else."

After Taylor left, Zack and I looked at each other.
"Suddenly I've lost my appetite," I said. "I'm going to go talk
to her now."

Taylor was curled up, still fully dressed, on the top of her bed with her cats. "Ready to talk?" I said.

She nodded. "Jo, what happened to Chloe the day she was assaulted?"

I sat down on the bed beside her. "You know everything that we know. A man picked Chloe up, gave her money, and assaulted her."

"And he ejaculated, but there was no penetration," she said.

"That's right but, Taylor, why are you asking about this?"

"Could you tell me where he ejaculated?"

My stomach was churning. "Between Chloe's breasts and legs," I said.

Taylor dropped her eyes and began stroking Benny, the old tortoiseshell she'd owned the longest and from whom she most often sought out comfort. "Vale wrote an essay for her Yale college admission package," she said. "It's called 'The Coin of the Realm.'"

"About the abuse of child actors," I said. "Roy Brodnitz told me about it. Vale wrote about child actors being taken advantage of by predators and not having parents or other adults in their lives to protect them."

Taylor's face was a mask.

"Vale was writing about her own experience, wasn't she?" I said.

Taylor nodded. "She just told me today, but I think I knew it all along," she said, and I could hear the heaviness in our daughter's voice. "That first night when Vale and I sat out on the balcony at Gabe Vickers's condo after the celebration for Zephyr, we were having a great time, but after a while, I realized I was doing all the talking. I apologized and asked Vale to tell me about her life. She said, 'I really don't have a life—just a lot of characters' lives.' I blurted out something stupid about nobody being able to live that way, and Vale told me that not having a life of her own makes it easier. As long as she knows everything that's happening to her is simply narrative, she's never upset. She can do whatever she has to, to survive."

"Taylor, I know you don't want to talk about this. Neither do I, but there's something very wrong about the dynamic between Gabe and Vale. He's overly possessive and when he's with her, his desire for her is obvious." The words began tumbling out. "I know that casting her in *The Happiest Girl* has worked well, but after promising Ainsley carte blanche, Gabe overrode her casting decision and put Vale in the lead. Everyone says Gabe is the best producer in the business. He must have known that casting Vale as Ursula could threaten the success of the entire project. Did he insist on giving Vale the role because he's in love with her?"

Taylor's voice was almost a whisper. "It's not love," she said. "It's something else."

"Obsession?" I said.

For a long time, Taylor remained silent. The only sound in the room was Benny's wheezy purr. My daughter's misery was palpable, and I longed to simply drop the subject, but I couldn't. "Taylor, are Gabe and Vale lovers?"

Her eyes flashing with anger, Taylor bolted to a sitting position. Realizing he'd been usurped, Benny hissed. "No," she said. "Not lovers—at least, not in any normal sense. She lies down naked. He masturbates and then ejaculates on her breasts and thighs. He's been doing it for months."

"And Vale agrees to this," I said.

"He doesn't ask," she said. "When it started, Vale knew that the other girl up for the role of Ursula was almost certain to be cast unless she went along with what Gabe wanted." Taylor's laugh was short and derisive, but her eyes were filled with tears. "Vale feels completely ashamed. Meanwhile, he says that since she's still technically a virgin, there's no harm in what they're doing."

"Taylor, I'm so sorry. You know that your father and I will do anything we can to help Vale."

"I know," she said, "and I'm so grateful for both of you. But you'd better go now. I'm starting to lose it, and I still need to call Vale and tell her that Gabe was almost certainly the man who assaulted Chloe."

Zack had reheated my dinner and poured me a glass of wine.

"You have to eat," he said.

After I'd soldiered through my dinner and drunk my wine, Zack and I cleared away the dishes away.

"Do you want to get it over with?"

"Might as well," I said.

When I finished telling him about my conversation with Taylor, Zack was angrier than I could ever remember him being. "Well, now we know," he said, and his voice was cold with fury.

"It's all going to come out," I said. "The attack on Chloe. The relationship between Vale and Gabe. Zack, I knew there was something wrong there. The way Gabe looks at Vale. His possessiveness."

Zack inhaled deeply. "Jo, if Gabe Vickers walked through that door right now, I'd kill him. That's exactly why we need time to think this through. We can't afford any missteps or that bastard will walk. Let's go tell Taylor that we want to handle this together with Vale. Taylor can call Vale and assure her that if she wants me to, I'll give the police this new information tomorrow morning. We can't hold anything back, but we can make sure that the police understand that protecting the privacy of the victims is essential. And I'll see Nick before I do anything else tomorrow morning." Zack rubbed his temples. "God, I am dreading that."

CHAPTER

14

It was difficult to imagine that any day could hold more pain than Monday had, but Tuesday was worse. It began with news of a tragedy. Pantera and Esme were just beginning to stir when Taylor appeared in our bedroom. She was wearing the flannel rompers she favoured for winter. Her hair was unbrushed and she was very pale.

"Something terrible has happened," she said. "Vale just called. Gabe Vickers jumped from the balcony of his condo. He's dead."

I could feel Zack's body tense. "It's hard to know how to react, isn't it? But Vickers's suicide does eliminate a lot of problems."

"He'll never do what he did to Chloe and Vale again," Taylor said softly.

Standing at the foot of our bed in her blue-and-white checked rompers, she looked very young. I moved closer to Zack and patted the place on the bed beside me. "Come get in here where it's warm, Taylor," I said.

She moved in next to me, but she lay on her back, staring at the ceiling, her body rigid. No one spoke. When, finally,

Taylor began to talk, her voice, usually so filled with life, was a monotone. "Lizzie found him," she said.

"Lizzie? The girl who came up to Vale the night of the dinner for Rosamond?" Zack said.

"Uh-huh," Taylor said. "When the weather is bad, Lizzie sometimes sleeps in that glassed-in vestibule that opens into the lobby—the place where guests key in the number of the apartment they're going to visit. Vale gave Lizzie the keycard for her condo, so she'd have a place to stay when it was cold, but she must have lost it, because she was in the vestibule this morning when she saw something fall. She thought someone had thrown out a coat. She went to get it and that's when she found him. She texted Vale, and Vale's with her now. I guess Lizzie's pretty out of it."

"Have they called the police?"

"Vale called 911 for an ambulance, but Lizzie freaked out when she suggested calling the police." Taylor paused. "Dad, Vale convinced Lizzie that the police wouldn't hassle her if she had a lawyer with her."

Zack said, "Are they still at the condo?"

"Yes. They're on the lower level. There's a workout room and spa down there, but the spa doesn't open until later, so there's no one around yet. There are police at the entrance and on the side of the building where Gabe is, so Vale suggested we use the delivery doors at the rear of the building. She has an access card, and she'll meet us there."

"Depending on the roads, I should be there in fifteen minutes," Zack said.

"I'm going with you, Dad," Taylor said.

"I'm coming too," I said. "If we get stuck, Taylor and I can shovel."

Zack had been a trial lawyer for almost three decades. Like most trial lawyers, he hadn't made many friends in the police department. Debbie Haczkewicz was the exception. When Debbie's son, Leo, was in a motorcycle accident that left him a paraplegic, he was despondent. Debbie credited Zack with showing her son that, while he would have to alter his life plans, he still had a life. Leo had become an ESL teacher, moved to Japan, married a colleague, and he and his wife had two little boys. Debbie was grateful.

During Zack's tenure as mayor, Debbie had served as chief of police, but she missed the camaraderie of her old job, and when a position opened in her former division, Major Crimes, she took it. That morning after Zack convinced her Lizzie would either take off or clam up if she had to face an officer without his support, Debbie agreed to give him a twenty-minute head start and that included travel time. We made it in ten.

Police cruisers were still arriving, but uniformed officers had already blocked off the semicircular driveway that led to the main entrance of the building. I dropped off Zack and Taylor at the delivery entrance and searched for a parking space. When I returned, Vale met me at the door.

She was composed as she moved forward to greet me. Whatever she was feeling about Gabe Vickers's death was hidden beneath years of training.

Her voice was controlled and expressive. "Thank you for coming," she said.

"I'm glad you called," I said.

"Zack tells me that we don't have much time, so please just follow me. Lizzie refuses to get in the elevator, so we're meeting down here. I should warn you, she's not in great shape, so don't push her too hard."

Lizzie was sitting on a black minimalist modular sofa outside the dimly lit spa. Vale sat down next to her, and Zack wheeled over to be close to them. Two white minimalist modular chairs faced the sofa. Taylor was in one, and I took the other. The chairs were as uncomfortable as they looked. Obviously, visitors were not encouraged to dally.

The contrast between Vale and Lizzie, side by side on the sofa, struck me hard. Vale's shoulder-length auburn hair was silky, her skin dewy, her brilliantly blue-green eyes clear. Every inch of her carefully nurtured body proclaimed that she was a highly valued young woman. Lizzie's brutally hacked black hair; her blotchy sallow complexion; her deeply shadowed, haunted eyes; and her rail-thin body sent a message that was equally clear: this was a throwaway girl. She and Vale had travelled along very different roads to reach that moment on the lower level of the shining condominium, and yet they had faced the same demons.

Zack had already begun talking to Lizzie. As she gazed at Zack, Lizzie's eyes were narrow and frightened, but Zack was reassuring. "As I've already said, there's nothing to be afraid of." He took Lizzie's hand. "If we play fair with the police, they'll play fair with us. Tell them everything. Don't hide anything. They always find out the truth and it's better if they find it out from us. If the situation gets too much for you, tell me and we'll stop. Okay?"

She nodded.

Zack texted Debbie and turned back to Lizzie. "Inspector Haczkewicz is on her way." Lizzie's hand tightened around his. Her nails were bitten to the quick. Zack's voice was gentle. "You've done nothing wrong, Lizzie."

"You don't know what I did before . . ."

"What happened in the past doesn't really matter now," Zack said. "What matters is that you're helping the police. Debbie knows that. She's not going to hassle you."

Inspector Haczkewicz was wearing a hooded black fleece anorak and black ski pants. She was tall with a thick, energetic frame and a determined stride. Even in street clothes

she exuded authority, but her smile as she introduced herself to Lizzie was warm.

Taylor stood so Debbie could sit to interview Lizzie.
Inspector Haczkewicz was old school. She used a coiled
paper notebook, and as Lizzie delivered her account of discovering Gabe Vickers's body in a breathless, childlike
voice, Debbie's pen flew.

When Lizzie finished, Debbie sat back in her chair.
"Thank you," she said. "That was very helpful. Just one
more thing." Her voice became low, almost hypnotic.
"Lizzie, I'd like you to close your eyes, and picture in your
mind exactly what happened when you went outside and
found Mr. Vickers."

"Zack says I don't have to talk about what happened
before," Lizzie's voice was wavering towards hysteria.

"Zack's right," Debbie said reassuringly. "Just try to
remember everything you saw and heard during those first
moments when you went outside. Don't rush."

Obedient as a docile child, Lizzie shut her eyes. Her body,
which had never stopped trembling during the interview,
grew still, and her face relaxed. Finally, she began to speak.
Her account didn't vary appreciably from what she'd said
earlier. When she'd finished, Debbie replaced the lid on her
pen, stood, zipped her anorak, and turned to Lizzie. "Thank
you very much," she said. "What you've told me could be
very helpful."

As soon as Debbie left the room, Zack picked up his
phone. I could see the tension in the set of his shoulders, and
instinct told me to get the girls out of the way. "None of us
has had breakfast," I said. "Why don't you three go to that
café across the street and get something to eat. Zack has
some calls to make and we'll join you after he's finished."

I walked the girls to the delivery door; when I returned,
Zack was still on the phone. "Well, thanks," he said. "I'll

give you my number again. Make sure he calls me when he gets back, but if he's not back in an hour, please let me know."

"What's the problem?" I said.

Zack rubbed the back of his neck. "I don't know. Maybe nothing, but, Jo, I have a bad feeling about where this is headed. Gabe had a lot going for him. He could have afforded gold standard legal representation. Vale is seventeen, above the age of consent. He could have easily argued that his relationship with her was consensual. What he did to Chloe was sickening, but even a halfway decent lawyer could have put together a winning case for him."

"So there was no reason for him to jump off that balcony," I said.

"No. We have to consider the possibility that Vickers's death was something other than suicide. I was watching Debbie's face, and I can guarantee that possibility hit her too. I just called Nick to reassure myself that he had no part in Vickers's death, that he'd been home all night and that he was still there."

"But he wasn't," I said.

"No," Mrs. Szabo said that Nick had dinner and watched a movie with Chloe, and then around nine o'clock, just after Chloe went to bed, he received a phone call. Mrs. S. says when the call ended, Nick was 'not himself'—her words. Nick has an exercise room in his garage. It's pretty rudimentary— treadmill, stationary bike, punching bag, weights—but Nick says it does the trick. Since he stopped drinking, that's where he goes to sweat off his emotions. Mrs. Szabo can see the light in the garage from her suite next to Chloe's room, and she said Nick was still out there when she went to bed.

"Sometime in the middle of the night, Nick knocked on her door, apologized for waking her, and said there was something he had to look after. Mrs. S. suggested he wait till morning, but Nick said it couldn't wait. She checked his bedroom when I called, and he wasn't there, and there was no light on in the garage. Mrs. Szabo is worried. So am I."

"If Chloe talked to him about the incident at the production studio yesterday morning, Nick might have put two and two together and determined that Gabe Vickers was the man who assaulted Chloe?" I said.

"God, I hope that didn't happen," Zack said. "But I can't imagine anything else that would have driven him out of the house in the middle of the night."

"Neither can I," I said. "But there's nothing you can do until you hear from him, so we might as well go across the street and join the girls."

Zack and I hadn't even made it to the delivery door when my phone rang. It was Roy Brodnitz, and it was clear from the moment he began talking that he was losing a battle to stay in control. "Jo, something terrible has happened, and Ainsley thinks we need a lawyer." He groaned. "I don't even know where to start."

"Take a deep breath," I said. "Zack and I know that Gabe is dead."

"Then it is Gabe," Roy said, and his voice was heavy. "Ainsley and I heard the sirens. We were at my place and could tell something had happened on the other side of the building. When we looked out the window, we saw the police and the body on the ground." The penny dropped. "Jo, how did you know it was Gabe?"

"I'll explain when I see you. Zack and I are on the lower level of your building. Can we take the elevator from here and get to you?"

"Take the one on the far left," Roy said. "I'll buzz you up to the twenty-sixth floor."

I texted Taylor to let her know our plans, then we headed up.

———

It's a truism that you cannot unsee what you've already seen. I would have given a great deal to unsee the images that met Zack and me when the elevator doors opened, mistakenly, on the twenty-seventh floor that morning.

Just a few days before, we had left a penthouse that was a sparkling showcase for earthly delights: succulent food; excellent drink; exquisite floral arrangements; and handsome people, beautifully dressed and glowing with the burnish of success.

Now the penthouse was a nightmare. The air was frigid. The sliding doors to the balcony from which Gabe Vickers had fallen to his death were open—the balcony was large, extending almost the full length of the living room—so the room was fully exposed to the elements. The wind had whipped snow onto the hardwood, and boot marks from the uniformed officers moving onto and off the balcony had already turned it to slush. Disposable coffee cups rested on glass tables that on Saturday night held champagne flutes. The dozens of Michelangelo roses that had filled the air with the scent of lemons were wilting in their cut-glass bowls. Lamps had been knocked over, and plates and glassware lay shattered on the floor.

Zack and I didn't have long to take in the nightmare. When a police constable spotted us, she was quick to approach. "You have to leave," she said. "This is the scene of an active police investigation."

My phone beeped a text notification. I checked the message. "We got off on the wrong floor," I said. "Roy apologizes. He punched in Ainsley's code accidentally. He'll meet us at the elevator."

As he adjusted his chair in the elevator, Zack's wheel ran over something. "What was that?" he said.

I bent down, picked up a plasticized keycard. "I'm guessing this is the keycard Lizzie lost," I said.

"Something lost is found. A good omen," Zack said. When we reached Roy's floor, he pressed the Doors Closed button and held it. "Jo, before we see Roy and Ainsley, what do you think happened in there? Cops don't go around knocking over lamps and smashing glasses."

"No," I said. "It seems Gabe did not go gently into that good night."

"Indeed," Zack said releasing the button.

There were four condos on the twenty-sixth floor, and when the doors opened, Roy was there, as promised. He was unshaven, but his jeans and checked cotton shirt were immaculate. As soon as I had learned of the role Des Love's *Aurora* played in Roy Brodnitz's life, I'd been reading about him in magazines and online. Roy was known to be brilliant but high-strung and erratic. I had seen evidence of his brilliance in *The Happiest Girl*, but his dealings with me had been marked by gentleness, sensitivity, and steadiness.

That morning his face was knifed by tension, and his usually relaxed baritone was taut with panic. "I'm so relieved you're here," he said "I'm totally at a loss about what to do. Ainsley and I still don't understand what happened."

Zack's voice was deep and calming. "Let's go inside. We'll tell you what we know, and then you can consider your next move."

The door to Roy's condo was open and Ainsley was waiting on the threshold. The night of the dinner party for Rosamond Burke, Ainsley had been a head-turner with her strawberry blond hair twisted into an elegant braid, her makeup skillfully applied, and her sea-green gown cut to flatter her dancer's supple body. That morning, stressed, without makeup, in khakis, a Duran Duran T-shirt and runners, her ponytail pulled through the opening of her Mets ball cap, Ainsley looked like the younger sister of the elegant woman who had hosted us at dinner. There were bruise marks on the backs of her hands, but she didn't mention them, and I didn't stare.

Ainsley offered us coffee, juice, and bagels that she said were probably stale. Zack and I passed on the bagels but accepted the coffee and juice gratefully, and the four of us settled around the kitchen table to talk.

As Zack related Lizzie's account of how she had discovered Gabe's body, Ainsley was stoic, but she and Roy exchanged a quick, anxious look when Zack said Lizzie had already talked to Inspector Debbie Haczkewicz from Major Crimes.

After he finished, Zack leaned forward, his powerful fingers spread like a starfish on the table. "So far, I've simply given you information that happened to come my way. Ainsley, Roy said you thought you might need a lawyer. I can advise you about that, but you'll have to answer some questions."

Roy and Ainsley looked at each other for a long minute. When Roy nodded, Ainsley began. Her voice was steady. "I'll answer your questions."

Zack smiled. "Good call," he said. "Are you ready?"

"Yes."

"All right, question one: Where did you spend last night?"

"Here with Roy, in his condominium."

"Why didn't you spend the night with your husband?"

"Gabe and I had quarrelled."

"What was the subject of the quarrel?"

"A marital problem."

"Debbie will push on that one," Zack said, "but your lawyer can try to shut her down. Next question: Did the quarrel become violent?"

"Yes."

"Who initiated the violence?"

"I did, but I left before it got out of control. Gabe was alive when I left. He might have had scratch marks on his face. Nothing more."

"When did you learn that Gabe Vickers was dead?"

"Jo confirmed it a few minutes ago, when Roy called her."

Zack sat back in his chair. "Ainsley, the sooner you talk to Inspector Haczkewicz, the better. I'm sure she's still on the property. Debbie is very, very good at her job. Don't try to shit her. Keep your answers short and precise, just as you did with me. Don't volunteer anything, until Debbie pushes, which she will, and then answer her question." Zack inhaled. "You'd also be wise to hire a lawyer. It can't be me, but I can recommend someone from another firm. Her name is Asia Libke, and she's as good as they come. Shall I call her for you?"

Ainsley glanced at Roy then looked back at Zack. "Please."

Zack opened his phone and called Asia. They talked briefly and Zack broke the connection. "Asia was on her way to work. She'll be here in ten minutes, so I'm going to call Inspector Haczkewicz and tell her you'll be ready to talk to her here in half an hour. That'll give you a little time with Asia."

"Thanks," Ainsley said. "Zack, I really appreciate your help. I know you're only here because of your family's friendship with Roy, but I am grateful."

Roy walked us to the elevator. "Is Ainsley in trouble?" he said.

"You're probably a better judge of that than I am," Zack said. "You know the truth."

"I have a question," I said. "Roy, how long has Ainsley known about what Gabe's been doing to Vale Frazier?"

Roy's expression was open and unguarded. "She had no idea until last night when Vale called and told her everything."

As soon as the elevator doors closed, Zack said, "So where does that little nugget of information leave us?"

"It connects some dots. As soon as Taylor told Vale that Chloe's attacker ejaculated between Chloe's breasts and her legs, Vale knew that Gabe was the attacker, because that's what he'd been doing to her. She called Ainsley and told her about what had been going on between her and Gabe, and that Gabe had assaulted Chloe Kovacs. The question now is, why did Vale call Ainsley."

"The simple explanation is retribution," Zack said.

"I don't believe she was motivated by revenge," I said. "We've seen how protective she is with Lizzie. As different as those two young women appear to be, they're both victims. Chloe was a victim too. I think Vale decided to put an end to it and so she called Ainsley."

"Thus precipitating the marital problem Ainsley and Gabe fought over," Zack said. "Incidentally, did you notice the bruises on the back of her hands?"

"I did," I said. "They looked painful."

"I'm sure the cops will get a picture of them," Zack said. "They're consistent with the pattern of bruising a victim makes on an assailant when he or she tries to fight them off."

"So Gabe was the victim?"

"At that point yes, but if Ainsley's telling the truth, Asia won't have any trouble stick-handling the situation," Zack said. "A wife gets a phone call from another, much younger woman, telling the wife that her husband has been taking advantage of her, doing the same things he did to her to at least one other innocent victim."

"Zack, do you think the phone call Nick received was from Vale?" I said.

"It's a definite possibility," Zack said. The elevator doors opened. Zack wheeled out and immediately checked his phone. "Three texts from Nick. He's fine. There was something he had to take care of, but he's home now. He's sorry to have troubled me. He's going to work. He'll fill me in when they're finished shooting at the end of the day."

"That has to be a good sign," I said. "If Nick's headed for work, that means he doesn't know Gabe's dead."

Zack shrugged. "Either that or that he knows how to establish an alibi with an old friend who may end up representing him."

CHAPTER

15

When she saw me walk through the door of the café, a wave of relief washed over Taylor's face.

I went to the booth where she, Vale, and Lizzie were sitting. "That took longer than we thought it would," I said. "I'm sorry if you were worried."

"How's Ainsley doing?" Vale said.

"This is a nightmare for everybody, but Roy's with Ainsley. She'll be all right. Zack's in the car waiting, so I guess we'd better pay the bill and get moving."

"Breakfast was good," Lizzie said.

Vale smiled at Lizzie fondly. "She actually ate something. Now for a shower and a change of clothes. One of the APs texted to say our call has been changed to ten o'clock, so the three of us are going back to my condo."

"Not me," Lizzie said. "I've got places to go."

Vale took her arm. "You're not going anywhere until you get into some warm clothes and find a coat of mine you want to wear."

Lizzie lowered her eyes. "I lost Taylor's coat," she mumbled.

"No worries," Taylor said. "It was just a coat."

"Taylor's right, Lizzie," I said. "It was just a coat."

When my daughter caught my eye, we both smiled. Many tears had been shed the October that Taylor discovered she'd shot up over the summer months and her much-loved coat was now too short. More proof that Zack and I didn't need that our daughter was becoming an adult.

We watched until the girls disappeared around the corner of Broad Street, and then Zack turned to me. "The less time we spend on these roads the better," he said. "I have a change of clothes at the office. I might as well go straight there."

After I'd dropped Zack off, I took the dogs for a run, made a pot of tea, and thought again of Catherine Parr Traill. Bewailing in abject terror took more vigour than I could summon. I did, however, have the energy to organize the placement of furniture in the new home office. The room we chose had been the previous owners' billiards room. It was large, and we had used the space as a repository for everything we couldn't find a place for. I took my tea and a pad and pencil into the former billiards room, snapped pictures of every item we no longer needed, and posted the photos with our contact information on I Will Help, an online group for people who have items to give to people who need them. Operation Shared Office was underway.

I had just begun measuring the room when Zack called. "Jo, I hate to ask, but I'm making myself crazy thinking about Nick. If I don't get some answers, I'm going to wheel over my joint in court this morning."

"That's an image that's going to stick with me," I said. "What can I do to keep your male parts intact?"

Zack chuckled. "Sorry about the image," he said. "But I am worried. Nick texted me that he's at work now, which should be reassuring, but something about the text just didn't sound right. I've been calling Taylor, hoping she'd be able to give me a first-person account of how Nick's doing, but her phone must be turned off. I'm due in court. Would you mind calling Taylor and leaving me a message after you've talked to her?

"I can do better than that," I said. "When Taylor rushed out of here this morning, she didn't take her satchel. It has her sketchbook and pencils in it, and it's a great excuse for me to visit the set. I'll call you after I see Nick."

"Thanks, Jo. I'll make it up to you. I'll leave early Friday afternoon and come home and help you with the office."

My response was quick. "You don't have to do that— really. Please. Don't even think of it."

"Okay, but at least let me take care of dinner tonight," Zack said. "Why don't I make reservations at the Sahara Club for the three of us?"

"*That* you can do! I could use a steak, but better make that reservation for four. I imagine Taylor will want to bring Vale along."

"Jo, I don't know . . ." Zack paused, measuring his words. "At first, I dismissed the call she made to Ainsley as impetuous, but do you think it's possible she was more calculated than that?"

"No. She must have felt Ainsley deserved to know the truth," I said. "We can't shoot the messenger."

"What if the message the messenger delivered caused someone to commit murder?"

"You're thinking about Nick," I said. "But, Zack, if she did make that call, I'm sure Vale believed she was doing the right thing. And we're not even certain she made it. Gabe was Vale's ticket to a great future. Exposing his crime would jeopardize her entire career. Whatever the case, she doesn't deserve to be treated like a pariah."

———

The road crews had been out, so the short drive to the sound stage was without incident. Taylor had told me that, at any given time, there are at least sixty people on a movie set, but Nick was easy to spot. He was the only one with his arm in a cast.

Our daughter was in her usual place at a small table just outside the activity on set. When I handed Taylor her satchel, she lit up. "Thanks," she said. "I'm totally lost without my art supplies, but I'm sorry you had to drive in this weather."

"Actually, the weather's improving, and the main streets are being cleared, so the drive wasn't bad. Besides, bringing you your satchel was just an excuse. Your dad and I wanted reassurance that Nick Kovacs was okay."

Taylor sighed heavily. "As you can see, he's not," she said. "His arm is broken, and his face is really a mess."

"I don't suppose he told you what happened."

"No, and I didn't want to ask. Jo, it physically hurts Nick to talk."

I winced. "And we can make an educated guess about how he sustained those injuries."

"Gabe Vickers," Taylor said quietly. Her brow puckered. "Jo, you don't think Nick had anything to do with Gabe dying, do you?"

"Nick is a gentle guy," I said. "Remember how he ran to help Shawn O'Day when Gabe gave him a nosebleed the night of Zephyr's celebration? Nick didn't know Shawn, but he made sure he was all right." I shook my head. "Anyway, I'll see what Nick says. You get on with your drawing, and please, stay in touch."

After I moved into Nick's line of vision, it didn't take him long to spot me and come over. He moved laboriously, obviously in pain. I held out my arms to him. "Consider yourself virtually hugged," I said. "How are you doing?"

He tried a smile. "Never better."

"Gabe Vickers?"

He nodded slowly. "Yeah."

"Nick, was it Vale Frazier who told you?"

"Vale? No." He was clearly surprised. "How would she even know? Some guy with no caller ID phoned me last night." He shrugged. "Or I think it was a guy. The voice was muffled. Whoever it was said, 'Gabe Vickers attacked your daughter, and he shouldn't be walking around.' I knew that going to Vickers's place would be a dumb move, and I tried to work through all the thoughts that were driving me crazy by taking my anger out on the punching bag, but . . ." He shrugged. "Anyway, I did go to Vickers's condo. When I confronted him, he didn't deny that he did it, so we started throwing punches at each other. We didn't stop until we were both seriously banged up, but, Jo, I swear when I left, he was alive."

"I believe you," I said. I touched his cheek gently. "Take care of yourself, Nick."

As Nick returned to his work, I spotted Ainsley, still in khakis, a T-shirt, ball cap, and sneakers. Her face was strained, but she was wholly focused on the scene they were shooting with Rosamond Burke. After a few minutes, she noticed me waiting and stepped back. "Let's take a break and start again in fifteen." She and Rosemond exchanged a few words, and then Ainsley joined me.

"I don't need to ask how it's going," I said.

"I'm hanging in," she said.

"This won't take long," I said. "Did Vale tell you about Gabe and Chloe Kovacs?"

Ainsley narrowed her eyes, sizing up me and my question. Finally, she answered. "Yes. After telling me all about how Gabe had been using her sexually since shortly before he cast her in the film, she told me that she also believed he attacked Chloe Kovacs because, just as he had with her, my husband had ejaculated all over Chloe's chest and legs." Her tone was dry as she continued. "I've heard rumours about Gabe and young girls before, though as far as I know he'd never been stupid enough to attack one the way he did Chloe. Anyway, I have always put the rumours out of my mind, but when I heard from Vale last night, I knew this wasn't going to go away. I was angry, and I was frightened, because the bad publicity could ruin our movie. I was also sick with disgust."

Ainsley's voice was steely. "Gabe had caused so much pain, and I knew there was worse to come. When I saw him, all I could think of was hurting him the way he'd hurt everyone else. I tried to hit him. He stopped me." She held out her hands. "Hence, the bruises.

"When I cooled off, I told him how we'd handle the problem. He was to return to New York ASAP and would no longer be publicly associated with *The Happiest Girl.* A press release would be issued saying that Gabe had withdrawn for medical reasons. Tobi Lampard, the production manager, would be made executive producer. Gabe didn't argue because he knew as well as I did that a sex scandal involving a child with a brain injury would kill the film. His last words to me were when I told him I was going to stay at Roy's. He said, 'Have him check his option contract for *Flying Blue Horses.*' Gabe was very calm." Ainsley closed her eyes and rubbed the back of her neck. "Joanne, he did not seem like a man about to commit suicide."

"What does Roy make of the reference to the option?" I said.

"I haven't told him yet. There's just been so much." Ainsley looked over at the set. "I'd better get back."

With that, the director returned to the task at hand.

My mind was swimming. All I wanted was to get into my car, press my forehead against the cool window next to the driver's seat, and try to make sense of everything that had happened since Taylor came into our room in the morning and said something terrible had happened. Just as I reached the door from Sound Stage 1 to the hall, the elegant and surprisingly strong fingers of Rosamond Burke, CBE, closed around my upper arm. "May I have a word with you, Joanne?"

"Of course, but let's go into the hall."

Rosamond was in costume and makeup for her role as Ursula's grandmother, a woman who dedicated her life to her conviction that, at our peril, humans neglect the lessons that bears can teach us. Rosamond, too, was a woman driven by her passions, and the inner light that emanated from her was igniting her performance. She had been an inspired choice for the role, and I knew Gabe Vickers had been brilliant to pursue her.

Rosamond's voice was low and urgent. "What's going on?" she said. "First one of the APs phones to tell me the call has been changed from eight to ten; Nick Kovacs comes in looking as if he's been run over by a lorry; Ainsley, who is always so effective, can't seem to put a foot right this morning; the crew are wandering about like lost sheep; and there are there are rumours going around that Gabe Vickers has left town or is dying or dead. I've been on troubled sets before, and I know that unless someone calls us together and explains the problem, we're going to lose a day of shooting. If Gabe Vickers is still in the city and alive, he's the one who should take charge."

"Rosamond, I'm afraid that one of those rumours is true. Gabe committed suicide this morning."

She took a deep breath. "Good God. Whatever made Gabe take his own life? He didn't seem the type."

I told Rosamond that I understood Gabe had been implicated in some sexual assaults.

Rosamond's bright blue eyes grew troubled. "I'd heard rumours about Vickers," she said. "But there are always rumours, and nothing I'd heard caught hold of me as something real."

Rosamond squared her shoulders. "But onward, ever onward. Gabe Vickers may be disgraced, but I certainly would not have wished him dead. And to give the devil his due, Vickers raised the money and chose the people who will bring what he termed his 'passion project' to an international audience." She turned to face me. "His death must be a blow for you too, Joanne. Gabe was putting together the financing for *your* endeavour, wasn't he?"

"I didn't realize my endeavour was public knowledge," I said.

"It's not, but Gabe has a reputation for getting the best people on board, and he'd already established his core: Roy and Ainsley, and I was told Gabe has already spoken with Vale Frazier's agent to sign her for the role of the young Sally Love."

"All that on the basis of some hastily scratched notes and a ton of ideas," I said. "Gabe Vickers was sick and twisted, but he really was a genius."

"Indeed," Rosamond said. "But to the matter at hand. Tobi Lampard, the production manager, has been part of every decision regarding this film. She has some very good people around her, and unless I'm mistaken she'll be Ainsley's choice to see the film through to completion."

"You're not mistaken," I said. "Ainsley just told me exactly that."

"Then Tobi's the logical person to make the announcement," Rosamond said. "She'll be in the Living Skies offices. I'll fetch her."

"You're a wonder," I said.

"No, just a worker like you—one who takes on whatever tasks come her way." Rosamond's tone was matey. "You're ancillary, Joanne, but Fate thrust you into centre stage, and you're performing well."

I checked my phone from the parking lot of the sound stage. Zack had called three times: twice to check on Nick, once to say he'd made dinner reservations for four at the Sahara Club. And a man from I Will Help had called to say they would take everything I had posted online, and their truck would be in our neighbourhood that afternoon. All I had to do was arrange a pickup time.

After I'd called I Will Help, I phoned Zack. Court was adjourned for lunch so I was in luck again.

"How's it going?" I said.

"Better than I deserve," he said. "How are you?"

"Ancillary but performing well."

"You're going to have to explain that."

"I'll save the explanation for our first martini," I said. "And, Zack, you may want to make yours a double. Sometime after midnight, Nick went over to Gabe Vickers's penthouse. They fought. To quote Rosamond Burke, Nick looks 'like he's been run over by a lorry.' He has a broken arm and his face is a mess, but he says Gabe was alive when he left. And there is one potentially good development. Although Nick's caller muffled his voice, Nick is relatively certain it was a man. Ainsley was on set when I was there, so I spoke with her too, and there's a new puzzle piece to deal with. Vale did tell Ainsley about what Gabe had done to Chloe. Ainsley had devised a plan for Gabe to leave town and completely dissociate himself from *The Happiest Girl*."

"Those are pretty mild consequences for committing a particularly ugly crime."

"They are," I said. "Zack, doesn't everything about this seem out of whack to you? Nobody I've talked to could believe Gabe was a man who would take his own life."

"Everyone has a tipping point," Zack said. "Maybe this morning, when he realized eventually someone would turn him in for what he did to Chloe, Gabe discovered his."

Maybe," I said. "Zack, thank you for agreeing to include Vale in our dinner tonight. She's so young, and for good or ill, Gabe was a large part of her life. Tonight will be hard for her. Having Taylor and us there might make it easier."

"Do you really believe the four of us can have dinner together and nothing that's happened in the past twenty-four hours will come up?"

"No," I said. "But we live in hope."

The pickup truck from I Will Help arrived right on time and removed everything from the room that was to be our office except a desk that Zack liked and the old cherry wood roll top desk and chair that belonged to my first husband when he was the province's attorney general. Ian's roll top from the legislature evoked memories of another desk I owned. In her will, Nina Love had left me her graceful Chinese Chippendale desk. It was lacquered black with gilt trim, and she kept a lacquered water jar on it. Painted fish swam on that jar—perfectly serene in their ordered, watery world. When my mother was at her worst, I would go to Nina and she would tell me to sit down and try to close out everything but the smooth passage of the bright fish as they swam around and around the jar. It always worked. That desk had been my refuge, and Nina had been my rock.

For fourteen years Nina's desk and chair had been in storage with everything else she had left me. Someday I would be strong enough to call the storage company and accept her legacy, but I knew today wasn't that day. Instead, I brought my laptop into the newly cleared space, pulled up the chair from the legislature, and wasted the better part of an hour looking at designer ideas for dream offices, most of which seemed to have views of either an ocean or Greenwich Village. I ordered the basics from an office supply store and decided our remaining decorating needs could be met through repurposing what we already had.

I was eyeing Sally's old worktable and deciding where to place it in the new space when Margot phoned.

"I'm not going to ask how your day's going," she said.

"A sensible decision," I said. "Hey, are you wearing your lawyer clothes?"

Margot's chuckle was low and salacious. "Are you fantasizing about me again?"

"Actually, I was hoping you could help me move some furniture."

"No biggie," she said. "I can move furniture in my underwear."

"Now I am fantasizing," I said.

"Put it on the back burner," she said. "This isn't one of our usual goof and gossip sessions. This is professional. Can I come over now?"

"Sure."

I was playing with the idea of using Sally's worktable as a partial divider between Zack's office area and my own when Margot arrived. She kicked off her boots and when I took her coat I saw that she was indeed wearing lawyer clothes: a smartly tailored grey pinstripe Merino wool suit, a white V-neck silk blouse, and a string of pale pink pearls.

"Can I get you something?" I said.

"Nope, I'm good. Let's talk. Have you got your Christmas tree up?"

"It's in the family room. I'll plug it in and we can talk there."

When Margot saw our tree, she sighed. "Your tree is so lovely. All the decorations on ours are cheap, cheerful, and unbreakable, and none is further than four feet from the ground. The rest of the tree is, in Lexi's words, 'bare nekkid.'

But I'm not here to talk trees," she said. "Gabe Vickers's decision to make his permanent exit from the planet seems to have put a burr under Zephyr Winslow's saddle. Since receiving the news about Gabe, she's phoned me at least a half-dozen times. To be fair, she's sunk a tonne of dough into *The Happiest Girl,* so she's worried about her investment, and with cause. The film will take a serious financial hit if Gabe Vickers's attack on Chloe Kovacs becomes public knowledge, as it inevitably will."

"So Zack has given you the full update," I said. "Look, this probably shouldn't go beyond us, but I talked to Ainsley this morning, and she seems to have come up with a strategy to tamp down the likelihood of a scandal."

"Already? She must be a cool one. Her husband jumps from the balcony of a twenty-seven-storey building and she's moved straight into damage control."

"The attempt at damage control started last night, before Gabe died. Ainsley found out about Gabe's assault on Chloe. Gabe and Ainsley fought and then she made some decisions. She told Gabe he would resign as executive producer of *The Happiest Girl* citing 'health concerns.' He would go back to New York and stay there."

Margot raised a perfectly shaped eyebrow. "Did Ainsley really believe the Regina police would let Gabe Vickers hop a plane and fly out of their jurisdiction."

"As far as she knows, the police didn't have any information to connect Gabe to Chloe's attack," I said. "Last night, it certainly seemed he could go wherever he wanted."

"Something's fishy here," Margot said. "Gabe could have walked away scot-free. He owned Living Skies, which meant he'd get a whack of the movie's profits, and his reputation was intact, so he could have gone back to New York and kept slithering around as a wheeler and dealer without missing a beat. He didn't stand to lose a thing, except perhaps his marriage, which I understand was one of convenience anyway, so to celebrate, he commits suicide. Does any of that make sense to you, Jo?"

"No. There has to be something more, but I have no idea what it is."

"We'll find out soon enough," Margot said. "And I should hit the road. Where's that furniture you want moved?"

"Are you going to start stripping?"

"Nope, I'm going to put on my coat, so my fancy suit is protected while we toil."

Margot and I had just moved Sally's worktable into the new office when the doorbell rang. It was Gale's Florist and from the heft of the delivery I was handed, I had a suspicion that we'd been sent a very big plant. Margot followed me into the kitchen and watched as I unwrapped a poinsettia that was the twin of the one we already had.

"That is spectacular," Margot said.

"It is," I agreed. "We have one exactly like it in the living room. Actually, Gabe Vickers sent us the first one."

Margot made a face. "That's a bit creepy."

I glanced at the card slipped between two bracts. "Creepier still, this one is from Gabe's widow, thanking Zack and me for our help this morning."

"Whatever the source, it's still beautiful," Margot said. "Let's take it into the living room and see how it looks." After we placed the second poinsettia on a table in front of an east window that caught the morning sun, Margot nodded approvingly. "Very nice, but you need one more."

"Why?"

"Because in decorating, you always follow the rule of three: one is meh, two is anal, three is a statement. A client taught me that."

"Was your client a decorator?"

Margot shook her head. "Decorating was his avocation.

He was a thief but a discerning one. He stole only the very best from the very best stores. You know those three woven leather pillows I used to have on the couch?"

"Whatever happened to them? They were beautiful."

"They still are, but they're in storage till Lexi loses her fascination with lipstick. Anyway, they were a gift from my client for getting him off. He told me that every time I looked at those pillows, I should remember the rule of three."

After Margot left, I went back to my drawing board. Newly obsessed with the rule of three, I worked for furniture arrangements that made statements. The time flew by, and I was startled when the grandmother clock chimed the hour and I realized it was time to leave for dinner.

Zack had work to catch up on at the office, so I picked up the young women at the sound stage and we drove downtown to the glass tower that housed the Falconer Shreve offices. Zack was waiting and after he transferred his body from his chair to the passenger seat, he collapsed his wheelchair and Taylor hopped out, picked up the chair, stowed it in the back of our station wagon, and we headed for the Warehouse District.

When we felt like splurging, the Sahara Club was one of our favourites. It was located in a sketchy neighbourhood, but during the two and a half years we lived in that neighbourhood we came to appreciate the restaurant's charms. From the strutting neon camels on the sign over the door to the muted lighting, ruby red leather banquettes, menus without prices, and the tender tunes played by the moustached gentleman at the baby grand, the ambience was strictly 1960s. The food was invariably terrific, and Zack said the martinis were almost as good as his.

As I pulled into the parking lot, I was looking forward to a pleasantly indulgent evening. The first hint of complication came when I spotted a silver BMW with a familiar vanity plate. I pointed it out to Zack.

"DANCE," he said. "So Zephyr's here. I saw Margot just before I left the office. She said Zephyr's been driving her crazy, but she didn't elaborate."

"She elaborated with me," I said. "But tonight that topic is verboten, so let's just breathe in the scent of that gorgeous wreath on the door. No plastic for the Sahara Club—that wreath is the real thing."

Taylor would drive home, so Zack and I both had a martini. After the first sip, Zack groaned with pleasure. "My old boss Fred C. Harney used to say a martini is the reward for one who bears the hope and burden of the day with grace."

Taylor regarded her drink thoughtfully. "I wonder what a virgin margarita is the reward for?"

"Keeping your parents out of the hoosegow for a DUI," Zack said.

Vale smiled. "Fred C. Harney sounds like a person worth knowing," she said.

"He was, and one of the best decisions I ever made was to article with him," Zack said. "I'd had other offers when I graduated."

"My dad was top of his class at the College of Law," Taylor said.

Zack's face creased with pleasure at our daughter's praise. "The U of S law school has a solid reputation and deservedly so," he said, "but when I graduated, I knew I still had a great deal to learn about the practice of law. In our first and only interview I realized that Fred C. Harney was the man who could teach me.

"He was brilliant, but he was a high-functioning alcoholic. His performance in court was inspiring—he was quick, articulate, and he knew when to pounce and when to hold back, but he had blackouts. My job was to sit next to him in court, watch everything that happened, and when court was over to go back to the office with him and give him a blow by blow of what had taken place. When I was finished, Fred C. would critique himself—always in the third person. 'He should have pressed that witness.' 'He should have cited *Haynes versus Olinski.* 'He should have realized at that point that his client was lying.' That sort of thing. Fred C. was the best. In law school, I'd learned about the theory and practice of law. Fred C. taught me how to be a lawyer." Zack picked up his menu. "Now, we should probably decide on what looks tempting—our server over there by the fireplace is starting to look anxious."

Zack and I ordered the Chateaubriand for two, and the young women decided to share an assortment of appetizers: escargot, stuffed mushrooms, scallops and bacon, Tuscan goat cheese, and then split the tableside Caesar salad for two.

It was a great meal. Zack told a couple of Fred C. Harney stories; Vale told us that when she auditioned for *The Happiest Girl*, Ainsley, Gabe, and Roy had liked what they saw of her audition tapes, but they wanted to see her in action. She walked into a rehearsal hall which was bare except for the table where Ainsley, Gabe, and Roy sat. Ainsley said, "You're a fourteen-year-old girl who transforms into a bear."

Vale's eyes were bright as she remembered. "It was a strange experience," she said. "I didn't have to think about it at all. My body just knew what to do, and I followed along. I forgot there were people in the room. I saw a wastepaper basket in the corner. I went to it and started pulling things out. Someone had left the wrappings from their lunch there. I pulled them out and sniffed at them, but there was nothing left on them. Then I found a yogurt cup that still had yogurt in it. I started licking, and then I crushed the cup, so I could get the rest. That's when I heard Gabe say, "You can stop now. We'll need to talk, but your chances of getting the part are excellent.""

Vale looked around the table. "Getting that part changed my life," she said simply.

We dawdled over supper and the girls had dessert so it was close to ten when we left. We were waiting for the bill when a group led by Zephyr Winslow exited the private dining room. They'd obviously been at a holiday party and the guests were merry, but Zephyr looked grim.

When Zack waved at her, she stared at him seemingly without comprehension and then she started towards us. She seemed unsteady on her feet and I wondered if she'd had too much to drink. She moved towards Vale. "Whore," she hissed, and then she seemed to collapse. The people with her were clearly alarmed, but Shawn O'Day was quick to act. He put a supporting arm around Zephyr, murmured, "Be quiet," and led her out of the restaurant.

"Are you all right?" I said.

Vale's expression was unreadable. "Do you believe what she said?"

"No," I said. "I don't."

"Even though you know about what I did with Gabe."

I nodded. "We know, and we don't think you're a whore. Not in the least."

Vale's smile was tinged with sadness. "Then I am all right," she said.

The server arrived with the bill. Zack protested, but Vale was adamant that the dinner was her treat. After she paid, she pulled out her phone. "I have to check on the time of the call for tomorrow." She read the text. "Not too early," she said. "I can sleep till seven."

She scrolled the other messages. "Nothing, nothing, nothing," she said under breath. Suddenly, she stopped and stared at the screen. "I only checked my messages once today. I must have missed this," she said.

Taylor read the words on the screen and then handed the phone to me. The text was concise: "Please forgive me. We can do this together. You will be my Sally Love." It was from Gabe Vickers.

"This was sent at three-thirty this morning," Vale said. "Lizzie called me at a little after five. Does that sound like a goodbye to you?"

"I don't know," I said. "But I want you to stay with us tonight. This is not a night to be alone with your thoughts."

Vale and Taylor were quiet on our way home, but they seemed fine when Zack and I said goodnight to them. Taylor held her arms out for a hug and then, after a moment's hesitation, Vale did too.

Zack and I didn't talk about the text till we were in bed. "Did Gabe's note sound to you as if he were saying goodbye?" Zack said.

"No," I said. "There was nothing valedictory about those words. The man who sent that text wasn't planning to end his life. He was preparing for the next chapter, and Vale Frazier was at the heart of it."

Gabe Vickers's text to Vale raised many questions, but neither Zack nor I mentioned them. Too much had happened that day, and we were tired to the bone. Soon after Zack got settled in bed, he fell asleep. I listened to his steady, even breathing and was both relieved and envious.

For what seemed like forever, I tossed and turned until finally, I fell into a dream-troubled sleep. Like all dreams, mine were fragmentary and disjointed, but one seemed to contain a logic that was just beyond my grasp. It started with a memory of a real event—Sally Love's fourth birthday party. In my dream, her young guests were watching Sally unwrap presents. Nina's gift to her daughter was a set of the Madame Alexander Little Women dolls, and Sally's friends were enchanted. Nina was introducing each of the dolls. When she held up a doll with brown hair and blue rickrack on her plaid dress, Nina said, "This is Jo—she likes to read, just like our Jo does," and I was thrilled when she handed me the doll. Nina picked up a blond doll wearing a pretty red-and-white checked dress and said, "This is Amy. She has beautiful blond hair like Sally, and she's her mother's little artist, just the way Sally is my little artist."

The next part of my dream had also been part of the real party, and my heart began to pound. Sally's face turned dark with rage, and she grabbed the Amy doll by the ankles and smashed her china face repeatedly against the edge of the table. Her voice was shrill with hysteria. "She is not me," she said. "I am my own Sally Love."

But the voice was not Sally's voice. It was Vale Frazier's, and it was Gabe Vickers who stood beside her. Vale repeated the words *I am my own Sally Love* and began gouging at his face with her nails but her nails had become like bear claws. She kept growling and clawing at him until his face was unrecognizable as human, and he fell to the ground. She looked down at him. "I am not your Sally Love," she said. Then she shrugged. "I didn't have to think about it at all. My body just knew what to do, and I followed along."

CHAPTER

16

The atavistic violence of the dream had filled me with a dread that still shadowed me when the dogs and I returned from our run. The scene that greeted me was comfortingly familiar: the coffee was made, the juice was poured, Pantera's and Esme's dishes were filled, and Zack was at the kitchen table checking his messages. I took off my parka and boots, drank my juice, poured myself a cup of coffee, and joined Zack at the table.

"So the day begins, and the inevitable must be faced," I said. "If Gabe didn't commit suicide, then he was murdered. So where do we go from here?"

Zack shot me a sour look. "And good morning to you," he said.

"Sorry," I said. "This has been gnawing at me all night."

"It's been gnawing at me too," Zack said. "Have you come up with anything?"

"Not much," I said. "Vale has to show Debbie the text Gabe sent her. It's not decisive, but it does reveal Gabe's state of mind an hour or so before he died, so it's relevant. And Zack, Vale has to tell Debbie about what Gabe did to her and her suspicion that Gabe might have attacked Chloe Kovacs."

"Agreed." Zack sighed. "There's certainly no shortage of people who might have helped Gabe over that balcony rail, especially if Gabe was as badly beaten up as Nick. Speaking of . . . Nick and I have to talk sooner rather than later. I'm assuming Gabe's condo building has surveillance cameras. In this weather, Nick wears that parka with his company's name on the back everywhere, and I'm sure the police will find the Kovacs Electric logo interesting."

"Zack, when I was speaking with Ainsley yesterday, she told me that Gabe's last words to her were to have Roy Brodnitz check his contract for *Flying Blue Horses*," I said.

"That, too, is significant," Zack said. "Because Roy's contract, like yours, legally gave Gabe Vickers and Living Skies a lot of control. When Falconer Shreve's entertainment lawyer and I were going over that, she explained that financing a movie or TV production often involves a number of production companies, and because the executive producer is the deal-maker he's the official contractor."

"As soon as Roy pitched the series to him, Gabe was determined to get the legal rights to produce it," I said.

"When Gabe and I talked about expediting the signing of the contracts, he told me he had an investor with very deep pockets in mind, but he needed to beat a rival producer with another project to the finish line."

"Did he offer any specifics?"

"No. Wheelers and dealers like Gabe Vickers always keep their cards close to their chest. He did say the six-part series would be a vehicle for Vale, and to be perfect as the young Sally Love, Vale needed—in his words—'to be just on the cusp of becoming a woman.'"

I shuddered. "That makes my skin crawl."

"Mine too, but it does provide another explanation for Gabe's eagerness to get you to sign the option contract.

Legally, Gabe could have taken the project to New York and produced it without the involvement of Ainsley or Roy. Gabe would have had to convince you, but he would have offered compelling reasons for you to let him proceed: you want the story told, and Vale will be passionate about playing the role of Sally at fifteen."

"But Gabe must have known that I wouldn't betray Roy. *Flying Blue Horses* was his idea. If he lost it, he would be devastated."

Zack frowned. "That's a bit melodramatic, isn't it? People in theatre have reverses just as people in any other business have reverses. It's a blow at the time, but you get over it."

"Most people do, but Roy invests a lot of his worth in his creative projects. I'm sure that's true of many artists, but for Roy more than most."

"Do you think Ainsley might have killed Gabe to protect Roy from being dealt another punishing blow?"

"I honestly don't know. Roy told me Ainsley married Gabe to ensure that *The Happiest Girl* was a success."

Zack whistled. "That's a significant line to cross."

"The loyalty between those two is primal," I said. "You know how fond I am of Roy. He's a decent man, but I believe Roy would cross many lines for Ainsley."

Zack drummed his fingers on the table. "There is another candidate who's less painful to consider. Zephyr's new escort, Shawn O'Day. Gabe humiliated him the night of the celebration for Zephyr. That must have stung."

"Yet he was strolling along the hall with Gabe and Ainsley a couple of days ago. Zack, there are so many loose ends here . . ."

"And the police will see where they lead. Jo, we have a solid police force. I saw that up close when I was mayor. You and I could save ourselves a lot of grief by letting go and letting them do their job."

"I'm not trying to do their job, Zack, but this isn't like that board game we play at the lake. We're not debating whether Colonel Mustard did the deed with a candlestick in the conservatory or Miss Plum used a dagger in the drawing room. We're talking about people we know and, in at least three cases, people we care about. At best, we might come up with a theory that would prove their innocence."

"And at worst?"

"At worst, we can help them prepare for what's to come. Zack, I had a terrible dream about Vale last night."

Zack listened intently. When I finished, he was clearly shaken. "Do you really think she could do it . . . ?"

"I don't know. My heart goes out to her, and I know yours does too. But we've both heard Vale talk about feeling dissociated from her actions, and Gabe used her—he used her body and he used her talent. And the tone of that final text he sent her was menacing."

"You will always be my Sally Love," Zack said the words with distaste. "God, Jo, I hope it's not her."

By the time Vale joined us in the kitchen, showered and wearing an outfit of Taylor's, Zack and I had deliberately switched to the more cheerful topic of what to get Charlie and Colin for Christmas.

Vale looked tired, but as always, she was controlled. "Taylor said to borrow what I wanted, so this is what I chose. She's sleeping in. She's coming over to the set later, but I've got that early call, so I'm taking off."

"If you want to stay and eat something, I can drive you," I said.

"As I told Lena, craft services is there for us 24/7, but thanks." Vale came over to the breakfast table. Her face was open, and her tone, gentle. "Thanks for everything. Both of you. I had a difficult night, and it was a great comfort seeing

Taylor in the next bed and knowing you two were in the house." She paused. "And that you still thought I was worth caring about."

When Vale left, Zack wheeled over to say goodbye. "Whatever happens, she needs to know we're behind her," he said.

"Yes," I said. "She deserves that."

Roy Brodnitz called at eight-thirty, sounding relaxed and at ease. "How are you?" he said.

"All things considered, I'm fine," I said. "And you?"

"Conflicted. I know I pushed for us to sign Gabe as executive producer of *Flying Blue Horses*, but Ainsley is like a part of me, and even with the stress of the police questioning her, Gabe's death seems to have lifted a huge weight from her shoulders. I didn't realize how much she was carrying. Of course, a weight lifted from her shoulders is a weight lifted from mine." He paused. "Now, if you're free for the next hour or so, there's something I'd like to discuss with you face to face."

When Roy arrived, he appeared rested, and he was freshly shaven and smartly dressed in pressed blue jeans and a cashmere crewneck, the same shade of blue-grey as his eyes. I'd made tea and we took it to the table overlooking the creek, which seemed to have become "our" spot.

He smiled his winning crooked smile. "Have the Vizslas been by yet this morning?"

"They're not due till ten-thirty."

"I only have an hour, so I'll have to catch them another time," he said. "Margot and Brock and I have been talking about getting Kai and Lexi a puppy. If you happen to see your neighbour, would you mind asking her if we could bring the kids by sometime when she's out walking Zoltan and Bela?"

"I'm sure she'd be delighted," I said.

"So would Lexi and Kai," Roy said. "Every child needs a dog."

"I agree. Did you have a dog?"

Roy shook his head. "No. That's why I know every kid needs one. Anyway, now to business. Rosamond asked to see what I'd written of *Flying Blue Horses* so far. As you know, there's not much, but she and I talked about what there is, and she's concerned that the balance is wrong between Sally's story and yours."

"And there's a good reason for that," I said. "Flying blue horses are more dramatically engrossing than a porcupine quill box."

"Don't sell yourself short, but that metaphor *is* useful because it points to the problem Rosamond flagged."

"Did she have a solution?"

Roy chuckled. "We're talking about Rosamond. Of course she had a solution. She believes the weight of the sisters' stories could be balanced by introducing a character like Ben Bendure, who'd known the Ellard and Love families from the beginning and who continued his relationship with both women throughout their lives."

As he talked about possibilities for structuring the script, Roy spoke with energy and zeal, and I found myself experiencing the thrill I felt when I realized that the dissertation of a student I was supervising was first rate, or that momentum was finally on our side in an election campaign.

"You look happy," Roy said.

"I am happy," I said. "This is fun, but I feel guilty."

"Don't feel guilty. My work always carries me out of myself."

"That's a blessing," I said. "Especially now."

"And it's one I'm grateful for," Roy said. "But, Jo, let's put the current situation aside and focus on the future.

Rosamond would like to be considered for the Ben Bendure role."

"Gender-blind casting?" I said.

Roy laughed. "No. There's no reason the filmmaker in our script can't be a woman, and it would be a crime to hide all Rosamond's womanly vibrancy in a khaki vest and walking boots. It'll be a great part to write. We have so much material to work with."

"I talked to Rosamond yesterday, and I was surprised at how far Gabe had already brought the project."

"Gabe had many skills," Roy said. "But despite John Donne's belief that that no man is an island, Gabe Vickers's death does not diminish me; it diminishes no one because he was a man without a conscience."

I felt the hairs on my neck raise. "Roy, I understand what you're saying, but be careful to keep your feelings about Gabe to yourself. This morning Zack and I were talking about the contracts you and I signed. If Gabe were still alive, he could have produced *Flying Blue Horses* without you or Ainsley. I didn't want that to happen any more than you or Ainsley did. Presumably, the option will now revert to his widow. We all had something to gain from Gabe Vickers's death, and that fact will be of interest to the police."

Roy's nerves were too close to the edge for him to hide his feelings. His face flushed with resentment. "You think Ainsley and I had something to do with Gabe's plunge over the edge of his balcony?"

I tried to keep my tone reasonable and reassuring. "Of course not, but there are details that don't point to suicide, and the police will be looking seriously into the behaviour of everyone who stood to benefit from Gabe Vickers's death."

Roy stood suddenly, his hands balled into fists at his sides. His eyes were blazing. "Ainsley could not have killed Gabe," he said tightly. "She was with me all night—every minute, every second. She was with me from the time she walked into my condo until we heard the ambulances, ran down the hall, and discovered that a person—who turned out to be Gabe—had jumped to his death. We weren't apart for a millisecond."

And with that, Roy stalked out of the room. I didn't follow him. I waited until I heard the door slam, and then I sat down, picked up my cup of lukewarm tea, and tried to assess what I had just lost.

I was still replaying the painful scene between Roy and me when Zack called to tell me that he'd just spoken to Debbie Haczkewicz and the shit was travelling towards the fan at warp speed. A preliminary autopsy on Gabe Vickers's body had shown that, in addition to the injuries he had sustained from his fall, there was evidence that Gabe Vickers had been badly beaten, and that he was self-medicating. His blood alcohol count was .10 per cent and he had ingested opioids at some point in the hours before his plunge.

"It was an ugly way to go," Zack said. "Given Vickers's injuries and the chemical-alcohol stew in his body, the medical examiner was surprised he was able to make it to the balcony."

"What was he doing out there in the middle of a blizzard anyway?" I said.

Zack's laugh was short and dry. "Having a cigarette. Gabe might have been six kinds of bastard, but he was considerate enough not to smoke in the house."

When the doorbell rang, I didn't rush to answer. I was relatively certain that whoever was on the other side was not the bearer of good news. My visitor was persistent, and finally I admitted defeat. When I opened the door it was, in Yogi Berra's immortal phrase, 'like déjà vu all over again.' The petite young delivery woman from Gale's Florist was on my porch holding a large and heavy plant. When I held my hands out to take the delivery, she grinned. "You and I have been to this movie twice before, right?"

"Right," I said. "I'm sorry I didn't come to the door earlier. I'm having a bad day."

"Happens to us all," she said. "Maybe the showgirl here will cheer you up."

I took the showgirl into the kitchen and unwrapped her. I checked the card. *Remember the rule of three. XO Margot.* I was smiling as I carried the plant into the living room and placed it in front of the third window in the room that offered decent light.

When I stepped back to see whether the arrangement of the poinsettias worked, I knew immediately that it did. The three plants with their dark green foliage and rich burgundy bracts made the room tastefully festive. Margot's client would have deemed them a statement, not a shout. I still had the florist's card in my hand, and without thinking, I tucked it under the new plant—a habit I'd fallen into two years earlier when Zack had been ill and the florist was constantly at the door. Keeping the card with the plant was a way of remembering who sent what when I wrote the thank-you note.

On impulse, I went to the first poinsettia we'd received, removed the card and read the message aloud. *"So a kingdom was lost—all for the want of a nail." Thanks for taking charge. Gabe.* The idea behind the old proverb had become an axiom in law. Zack said that his mentor had taught him early that the failure to correct some initially small problem could lead to successively more serious problems and ultimately to a dire outcome.

The note on the card was a powerful message, but it had not been intended for Zack and me. Gabe had ordered two poinsettias from the florist, and the cards had been switched accidentally. When I saw the twin of our plant in Zephyr Winslow's living room the morning we had tea, I had known at once that the message we'd received had been intended for her. At the time, the mistake had seemed inconsequential. Now I wasn't so sure. The poinsettias had been delivered the morning after Shawn O'Day had threatened to reveal what he knew about Gabe's sexual perversions. Shawn very quickly became Zephyr's constant companion.

The night Zephyr summoned me to her home, she had an agenda: she had been determined to sow doubts in my mind about Vale Frazier. Her modus operandi had been long on innuendo and short on specifics, but in retrospect, its timing was significant. Zephyr's call had come just hours after the journalist from *Nexus* had interviewed Vale and Taylor. Gabe Vickers had been present at the interview, and Vale saying that she was absolutely open with Taylor had been a red flag he couldn't afford to ignore. If Vale revealed what had been going on with her and Gabe to Taylor, what was to stop the news from spreading? The consequences could be catastrophic to *The Happiest Girl*. He needed an ally and Zephyr, as the anonymous bankroller of the project and a major funder of the Saskatchewan film industry, had a vested interest in keeping a lid on any scandalous rumours associated with the project.

But what if Zephyr had found out that Gabe was about to leave Canada, that after all her efforts to contain his secrets, after all her investment in him and the film studios, he'd been careless—and criminal? If Gabe were to flee Canada, Living Skies would follow shortly after *The Happiest Girl* was completed. That would be a blow to the resurgent Saskatchewan film industry, and to Zephyr Winslow herself. Had Zephyr once again taken charge and this time stopped Gabe? The pieces were all there, but they were not firmly in place.

Zack's advice that we step back and let the police do their job was the sensible course of action, but the police didn't know about the message on the florist's card. The least I could do was drop it off at the station, explain my concerns about Zephyr's involvement with Gabe Vickers, and let the experts draw their own conclusions.

I put on my coat and boots and took my shoulder bag from the hook by the door. When I opened the bag to drop in the note that had come with the poinsettia, I saw the plastic keycard I'd picked up from the floor of the penthouse elevator barely an hour after Gabe died. I recalled that Lizzie had lost Vale's keycard. In the turmoil that morning, no one had asked Lizzie where and when it had disappeared. My nerves twanged.

That morning, as the five of us had sat in the shadowy light of the spa waiting room, something had been weighing heavily on Lizzie's mind. In assuring Lizzie that she had nothing to fear from the police, Zack said, "You've done nothing wrong." Lizzie tried to correct him, saying, "You don't know what I did before." Zack assumed, as I did, that she was talking about something much earlier in her life, and he said, "What happened in the past doesn't really matter now."

Remembering how Lizzie's dark eyes had continued to dart anxiously despite Zack's attempts to calm her fears, I was certain that when she told him he didn't know what she'd done before, she was talking not about the distant past but about the minutes before Gabe went over the rail of the balcony. In her interview with Debbie Haczkewicz, Lizzie became agitated when Debbie asked her to picture exactly what happened that morning, and she repeated Zack's assurance that she didn't have to talk about what happened "before." Only when Debbie agreed that all Lizzie needed to talk about were the first moments after she went outside did she relax. Lizzie had never been asked about where she was and what she was doing during the early hours before Gabe fell to his death. It was time we heard her story.

Zack was still in court, so I sent a text: "Closer to discovering what happened on Gabe's balcony the night he died. Call ASAP."

Fired up by the prospect that Lizzie had information that would shed light on the circumstances surrounding Gabe Vickers's death, I drove to the production studios. Tobi was on set. I gestured to her and explained that it was imperative that I talk to Vale. Tobi waited for Ainsley to call a break then spoke briefly to her and when Ainsley nodded assent, Vale approached me.

She was in costume: blue jeans, walking boots, and the colourful Fair Isle sweater that Ursula wore throughout the story because her grandmother had knit it for her. When I showed Vale the keycard I'd found in the elevator and said I was certain it was the keycard Lizzie lost, Vale's face remained impassive, but I could feel her anxiety. I wasn't surprised. Lizzie's behaviour was unpredictable.

Taylor was in Vale's dressing room working on a sketch and we joined her there. After I explained again the circumstances under which I'd found the keycard, Vale's brow furrowed. "I'm not sure this is actually my keycard," she said. "Gabe gave me one for his and Ainsley's penthouse too, and Lizzie could have picked it up at my place."

As she twirled a strand of her auburn hair, Vale was thoughtful. "It sounds ridiculous, but I haven't had time to get any sort of perspective on what happened. I didn't learn about Chloe's reaction to seeing Gabe until late in the day. Lizzie told me what happened when we took a break just before dinner.

"That's when I called Taylor and asked her to find out exactly what the man who attacked Chloe did to her. When Taylor told me what she'd learned, I knew immediately that

Gabe was the man. I told Tobi I thought I was coming down with the flu and needed to go home. Lizzie came back to the condo with me. She was hovering. I told her there was a problem that I had to work through and asked her to get herself something to eat and go into the bedroom and watch TV."

"How long did Lizzie stay with you that night?" I said.

Vale shrugged. "I don't know. After Gabe showed up, there was just so much emotion."

"Had you asked him to come?" I said.

"He was the last person I wanted to see. I was sitting at the table trying to focus on my pages for the next morning and he just came through the door."

"He had his own key?" I said.

Vale's voice was thick with disgust. "Of course. His schedule was erratic, and he said he wanted to take advantage of every chance to be with me. Anyway, that night he said that if rumours started circulating about him not to believe anything I heard, that I was the most important person in his world, and that we were going to make amazing movies together.

"I told him I couldn't talk about what we were going to do together until he explained what had happened with Chloe." Vale's extraordinary turquoise eyes were brimming. "I didn't want to think that he had done this to her, Joanne. I think I would have accepted almost any explanation Gabe offered, but he actually laughed when I confronted him. He said he'd just acted on impulse and she probably didn't even understand what had happened." Vale's complexion flushed with anger. "I couldn't believe he had done something so vile and said something that cruel. I told him that we both knew it was too late to replace me in *The Happiest Girl*, but our personal relationship was over.

"That's when he lost it. He'd been in control until then, but he begged me to forgive him, and he cried. I cried too. He said his need for me had ruined his life and I told him it had done the same thing to me. We both said hurtful things. It was loud and it was ugly. Lizzie gets very upset by conflict. That must have been when she slipped out of my condo. I didn't hear from her again until she texted me the next morning to say she'd found Gabe's body." Vale covered her eyes with her hand. "That's it, I guess."

"Unfortunately, this isn't over, Vale. Lizzie told you that she spent that night in the vestibule at the front of your building because she'd lost her key. The vestibule would have provided shelter, but it was unheated and the temperature outside was thirty below zero. When we met you and Lizzie the next morning, she had been inside for less than half an hour, but nothing about her suggested that she'd spent hours in an unheated space when the temperature outside was thirty below."

"You think she wasn't outside," Vale said.

"I don't know," I said. "There are just too many unanswered questions. That's why we have to find Lizzie."

"It won't be easy, Vale said. "I've asked, but she won't tell me where she lives. She says she needs her space. She never mentions any friends. Everything she gets she gives to strangers. I think she mostly just hangs out at the library and at the food court at that mall downtown."

"Cornwall Centre," Taylor said.

Vale nodded. "Lizzie likes the library because they never hassle her, and as long as she has a drink or something to eat on her table at the food court, they leave her alone." Vale frowned. "And she likes this place she calls 'the ladies.' The first time Lizzie mentioned it, I thought she was referring to a public washroom, and I told her to steer clear. But she said 'the ladies' isn't a bathroom, just a place that makes her feel safe, so I didn't press her."

Taylor and I exchanged glances "We know where to find *The Ladies*," I said.

The buzzer in Vale's dressing room sounded. "I'm wanted on the set," she said.

"Jo and I will see if we can find Lizzie," Taylor said.

"She's so vulnerable," Vale said. "I'd prefer not to involve her."

"We don't have a choice," I said. "Right now, a cloud is hanging over a number of innocent people. I think Lizzie has information that can help dissipate it."

The three of us walked together to the end of the hall. Vale was clearly troubled. Taylor put her arms around her. "Don't worry," she said. "This will work out." Vale turned so that her face and Taylor's were almost touching. For a few moments, they simply looked at each other, and then, very gently, our daughter kissed Vale's lips.

Taylor and I didn't mention the kiss as we drove downtown. We went to Central Library first, the largest of the city's libraries, with diverse patrons. As always, Central was filled with people in search of answers, questions, new worlds, fresh perspectives on old worlds, and just plain diversion. Also as always, there were those, like Lizzie, who simply sought a haven where they could be safe, warm, and treated with dignity. Taylor and I split up to search. She took the children's library in the basement. I took the library's second floor, and we checked the main floor together. Our search was thorough, but we came up empty.

The parking space we found in the mall's parkade was on the second floor, home of the food court. The place was crowded, noisy, and redolent of the aromas of food courts in malls throughout Canada and the U.S. Scores of people loaded down with holiday packages were arriving, lining up, elbowing for tables, savouring their Orange Julius drinks and New York Fries, dumping their trays, and leaving, but Lizzie was not among them.

When we admitted defeat and left the food court, Taylor was philosophical. "Looks like *The Ladies* will have to come through for us," she said.

The sculpture my daughter and I were headed for had been installed when the Cornwall Centre mall opened in 1981. Its official name is *Regina*, but most people just call it *The Ladies*. It's a lovely and welcoming piece. Three larger-than-life women, dressed in the kerchiefs and outfits of their homeland, are standing with their children, looking out at this new land where they will make a life. Situated in a space designated for lounging and visiting, the sculpture's warm colours and the soft curves of the women's bodies make it an ideal place to meet friends or to chat.

As Taylor and I stood side by side on the escalator carrying us to the main floor, I said, "When you were little and we came to the mall, I always told you that if you got lost, I'd be with *The Ladies*, waiting for you."

Taylor's expression was tender. "I remember. You were always there."

"I still am," I said.

"I know," Taylor said. "And that means a lot, but I'm not lost, Jo. I've found a place where I'm very happy." Taylor's smile was poignantly self-mocking. "It seems I belonged with the ladies all along."

"With women or just with Vale?" I said.

"I don't know," Taylor said. "Neither does she. This relationship is a first for both of us, and we're just at the beginning. Bringing two lives together in the right way will be a lot of work."

"You have all the time in the world," I said, "and if you and Vale are meant to be together, it will be worth the effort."

"We think that too," Taylor said. "And look, there's Lizzie just waiting to be found."

———

A journalist friend once told me that if you ask the right question, everybody has a story they want to tell. With Lizzie the right question was simple. "What happened the night Gabe Vickers died?"

On the drive back from the mall, Taylor sat in the back seat with her. It was a good decision. Lizzie was nervous about telling her story, and Taylor was able to convince her that if she shared her concerns with us, we could deal with them.

Lizzie's requests were easily met. She wanted to talk in a place where she felt comfortable, so we met at Vale's condo. She was adamant about wanting Vale and Zack there, and equally adamant about not wanting Debbie present. Taylor texted Vale and she said she'd wait for us at the main entrance to the production studios. It was all very low-key. Vale made us herbal tea while we waited at the condo for Zack to arrive, and we began as soon as he joined us.

He asked Lizzie if he could make a video of the interview on his phone and send it to Inspector Haczkewicz. He explained that getting Debbie involved immediately would let her know that we were all on the same side and that talking to us would give Lizzie a chance to get used to the questions Debbie would later ask.

Lizzie agreed, and so we began. Zack was skilled at questioning witnesses, and his voice was deep and encouraging as he led Lizzie through her story.

She was fuzzy on questions of time and on the exact wording of the conversations she overheard, but Lizzie's story had the ring of truth, and I could tell by looking at Zack, Taylor, and Vale that, like me, they believed what Lizzie was saying.

From the outset, it was clear that Lizzie's actions that night were rooted in her gratitude to Vale for caring about her. When Vale asked her to leave the sound stage with her, Lizzie was proud that Vale had chosen her to be the person to take care of her. Lizzie hadn't been hurt or angry when Vale bristled at her hovering and suggested she get herself something to eat and go into the other room to watch television. She understood how much people need to be alone sometimes.

Lizzie had heard Gabe come into the condo, and believing that Vale might need her, she had opened the bedroom door a little so she could be there if Vale called. Lizzie said she'd always hated it when her mother and her mother's boyfriend began yelling because things got broken and people hurt and the police would come and make everything worse. When Gabe and Vale raised their voices at each other, she felt sick to her stomach, so she hid in the bedroom's walk-in closet.

After Gabe left, Lizzie opened the closet door a crack, but she stayed inside. When Vale called her name, Lizzie didn't answer. She still felt scared, and when she heard Vale crying in bed, she curled up on the closet floor and covered herself in one of Vale's robes and fell asleep. She didn't know what time it was when she woke up. Vale was sleeping, and everything was very quiet, and Lizzie wanted to be somewhere far away where nobody was crying or angry.

She crept out of the closet, picked up her phone and the keycard Vale had given her, and tried to leave. She got into the elevator and swiped the keycard, but when the elevator doors opened, she wasn't in the lobby. She was in a penthouse and she knew right away that something had happened. The lights were still on, and the room was very cold. Lamps and chairs had been knocked over and there was broken glass on the floor. Then she noticed the doors to the balcony were open and she went to shut them.

That's when she saw Gabe. She called to him, but he didn't answer. It was freezing and he wasn't wearing a coat. She thought he would die if he didn't come inside, so she stepped out onto the balcony and called his name again, very loudly. When he still didn't answer, Lizzie thought he must have passed out. He was leaning over the railing of the balcony with his head down, as if he was throwing up. It seemed like most of his body was over the railing. She thought the best way to get him down would be to pull him by the legs. She tried, but he didn't budge, so she pulled harder. The floor of the balcony was icy. Lizzie lost her balance, slipped, and fell into Gabe. Then he tipped over, and all of a sudden, he was gone. She looked down. The security lights were bright, and she could see him on the sidewalk beside the building.

She knew she should get help, but she didn't want to get in trouble and so didn't call 911. Instead, she got into the elevator, and this time made sure she pressed the button marked L for lobby. There was nobody in the lobby, so she ran outside to see how badly hurt Gabe was. She knelt beside him and called his name, but no matter how many times she called his name, he didn't answer. That's when she knew he must have died. Her story finished, Lizzie leaned towards Zack. "Is that enough?"

Zack smiled and took her hands in his. "Yes," he said. "That's enough, at least for now. Lizzie, after Inspector Haczkewicz sees the video we just made she'll want to talk to you again."

"Right now?"

"No, later, but I'll talk to her first."

"Am I in trouble?"

"No, I think Debbie and I will be able to work this out."

"And nothing's going to happen to Vale?"

"No, Vale will be fine. Lizzie, I wonder if you and Taylor could go to the bedroom for a minute and let me talk to Joanne and Vale."

Vale had clearly been shaken by Lizzie's account, but she was composed. "Zack, how can you possibly work this out?"

"I can't do it alone, but I think we have logic and science on our side. As far as I can tell, three separate factors contributed to Gabe Vickers's death. After he and Nick Kovacs fought, Gabe was badly hurt, but Nick was also badly hurt. If Gabe had gone to Emergency the way Nick did, the medical people would have given him the treatment he needed. I'm guessing Gabe didn't go that route, because he knew that as soon as he walked into a hospital, he'd be confronted by questions he didn't want to answer.

"We're already aware of the fact that Gabe used prescription drugs and alcohol to deal with the pain from his injuries, and that given the lethal mix of drugs and booze sluicing through his veins, the medical examiner was amazed that Gabe made it to the balcony at all. There was vomit on the ground in the area near where he landed, so Lizzie's guess that Gabe had leaned over to throw up and passed out was right.

"The third factor is that he went over the balcony railing and plunged head first onto a concrete walk from a considerable height."

"And he went over the railing because Lizzie slipped and fell against him," Vale said, and the fear in her voice was palpable. "Zack, the only reason she was in this building tonight was to care for me. Do you believe that what happened was an accident?"

Zack's voice was steely. "Yes, that's what I believe, because that's what Lizzie says happened. And the truth is that if she had never set foot in the penthouse, the outcome would have been the same. Gabe Vickers would have died of exposure.

"Coroners have a phrase they use on death certificates to describe the cause of a death like Gabe Vickers's. They call it 'death by misadventure,' which is primarily due to an accident caused by a dangerous risk taken voluntarily. Knowing the risk, Gabe Vickers voluntarily attacked Chloe Kovacs. Knowing the risk, Gabe Vickers chose to self-medicate rather than seek professional help when he was injured after his fight with Chloe's father. Knowing the risk, he chose to go to the balcony for a cigarette. What happened next was an accident that occurred because of a series of dangerous risks that Gabe Vickers undertook voluntarily. A textbook case of death by misadventure."

Vale leaned forward and put her head in her hands. For close to a minute, she stayed that way, absolutely still. Finally, she straightened. "It's almost over," she said. She turned to Zack and then to me. "You've both been so steadfast through all this. I don't know how to thank you."

Zack smiled. "Hey, no need for thanks," he said. "It's all in the family."

CHAPTER

17

Having Gabe Vickers's death declared "a death by misadventure" involved a meeting with Linda Fritz, Zack's favourite Crown prosecutor. Linda was smart and sensible and when she and Zack met for lunch, she was quick to agree that, given the evidence, death by misadventure was a sensible conclusion. Zack spent the rest of their lunch trying to convince Linda to join him on the dark side and become a trial lawyer at Falconer Shreve. I was keeping my fingers crossed. I liked Linda, and Zack's determination to add her to the firm's trial law division was proof that he was serious about cutting back on his hours.

The news that Gabe's death would not be the subject of a lengthy and publicity-generating trial lifted a burden from Ainsley Blair's shoulders. There would be whispers about the underbelly of Gabe's life, but by the time *The Happiest Girl* hit theatres, the rumours would be forgotten. As the new head of Living Skies, Ainsley was busy arranging financing and sending out feelers about casting and film crew positions for *Flying Blue Horses*. She was doing that, in addition to putting in twelve-hour days directing the movie. I recognized the signs. There were times when the only antidote to guilt and pain was exhaustion, and Ainsley was running on empty.

Roy was clearly concerned about his longtime collaborator and friend. He spent most if not all of his free time by her side, and his relationship with Brock suffered. In the immediate aftermath of Gabe's death, Roy had been dismissive of its effect upon him. Although he claimed that he was not "diminished" by Gabe's death, as a man whose nerves were perilously close to the surface, Roy was haunted by his memories of the horror surrounding Gabe's final hours. He had forgiven me for my fumbled caution about how he spoke about Gabe, and we continued to work together on ideas for the series, but the gusto he had brought to the project was gone.

Nick Kovacs was recovering well from the physical injuries he'd suffered during his fight with Gabe, but he blamed himself for Gabe's death. No matter how often Zack or Henry Chan took him through the sequence of events that led to Gabe's fall from the balcony, Nick was convinced that if he had "handled the situation better," Gabe would still be alive.

When Zack finally laid it down for Nick, I was in the next room, but I had heard his words. "So let's run through this again," he said. "Instead of going to the penthouse, you stay in your garage pounding the shit out of your punching bag. Not much changes for you. When you wake up the next morning, you're probably a little stiff from all that punching, but you're still sick with rage at what happened to Chloe. Gabe, on the other hand, wakes up feeling like a million dollars because he's free to walk out of the condo, lure the next innocent child he finds down an alley, and make her watch as he jerks off and blows his wad all over her young body. Nick, next time you start beating yourself up, think of that child."

When Nick and Chloe came out to stay with us at the lake for a few days between Christmas and New Year's, Nick's cast was off his arm and he seemed at peace.

Zephyr, on the other hand, remained Zephyr. Plans for the day set aside to celebrate the renaming of the Saskatchewan Film Production Studios were in full swing, and Zephyr was in her glory. We learned from Debbie that on the day of Gabe's death, the police had interviewed Shawn O'Day. On the snowy morning that Chloe erupted, O'Day had been at the film studios as an emissary for Zephyr—a role that forced Gabe to extend a cordial welcome to him. Shawn admitted to making the phone call to Nick Kovacs that was the impetus to the tragedy. O'Day told the police that his intent was simply to get the powerful producer with deviant sexual interests off the streets with minimal publicity.

After she confessed what had happened in the minutes leading up to Gabe's death, Lizzie had frightened us all by disappearing for close to a week. When the police found her, we learned she had joined a large evangelical church on the outskirts of the city, and she'd been born again. She told Vale, "My church will take anyone and everyone and they wash us all clean. I feel clean, and they've found me a place to live. Right now, I'm working in their cafeteria, but they're going to get me on a life-affirming path. I'm filled with joy. Praise Jesus." Indeed.

Vale checked out the mega-church. The principal tenet of its theology appeared to be that God rewards those who believe by showering them with riches, but the church itself was legitimate. Lizzie was safe and happy on her life-affirming path, and all of us who had grown to care for her were grateful.

The shooting schedule of a movie takes precedence over everything else, so because we wanted Rosamond and Vale to be part of our Christmas, we made our plans accordingly.

The cast and crew of *The Happiest Girl* had been working punishing hours, five days a week for eight weeks. Christmas Eve fell on a Sunday, what would ordinarily be a day off. Since Christmas was Monday, the cast and crew worked Christmas Eve day from seven in the morning until two in the afternoon and were free until the morning of Wednesday, December 27, at seven. It was a work schedule worthy of Scrooge before his epiphany, but no one complained.

Our family has always been traditional about Christmas. We opened one present Christmas Eve, and shook out stockings and opened the rest of the gifts on Christmas morning. Christmas Eve dinner had always been roast beef and Yorkshire pudding with Zack's partners and their families, but this year there were changes. Noah Wainberg and his daughter, Isobel, and his grandson, Jacob, were spending Christmas in Vancouver, and Gracie Falconer and Rose Lavalee, the woman who had raised Gracie, were joining them.

Rosamond Burke was also a Christmas traditionalist, but her traditions were definitely Dickensian. As soon as she signed the contract to play the grandmother in *The Happiest Girl*, Rosamond had her assistant search out the best venue in Regina to host a dinner on Christmas Eve. Our family always attended the 5:30 children's service at St. Paul's on the twenty-fourth, and Rosamond was Church of England, so the cathedral was fine with her. After church, Rosamond, Vale, and our family, except for Peter, Maisie, and the twins, who were busy establishing their own traditions at the farm, gathered together at the Scarth Club, an old and handsome establishment that knew how to do Christmas well: holly, ivy, a fat goose, plum pudding, and after dinner a group of carolers.

Vale stayed with us overnight, so when Zack, Taylor, and I made our Christmas morning rounds to see what Santa left the grandkids, Vale was with us. Being with young children on Christmas morning and tromping through the snow on a Saskatchewan farm to feed animals were new experiences for her, and she drank them in. After dinner at our house, all the family, including the twins, gathered in front of the tree and, at Rosamond's request, we read out loud Dickens's *A Christmas Carol.*

Rosamond began, and from the moment she read the opening lines of stave 1—"Marley was dead: to begin with. There is no doubt whatever about that"—she had her audience in the palm of her hand. The book Rosamond brought to read from was an old one—large, bound in maroon leather, and heavy—and we passed it around with care and reverence.

As Rosamond described the visitation of Marley's ghost in her powerful, melodious voice, Charlie and Colin were mesmerized. They drifted off as their father read about how the Ghost of Christmas Past transported Scrooge through time to see his own miserable Christmas as a child. The twins continued to doze through staves 3 and 4, but they awoke with a start as Zack boomed out Scrooge's joy at discovering the meaning of Christmas in stave 5. As he read how it was always said of Scrooge "that he knew how to keep Christmas well, if any man alive possessed the knowledge. May that truly be said of us, and all of us!" Charlie and Colin looked at their grandfather with new eyes. This was the man who ate their mushy broccoli with gusto. We lived in a world of wonders.

Our family had decided to limit gift-giving that Christmas and donate what we would have spent on each other to April's Place. The grandkids received gifts and the rest of us exchanged stocking stuffers.

There were, of course, gifts for Rosamond and Vale. During her time on set, Taylor had been sketching portraits of the cast and crew. She was working in conte, a kind of pastel/crayon hybrid that combined the softness of pastels with the vibrancy of crayons. Ultimately, there would be contes of each person who contributed to the making of *The Happiest Girl*. But Taylor had completed two pieces as surprises for Vale and Rosamond. Each captured the two actors during a pivotal moment for her character. Vale's was of Ursula picking snowberries on the tundra with her grandmother. Rosamond's was of the grandmother and Ursula just before the grandmother's final transformation from human life to something beyond human understanding. Predictably, both Rosamond and Vale were thrilled.

My gift to Vale, a boldly illustrated version of *Alice's Adventures in Wonderland*, proved to be an unexpected hit. The book featured hundreds of collages by Andrea D'Aquino that fascinated Vale. After everyone left, Vale took me aside and pointed to some of the images that she found most arresting. "Look how D'Aquino tears up pieces of discarded paper and reconfigures them to produce these amazing effects," she said. "Her art is a perfect representation of the text."

"I hadn't thought of that," I said.

Vale's face was shining. "Think of Alice's line after she's gone down the rabbit hole. She says, 'Who in the world am I? Ah, THAT'S the great puzzle.' At the end, in order to find an answer, Alice has to put the pieces of herself back together in a new way." Vale paused. "You gave me this book because you know that I have to do that too."

I smiled. "I suspected you might be thinking along those lines."

Vale nodded. "Joanne, when did you discover who you were?"

"I'll be sixty-one on my next birthday," I said. "That's sort of my target date."

Vale grinned. "So it's not too late for me to work this out?"

I touched her arm. "It's never too late," I said. "At least that's what I'm counting on."

On January 30, Rosamond Burke boarded a plane for Toronto and a connecting flight to London. She would be home for her February 1st birthday. A day later, Taylor drove Vale Frazier to the airport to catch a flight to Vancouver, where Vale would begin work on her next film, a tender love story between exchange students from warring countries. She and Taylor had committed the schedules for flights between Regina and Vancouver to memory.

Principal photography, the middle phase of movie production, was finished. Sets had been struck; props and costumes were stored; actors, musicians, dancers, and production people had moved on to other jobs. The banner reading, "Welcome, *The Happiest Girl*!!!" had been removed from the entrance to the production studios. Rumour had it that a zombie movie would begin shooting there in March.

The Happiest Girl would now go to Vancouver for post-production. Because computer-generated imagery would be a significant part of the film, Tobi Lampard had scheduled six months for this final phase in the making of the movie. With luck, the movie would be in theatres the week before American Thanksgiving, an ideal release time for a film with high expectations for success.

By the end of the year, the movie that for three months in mid-winter had shaped our lives would be shown in thousands of theatres in scores of countries. People none of us would ever know would heap praise or scorn on it, be moved by or indifferent to it, argue about it or dismiss it out of hand. *The Happiest Girl* no longer belonged to us.

At the end of February, Taylor and I went to Saskatoon. Father Gary Ariano was teaching at St. Mike's in Toronto for the semester, so our plan was to visit Ben Bendure and to see Sally's old studio on the bank of the South Saskatchewan River. As Roy and I had, Taylor and I met Ben in Izaak Levin's former home on 9th Street. I had been concerned about Taylor's reaction to the shrine Izaak Levin had created to honour the woman he loved. After several futile attempts to explain the complexity of Izaak and Sally's relationship to Taylor, I realized that I didn't truly understand it myself and gave up. But from the moment we entered Izaak's house, Taylor's attention was not on his feelings for her birth mother but on the diversity and quality of the art he had gathered to honour her.

Taylor, too, had been intrigued by the rich textures and playful juxtaposition of elements in the collages Andrea D'Aquino created for *Alice's Adventures in Wonderland*, and she was immediately drawn to the collage of Sally that Izaak had given the place of honour on the wall facing his favourite armchair. I wanted Ben and Taylor to have some time alone, so while they explored the house, I sat in Izaak's favourite armchair, marvelling at the skill with which the artist had captured Sally's boldness and her vulnerability.

Ben had invited us to another picnic lunch at his condo, but when we were standing at the door with our coats on, Taylor returned to the living room for a final look at the collage of Sally.

When my daughter rejoined us, Ben said, "I'd like you to have that piece."

Taylor beamed. "And I would love me to have that piece," she said. "Thank you so much."

"It's my pleasure," Ben said. "And it introduces a subject I was hoping we could talk about at lunch. Taylor, I'd like to know what you think I should do with the art in this house."

It was a big decision, and over lunch, the three of us had a lot of fun floating ideas about how best to deal with Izaak's extraordinary collection. When Taylor and I left, nothing had been decided but Taylor wanted Vale to be part of the discussion. Vale was coming to Regina for Easter, so we invited Ben to join us then. The process was underway.

The current artist-in-residence had arranged to spend the afternoon elsewhere so that Taylor and I could take our time looking at Sally's old studio. It was one of those late-winter days when you can smell the earth warming and the promise of spring is in the air. As soon as we stepped out of the car, we heard the crack of ice breaking up on the river.

The studio was filled with the tools of a working artist, and Taylor was pensive as she moved carefully through the stacked canvases, tins of turpentine, canvas sleeves filled with paintbrushes, and tubes of paint laid out in an order Taylor recognized immediately. "Look, Jo. Whoever works here arranges their paints in the same order I use—reds and yellows on the left, white in the middle, and blues and greens on the right. Warm colours to cool colours," she said.

"So you feel at home here," I said.

Taylor smiled. "I feel at home anywhere there's good light, space to work, and the supplies I need." She walked over to the window, took out her phone, and made a video of the riverbank, still patched with snow, and of the rushing river.

"The woman I spoke to in the Fine Arts Department says the current artist-in-residence will be finished by July 1st. The university hasn't committed to anyone else, so you could take possession then."

"It really is perfect," Taylor said. "The view, the space, the light, and it's really kind of a thrill to think of Sally making art here . . ."

Like her birth mother, Taylor had a mouth so expressive that I could read her mood by studying it. That day, a glance at the line of her lips told me all I needed to know. "But this isn't where you want to be," I said.

Taylor shook her head. "Remember that story you used to read me about the dog in the manger?"

"I do. It's in our book of Aesop's fables."

"I used to be so scared of the mean look on that dog's face as he lay in the manger full of hay, taunting that poor hungry ox," Taylor said. "The dog had no use for the hay, but whenever the ox tried to eat, the dog bit him."

"You already have two studios—the one out back in Regina and the one at Lawyer's Bay. You don't want to be the biting dog," I said.

"I don't," she said. "Jo, I knew the moment I walked into this place that whoever was working here loved it. Sally would want her studio used all the time by people who loved it."

"You're right," I said. "She would."

"And I don't even know where I'm going to be. If my relationship with Vale develops the way we hope it will, she'll be travelling for her work. Her film in Vancouver will wrap by the beginning of May. Ainsley is hoping to shoot some of the outdoor footage for *Flying Blue Horses* up north in the summer."

"Roy asked me to suggest something here in Saskatchewan," I said. "The Artists' Colony at Emma Lake looks much as it did sixty years ago, and its beach is as pristine as the beach at MacLeod Lake was when I was growing up."

"I can hardly wait to see it," Taylor said. "Anyway, after they're through filming up north, Ainsley's planning to get as much as she can get done with Rosamond and Vale at the sound studios in Regina before they both have to leave on the publicity tour for *The Happiest Girl* at the end of October."

"Roy says the tour will last till Christmas," I said. "That's pretty intense."

"It is, but it's part of Vale's life, so it will be part of my life too. Most of what Vale will be doing till the end of November will be in the U.S. and Canada. I've already made lists of the art I want to see and the galleries I want to go to. Then, two weeks before Christmas we're going to Europe so Rosamond and Vale can do publicity where Rosamond is best known."

"But you'll be home for the holidays?" I said.

Taylor moved closer to me. "Rosamond says London is a fairyland at Christmas. Vale and I are hoping you and Dad will join us there." Our daughter saw the fear in my eyes and misread it, at least partially. "Don't worry, you don't have to fly, Jo. There are some beautiful ships that will bring you safely across the ocean."

I tried to keep my tone light. "I guess I just need some time to get used to the idea," I said. "Actually, there are quite a few things I'm going to need time to adjust to."

Taylor's voice was anxious. "Is my being with Vale one of them?"

"Not at all. Your dad and I agree that you and Vale are good together. It's just that all of a sudden you'll be part of a world that I don't know or understand."

"I don't understand it either," Taylor said. "But I want to. I want to see what's out there." She took my hand. "If you and Dad come for Christmas, you could see what's out there too." She paused. "Promise me you'll think about it?"

As Taylor faced me, her eyes shining with passion and anticipation for the adventures ahead, a memory of Sally flashed through my mind. We had just reconnected after our long separation and were having tea in my kitchen one evening, after my children had gone to bed. Sally was regaling me with stories about her travels. She had an eye for the telling detail and it was a pleasure to listen to her, but as the two of us were laughing, I felt a sudden stab of heartache. Sally must have felt it too, because she stopped mid-sentence and fell silent. As the silence between us lengthened, we looked into each other's eyes. Finally, I said, "We should have been together, Sally."

She reached across the table and put her hand on mine. "I know, and, Jo, I would give anything to have shared those years with you, but the distance between us was only physical. You've always been in my heart—and I was always in yours." Her eyes were brimming, but the corner of her mouth curled towards a rueful smile. "After all, who else could have stood it in these battered hearts."

That was Sally.

Being with Taylor in the studio where Sally had finally settled to make her life's work, I felt the same sweet sadness I had felt fourteen years earlier when my sister and I had talked of the years together we had lost. Taylor had decided what her first steps away from us as an adult would be, and I was struck again by the painful truth of C.P. Snow's observation that the love of a parent for a child is the only love that must grow towards separation. But as Sally had pointed out, the distance between Taylor and us would only be physical. Taylor's family, including both her mothers, would be with her every step of the way.

ACKNOWLEDGEMENTS

Thanks to:

Kendra Ward, my editor for her quiet intelligence and her firm but gentle guidance;

Ashley Dunn, for being at her desk when I needed her most;

Kelly Joseph for her reassurance and unfailing kindness;

Heather Sangster for giving the manuscript that final, essential polish;

Jared Bland, for his commitment to the writers of M&S, a publishing house that has always put writers and readers first;

Naima Kazmi, MD, for being everything a family physician should be;

Wayne Chau, BSP, for his professionalism and his great sense of humour;

Kai Langen, Madeleine Bowen-Diaz, Lena Bowen-Diaz, Chesney Langen-Bell, Ben Bowen-Bell, Peyton Bowen, and Lexi Bowen, who introduce us to their brave new worlds with patient kindness;

Ted, my love of almost fifty years, for going the distance with me; and

Esme, my constant companion.

Several of the pieces of art made by or owned by my characters have been described in earlier novels in the Joanne Kilbourn Shreve series.

Pages 182–183: Sally Love's *Erotobiography*
Pages 144–145: The fire scene at womanswork gallery
Pages 32–33: Sally Love's *Perfect Circles*
Page 102: The mural at St. Thomas More College
Pages 137–138: The artwork in Izaak Levin's home
Are described in *Murder at the Mendel*
First published by Douglas & McIntyre Ltd., 1991.
    First M&S paperback edition, 1992.

Pages 13–14: Taylor Love Shreve's *Two Painters*
Is described in *The Gifted*
Published simultaneously in the United States of
    America by McClelland & Stewart, a division
    of Penguin Random House Canada, 2013.